FRANCE

UNDER

ATTACK

TED HALSTEAD

BOOKS BY TED HALSTEAD

The Second Korean War (2018)
The Saudi-Iranian War (2019)
The End of America's War in Afghanistan (2020)
The End of Russia's War in Ukraine (2020)
The Russian Agents Box Set (2020) - A collection of
the four books listed above
The Second Chinese Revolution (2021)
China Invades Taiwan (2021)
The Indo-Pakistani War (2022)
China Conquers Taiwan (2023)
The Russian Agents Box Set 2 (2024) - A collection of
the second four books listed above

All books, including this one, are set in a fictional near future in which Vladimir Putin is no longer the Russian President. Some events described in these books have happened in the real world, and others have not.

To my wife Saadia, for her love and support over more than thirty years.

To my son Adam, for his love and the highest compliment an author can receive- "You wrote this?"

To my daughter Mariam, for her continued love and encouragement.

To my father Frank, for his love and for repeatedly prodding me to finally finish my first book.

To my mother Shirley, for her love and support.

To my granddaughter Fiona, for always making me smile.

All characters are listed in alphabetical order by nationality on the very last pages, because that's where I think the list is easiest to find for quick reference.

CHAPTER ONE

Abandoned Libyan Military Base
Southern Libyan Desert

"It's all clear. Nothing's moving for dozens of kilometers in any direction. And the bunker door is hanging wide open. I say let's go in and see if they missed anything."

Anatoly Grishkov tried to keep his astonishment off his face, but doubted he'd been successful.

The man who had been speaking, Henri Fournier, was not the detachment's commander.

Thankfully.

But, Henri was the team's only member of French intelligence, more formally called the Direction générale de la Sécurité extérieure, or DGSE.

Grishkov knew Henri was in his late twenties, though he looked even younger. His unkempt dark hair framed a face that Grishkov thought unlikely to need frequent shaving.

They were in the Libyan desert because the DGSE had learned a weapon was here that would be used to launch a terrorist attack on Paris.

Nuclear? Chemical? Biological?

The DGSE thought nuclear was the most likely option, but they didn't know for sure.

Still, that guess helped explain why Grishkov had been persuaded to join this expedition. Before his recent retirement to southern France with his wife Arisha, Grishkov had worked for Russian intelligence.

Not so long ago, Grishkov had been the lead homicide detective for the entire Vladivostok district.

Before that, Grishkov had served in the Russian Army in Chechnya at the height of the war in the 1990s. He'd always thought his short stature was one of the reasons he'd survived, when so many of his fellow soldiers had not.

He was simply a smaller target.

As Grishkov aged, he looked more and more like his father, who had also been a policeman. Like him, he was stockier and more muscular than the average Russian, with thick black hair and black eyes.

Grishkov had only been convinced to join the DGSE for the duration of this mission because his two sons were attending university in Paris.

He knew without having to ask that warning his sons or simply moving them out of Paris was not an option the DGSE would accept.

Not unless Grishkov was willing to move his entire family back to Russia.

Where his draft-age sons would likely find themselves performing their military service within days of arrival.

Grishkov's wife Arisha had been very clear that would be unacceptable. Having barely survived his time in the Russian Army, Grishkov wasn't inclined to argue the point.

Grishkov had been told the DGSE wanted him because he had previously been part of FSB teams that had successfully located and dealt with stolen nuclear weapons. That made sense, as far as it went.

Still, Grishkov thought that wasn't the only reason. So far, though, he had no idea what the DGSE's other motives might be.

Grishkov looked curiously at Captain Giraud, their detachment commander. A regular French Army officer, Giraud had spent nearly his entire career in Africa. Djibouti, Chad, Mali, and Niger were some of his most recent deployments.

Had he learned anything there?

Apparently he had.

Because now Giraud turned toward Grishkov.

"So, I can see on your face that you are not as eager as Henri to begin exploring that bunker. But he does have one point. That is the whole purpose of our mission. So, why the hesitation?" Giraud asked.

Grishkov frowned and tapped the side of his sniper rifle's SCROME J8 telescopic sight.

"Captain, I see a metal box that looks much newer than the rest of the bunker door. They tried to paint it to match but didn't do a very good job. Or maybe they did their best, but had to leave before the paint finished drying."

Henri shook his head. "Even if that means whoever came before us rigged some sort of explosive charge to the door, can't we count on Felix to deal with the problem?"

Grishkov turned to look at Felix Weber, who was weighing his response before he spoke.

Not a surprise. Grishkov doubted Felix had said more than a dozen words in total during the mission so far. He had a well-muscled physique that suggested he was no stranger to a gym, and close-cut blond hair.

A sergeant in the French Foreign Legion, Felix was born in Germany. However, Grishkov had seen in the files he'd been allowed to review just before the mission that Felix had been naturalized as a French citizen.

That happened after Felix was wounded, under a provision known as "Français par le sang versé" or "French by spilled blood."

Grishkov knew that simply having been wounded wasn't enough. It had to be in a "battle for France." Those details, though, had been redacted in the file furnished to Grishkov.

Felix had also been the helicopter pilot who had brought them to this part of the seemingly endless Libyan desert. Grishkov had seen from his file that he'd been commended several times for his courage flying under fire.

Finally, Felix shrugged. "I saw it too. Grishkov is right. The box probably has embedded sensors of multiple types. They will trigger a detonation as soon as someone approaches within the blast radius of the explosives set nearby. The connection between the box and the explosives is most likely by radio signal. But there could also be a wired connection we can't see from here."

Giraud sighed and thoughtfully rubbed the grey stubble that had appeared on his face since flying to Libya. "Is there any way to disarm the device safely?"

"Captain, I have a radio jammer that might work. But it may not. If it doesn't, I'll never get close enough to deal with any wired connection that may be there as a backup," Felix replied.

Grishkov nodded. "I saw these for the first time in Chechnya, always from a respectful distance. After explosives linked to these sensor boxes had already taken out several Russian Army units. I'm sure that the technology they contain has only improved in the years since."

"Suggestions?" Giraud asked, looking at them in a way that said they were all free to speak.

Grishkov tapped the FR F2 sniper rifle he had by his side, already set up in its standard bipod-stock configuration. The FR F2, from the French name Fusil à Répétition modèle F2, had been the standard French military and police sniper rifle since the mid-1980s.

Until it had recently been replaced by the FN SCAR-H. On paper, the FN SCAR-H was superior to the FR F2 in every way. Giraud had pointed this out to Grishkov before their departure, and Grishkov had nodded his understanding.

But then Grishkov explained that he had used the FR F2 before and found it performed well. Grishkov also noted that since they had to leave without delay, there would be no time to become familiar with a new weapon.

Fortunately, several FR F2s were still in stock and awaiting disposal.

It was now time for Grishkov to justify his choice.

"I can take out the box from here," Grishkov said. "We should be safe from even a massive charge with heavy debris at this distance. And if shooting it doesn't result in an explosion, we'll know we can proceed without risk."

At first, Giraud said nothing in response. Instead, he looked toward the bunker. Giraud was clearly gauging the distance between it and the low sand dune that currently served as their observation point.

It was over a kilometer away.

Then Giraud looked at Grishkov and his FR F2.

Finally, Giraud shrugged and said, "Proceed."

Grishkov was still prone from his earlier observation, and his right eye was immediately pressed against the rifle's scope.

Grishkov's right hand reached for the trigger and then stopped.

"I strongly recommend you all get below the edge of this dune. And put on your helmets. I should have said I *believe* we're safe here, but the truth is we have no idea how strong the explosion might be."

Everyone but Grishkov moved down from the dune's crest, with only Henri muttering something that Grishkov didn't quite catch.

Grishkov's French was still far from perfect, but he thought he heard something that sounded like "old woman."

Then Grishkov pulled the trigger and immediately rolled sideways down the side of the dune, keeping a firm grip on his rifle.

Almost at once, Grishkov found his head in Giraud's lap.

"Cozy?" Giraud asked with a smile. Grishkov was close enough to Giraud's face to see the individual strands of graying stubble that had begun to poke out of his cheeks and chin.

At the same instant, the sound of a massive explosion reached them.

And shook the earth around them.

Pieces of metal hissed over their heads.

And then began to fall around them like rain, thudding into the soft sand.

Henri yelped and then lay still.

Seconds later, all was quiet.

"Henri, are you injured?" Giraud asked.

"No," came Henri's immediate response. "The shrapnel was hot, and a piece burned through my pants. But I think I'll get off with no worse than a blister."

Giraud grunted and pointed at Henri's helmet.

Its top sported a dent containing a large metal fragment.

Henri took off the helmet and his eyes widened as he saw it.

Then he turned to Grishkov.

"I'm man enough to admit when I've been wrong. Your advice was good. I'll make a point to listen to it from now on," Henri said.

Grishkov nodded but said nothing. Instead, he poked his head over the dune's crest and looked toward the distant bunker. All the other team members quickly joined him.

All that was visible now was smoke rising from a hole in the desert.

Giraud turned toward Grishkov.

"Yes, indeed, your advice was good. So, do you think it's safe for us to sift through the rubble?" Giraud asked.

Grishkov shrugged. "If they left any other surprises, like mines between here and there, the explosion likely would have triggered them. Also, I'm betting that a detonation of this scale wasn't caused by just whatever explosives were set here recently. The bunker must have had a substantial stockpile there already."

Giraud nodded thoughtfully. "So, eliminate any investigators who might follow them. As well as any evidence they might have left behind. A good plan."

Having just finished bandaging his wound, Henri looked up from his leg and glanced at his helmet. "Yes, one that almost worked."

Giraud smiled. "Well, but not quite. Thanks to Monsieur Grishkov, we're still here. Let's see if there's anything left to find."

He stood up, and the rest of the team followed him.

They were about halfway when Felix walked past him, holding

a small box in his left hand. A cord was attached, and something that looked to Grishkov like a microphone was at its end. Felix held that device in his right hand and was slowly swinging it from side to side.

"Captain, let me take the lead. This way, I can warn you if the explosion has scattered any radioactive materials," Felix said.

Giraud nodded, and said, "Very well."

Grishkov looked at the device curiously. Its side bore the name of a German company, and a small streak of rust on one side testified to its age.

Felix noticed. Without looking back and continuing to wave the sensor from side to side, he said, "Yes, it's old. But I know it works."

Grishkov nodded gravely and replied, "I knew there was something I liked about you."

Nothing more was said until they had reached the smoking hole where the bunker had been before the explosion.

Up to now, the box Felix held had been silent. Now, it began to click. Not rapidly and not loudly, but enough to get their attention.

Giraud asked, "So, are we in danger?"

Felix shook his head. "Not if we leave soon. But unless anyone wants to climb into that hole, I think we've seen all there is to see. I will collect a few samples for analysis back at headquarters, and then I recommend we leave."

"Very well," Giraud replied. "So, do you believe a nuclear weapon had been stored here?"

"Based on these readings, that's impossible to say. Radioactive material, certainly. But a working nuclear device? There's no way to be sure. Once the lab at headquarters completes its analysis, we may know more," Felix said.

Then Felix pulled a small box from his pack, along with a thick pair of gloves and a small pair of metal tongs.

Grishkov could see when Felix opened the box that it was a dull gray color inside. Lead-lined.

Moments later, Felix filled the box with some of the fragments scattered around them and placed it back in his pack.

"Time to go," Giraud said. They wasted no time in leaving.

So, Grishkov thought, they had learned two things.

A nuclear weapon might have been stored at the bunker.

And if so, whoever had removed it wanted no interference with its use.

CHAPTER TWO

Société Générale de Transport International Headquarters
Paris, France

"Your people have to be more careful with their communications," Roland Dubois said with a scowl. "It wasn't easy for me to slow down the team we just sent to Libya."

Khaled Madi shrugged. "That service is why we are paying you, after all."

Dubois' scowl deepened further, and he was obviously struggling to keep his temper in check.

Madi watched Dubois with no small amusement. The man was a minor French politician, appointed to head the DGSE as part of a complicated deal between center-right parties. Pudgy and with thinning hair he kept in a ridiculous comb-over, Dubois' appearance was the opposite of impressive.

Part of Madi's contempt for Dubois came from his awareness that he, on the other hand, was handsome. Slim, with regular features, brown eyes, tan skin, and curly brown hair, Madi had never encountered difficulty attracting female companions.

Handsome was not only Madi's opinion. A magazine had even included him on its list of "Ten Most Eligible French Bachelors."

There had been a long stretch when the DGSE's leadership had been largely military. Then, its heads had been a series of retired diplomats.

It was fortunate for Madi that politics had put the exact leader he needed in charge at the DGSE at just the right time.

One who was weak. And greedy.

In a tone barely under control, Dubois finally ground out, "If I am found out, all the money you've spent will have been wasted. You must understand that the men working for me are not fools."

"Understood," Madi said at once. And meant it.

Dubois might not be the sharpest tool Madi had available.

But Madi knew the truth when he heard it. Dubois couldn't give one order after another that turned out to be precisely the wrong one without drawing suspicion.

"Don't forget," Madi added, "that when the bomb goes off, you will get the credit for discovering who was responsible."

It was a well-timed reminder. Dubois' scowl eased, and at last, he nodded.

But almost at once, Dubois's scowl returned.

"You said that once the bomb explodes, you will use your prior knowledge of the event to profit handsomely in the stock market. But how can you do so and avoid suspicion? Yes, your headquarters is here in Paris. But I guarantee many offices will be looking for suspects among those who made money in the market, and most will have headquarters here, too. This probably includes my organization, which has many financial experts. Tasked with tracking money tied to terrorism, which this certainly will be," Dubois said darkly.

"Don't lose sight of what we already discussed," Madi replied. "Not only will you get the credit for uncovering the source of the attack. The DGSE and all the other national security offices will see massive budget increases as a result. This bomb will be a wake-up call that politicians on the left will be unable to ignore. As for how I will avoid suspicion, are you sure you wish to know?"

Dubois opened his mouth and then closed it.

Good, Madi thought. At least he has some tiny bit of sense. All knowledge came with some risk.

In this case, that Dubois might inadvertently reveal it. And at the same time, his complicity in the attack.

But to Madi's disappointment, Dubois slowly nodded. "Yes," he said. "I must know."

"Very well," Madi replied. "My stock portfolio has remained largely unchanged for many years. Of course, shares in my own company are the largest single component. After the explosion, much of what is normally produced throughout a large area of central France will either be rendered unsellable due to contamination or not be produced at all, correct?"

"I suppose so," Dubois said, his eyes widening.

Excellent, Madi thought. Not too bright, but not a complete idiot either.

"Bulk goods to replace them will have to be imported, mostly by ship or truck. My company has a large market share of both. That has been true for many years, so no one will believe that gives me any special motive. But that is not the only reason I am sure I will avoid suspicion," Madi said.

"Yes? And the other reason?" Dubois asked, leaning forward.

Madi smiled. "Because I have been buying stock in solid companies that produce goods in central France for months. Precisely the ones that will see the largest fall in value due to the explosion."

Dubois nodded. "And I suppose your stock purchases in those other companies will be enough to divert suspicion. But still, leave you with a tidy profit from handling the increased import shipments and the rise in your stock price."

"Well put," Madi said approvingly. "Have I put your concerns to rest?"

"You have," Dubois said as he stood. Madi stood as well, smiling.

"Here's hoping we can keep these meetings to a minimum," Dubois added as he walked to the door of Madi's office.

Once Dubois was gone, Madi's smile remained.

But now it looked considerably less pleasant.

That was because Madi was now thinking about just how right Dubois was about the need to reduce the number of future meetings.

Madi would probably have to speak with Dubois again before this business was finished. So, for now, Dubois was safe.

But once Dubois had fingered ISIS as the terrorists behind the dirty bomb's explosion in Paris, he would become a loose end that had to be dealt with.

Fortunately, the ones to blame for Dubois' death would be easy to identify.

ISIS again, of course. And what better proof of how great a threat ISIS posed and how thoroughly they had to be eradicated?

Ironically, ISIS had started the chain of events that would lead to their undoing. One of their new recruits happened to be one of the very few who knew that Khaled Madi had started out life with a different name and a famous father.

Muammar Gaddafi.

Of course, Madi had not been one of Gaddafi's legitimate children. But for reasons Madi had never understood or questioned, he seemed to have been one of his father's favorites.

When Madi had barely been a teenager, Gaddafi took him on a trip. It was to show him a weapon that, Gaddafi had said, would "make their enemies tremble."

Madi had made all the noises to show he was impressed, as he knew his father expected. In truth, though, he hadn't really understood what he was seeing. Shiny metal. Serious-looking men in white coats.

And, of course, armed soldiers. That was nothing new at all. There were plenty of them in Tripoli, too, and everywhere Madi had been in Libya.

Still, Madi knew from watching his father that this place was special. So he listened carefully to the men talking and picked up two details.

The name of the base. As well as the name of the nearest town.

Not long after that, Gaddafi decided to send Madi to a French-language boarding school in Geneva, Switzerland, under the assumed identity of "Khaled Madi," accompanied by one of Gaddafi's female bodyguards, Rania.

Called in Arabic "ar-rāhibāt ath-thawriyyāt," by the literal English translation "the Revolutionary Nuns," or more commonly "the Amazons," these female guards had attracted much attention both inside and outside Libya.

On the one hand, they had received military training and did guard Gaddafi. One of his female bodyguards had been killed and seven others wounded when rebels ambushed Gaddafi's motorcade near Derna, Libya, in 1998. Press reports claimed that the dead guard had thrown herself across Gaddafi's body to shield him.

On the other, many reports said that Gaddafi and his top associates sexually abused the Amazons.

Madi didn't know whether that was true. He had always suspected that his guard Rania was his mother, though she had always denied it.

Until three things had happened.

First, Madi graduated and used the trust fund supplied by his father to start a successful business career in France. Rania had given Madi the names of security and computer experts to recruit, who had done much to fuel his rise.

Madi knew that an ordinary bodyguard would not have had such knowledge.

Next, Gaddafi had been killed in 2011 after being captured by Libyan rebel forces. Forces aided by an American Predator drone and French Mirage 2000 fighters.

Finally, Rani had been struck by cancer.

Madi was already wealthy and brought in the best specialists available. None of them could stop the cancer's spread.

In the end, Rani admitted that, yes, she was Madi's mother and that the relationship that resulted in Madi's birth had been her idea, not Gaddafi's.

Madi wasn't sure why, but he believed her. And he knew that was just as important to him as it had been to his mother.

When someone calling himself "Hassan" and claiming to be with ISIS contacted Madi online, it had been a simple blackmail threat. Pay us, or we reveal that Gaddafi was your father.

After an initial moment of panic, Madi collected himself and alerted his security team to the threat. First, they confirmed that it was indeed ISIS that had made the threat, in part because tracing the online contact back to a geographic location had proved impossible.

Even for Madi's team, which included world-class hackers working with the latest equipment.

His hackers had told Madi that even if he sent ISIS payments online, they could not locate the recipients.

That's when inspiration struck. What if, Madi asked, ISIS were to send payment to him?

Madi would always remember the expressions on the faces of his security team at that moment. They ranged from startled, to puzzled, to evident concern for his sanity.

Yes, indeed. Why in the world would ISIS ever send money to Madi?

Well, Madi was asking because he had remembered that base in the Libyan desert. Gaddafi had told him that anyone who didn't know where to look would never find the bunker where the weapon was stored.

But was that still true, even years after Gaddafi's death?

Madi had given his security chief Tareq the information he recalled from his trip to the base with Gaddafi all those years ago. Tareq had confirmed that though the base's aboveground structures had all been thoroughly looted, the bunker Madi remembered had been covered by sand and remained undiscovered.

In fact, Tareq said, digging equipment and a capable crew would be needed to shift enough sand to allow access to the bunker.

That was enough to let Madi make ISIS a counteroffer. He would pay ISIS nothing.

Instead, ISIS would pay Madi the equivalent of fifty million American dollars in cryptocurrency for the location of a dirty bomb designed to spread nuclear material using conventional explosives.

Extracting the device from the bunker and transporting it to ISIS' preferred target was not included in that price.

For another 50 million, Madi promised to see the bomb safely transported to Paris, where it would be detonated.

Of course, Madi had added, he planned to be elsewhere when that happened.

"Hassan" had asked why Madi had selected Paris as the target. As always, Madi believed the most effective lie stuck to the truth as far as possible.

Picking the city where his company had its headquarters would help divert suspicion from Madi.

Madi thought the French should pay a price for the help their Mirage 2000 jets had given to the rebels who had killed his father.

His transport company had assets in both Spain and France that would make it easier to transport the bomb to Paris as a target.

All true.

None of it was the real reason Madi had decided to use this particular plan. One that would turn ISIS' threat to reveal his father's identity to Madi's advantage.

Madi was one of the fifty wealthiest men in France. By many calculations, the richest born outside France. Though he had become a French citizen years ago, nobody in the French elite considered Madi truly "French."

No. Madi had not been born in France. His parents were not French. He had not attended French schools.

Madi would always be an outsider. Just like everyone in France who had not been born there. Or whose skin was not white.

Or both.

Only the Saadé family had ever broken into the ranks of the truly wealthy in France despite being foreign-born. In many ways, though, they had been the exception that proved the rule.

The man who had established the family fortune, Jacques Saadé, had been born in Lebanon and raised in Syria at a time when both were French protectorates.

So, an origin that was not quite French. But much closer than someone like Madi.

And just like Madi, the Saadé family had made its money in transport. A business looked down on by the wealthiest French families, who had made their fortunes in fields like fashion and luxury goods.

Madi had dealt with the French elite many times, both business and political. Unfailingly polite?

Absolutely.

Not a word that could be construed as racist? Or condescending?

Never.

At least, to Madi's face.

But behind his back, he knew things were very different.

So, was Madi willing to take risks to increase his wealth many-fold?

Of course.

Even more, though, Madi was looking forward to seeing many of the most wealthy families in France brought down a peg or two.

Or three or four. The knock-on effects of a dirty bomb explosion in central Paris were hard to calculate. They might be even more severe than he thought.

Yes, on Madi's darkest days, he had fantasized about nuclear-tipped cruise missiles striking the Eiffel Tower.

A dirty bomb explosion instead, though, would have a much higher concentration of highly radioactive material. Plus, detonation at ground level would make the spread of contamination far more severe.

So, not so spectacular as an attack from the air.

But for Madi's purposes, even more effective.

At its height, ISIS had been estimated to control assets worth about two billion American dollars. Even now, after many setbacks, the fifty million dollars in cryptocurrency they had already paid Madi was easy for ISIS to afford.

That first fifty million dollar payment from ISIS had served two purposes.

First, it had given Madi an untraceable source of funds to carry out the bombing.

Just as important, it had allowed Madi's hackers to backtrack the cryptocurrency funds received from ISIS to a precise physical location in the Syrian desert.

Of course, Madi had confirmed this. It had proved surprisingly easy.

Commercial satellite imagery for almost any set of GPS coordinates was available to any large company. At a resolution surpassing what had been classified "Top Secret" during the Cold War years.

But what if the ISIS command center had moved by the time the bomb exploded, and Madi's second payment was due?

Madi had thought of that, too. He had insisted on a "good faith" payment of five million dollars as soon as the bomb was in place and ready for detonation.

And once it had exploded, did Madi expect to receive the remaining forty-five million dollars?

Well, he certainly wasn't counting on it.

But that was fine. Because ISIS would have given him something far more valuable.

A scapegoat. Someone had to be blamed for the attack. Madi might have done everything possible to cover his tracks.

But unless a culprit was found quickly, even Madi's best precautions might not be enough.

The ability to promise a targetable ISIS location had even given Madi an unplanned advantage.

Madi had met Roland Dubois at one of the parties he was expected to attend as a company head. Hosted by a political party, it was a fundraiser Madi would have preferred to avoid.

But if Madi wanted his company to be considered for certain government contracts, he had little choice.

It was a chance meeting that Madi took as a sign his plan was meant to succeed. Never religious, Madi was still a man who sincerely believed in luck.

Both good and bad.

Madi was sensible enough to know that he had been blessed with more than his share of good fortune so far in life.

Finding a man at the head of the DGSE as weak and greedy as Roland Dubois? A stroke of luck indeed.

Dubois was in a position to inform Madi of what the French government knew almost as soon as they did. And even to slow down anyone who might act against Madi's operatives.

Though Dubois was right. They would have to be more cautious from now on.

Because if the years had taught Madi anything, it was this.

Even the best luck could only be pressed so far.

CHAPTER THREE

Southern Libyan Desert

Samir Ali grimaced as he looked over the collection of equipment on the trucks. It didn't help that a brisk wind was spraying liberal quantities of Libyan desert sand into his face.

Fortunately, the large black sunglasses that allowed him to see despite the blinding midday sun also protected his eyes from the blowing sand.

Ali could still feel grit scouring his cheeks, but that didn't trouble him. After decades of hauling oil drilling equipment all over Libya, Ali thought his skin had become as tough as any other desert creature's hide.

Maybe tougher.

With, many said, a personality to match.

Like his long-dead wife. Or his sons, who had grown up years ago and moved away from Benghazi, where Ali had a small apartment.

One that Ali rarely saw. Unless he was moving equipment with his truck, he had no money to eat.

"You expect me to fit all this on my truck in one trip? Look, get rid of this thing, and I think I can do it. Otherwise, no deal," Ali said.

With that, Ali gestured at a massive metal object of a type he'd never seen. It was half a cylinder with a flat bottom. Above the metal bottom, a metal sheet curved upward for about a meter before sloping back down on the other side to produce the half-cylinder.

The largest rivets Ali had ever seen secured the curved metal sheet to the bottom.

The metal wasn't steel. It was too shiny, and there wasn't a speck of rust on it.

Well, on the metal sheet, anyway. The rivets were another matter. They were ordinary steel, and now each a solid mass of rust.

Whatever the object was, it was old.

Really old.

Ali pitied whoever tried to pull the contraption apart without damaging whatever was inside.

Fortunately, not his problem.

He knew why Abdul had come to him. Ali's truck was old.

But it was well-maintained. Just like the small but powerful crane on the back of his truck.

Out here in the southern Libyan desert, Ali was Abdul's only option if he didn't want to do the job himself.

Ismail Abdul shook his head, and took another long drag from the cigarette that always seemed to be hanging from his mouth.

Ali had noticed Abdul always smoked the same brand, made by a British company called Dunhill.

Why? Because in North Africa it was rare and expensive? Or because Abdul truly thought it was the best?

Ali had to admit the cigarettes did have a distinctive smell. And Abdul smoked enough of them that his clothes always carried the smell, even when a lit cigarette wasn't jammed in his mouth.

Not that it really mattered, Ali thought. He had agreed with his father about very few things before his passing many years ago. But on one point, they were in complete accord.

Sooner or later, cigarettes would kill you.

"That's the most important piece of equipment we need to be transported," Abdul said. "Put it on your truck first, then do your best to add as many other items as possible. Try to load as much as you can, to make a decent match to the shipping documents."

Ali looked at Abdul suspiciously and said, "I've been hauling oilfield equipment around this desert longer than you've been alive. I've never seen anything like this. What is it, a bomb?"

Ali watched Abdul closely to see his reaction. Ali hadn't survived traveling alone in the desert for all these years by being stupid. Or by being unable to read people.

If Abdul lied to him now, he'd know.

Fortunately, Ali could see that Abdul was genuinely startled by the question.

"A bomb? No, of course not! I had to use dirt tracks that didn't even qualify as roads to get here from where I picked up this load. Plenty of bouncing up and down, I can tell you. Would I have done that with a bomb in the back?" Abdul asked.

OK, that sounds like the truth, Ali thought. But...

"Where was the pickup point?" Ali asked.

Abdul promptly named a village about two hundred kilometers away.

Ali grunted. He knew it. Small, near a now-abandoned oilfield.

Yes, it wouldn't have been an easy drive. And one no sane man would have made carrying a bomb.

Ali still didn't like it. In the desert, it was the unknown that would kill you.

And this shiny hunk of riveted metal was definitely unknown.

But Ali needed the money. And Abdul sounded desperate.

How desperate, Ali wondered.

"I'll do it for double the price you offered. Not a dollar less," Ali said.

American dollars, of course. Ali had never accepted anything else, even when Gaddafi was still in power. Russian-printed Libyan currency issued since 2016 under the supposed authority of Benghazi's new rulers had just reinforced that policy.

The squawking from Abdul that followed told Ali "double" would cut quite a bit into Abdul's profit from the deal. But apparently, not too heavily.

Because finally, Abdul said, "Agreed. Half now, and half upon delivery."

Ali nodded. Those were standard terms.

Then Abdul lifted one finger and smiled. "And here is a sweetener for the deal, that I was told only to offer after you agreed. Make delivery in Tangier by the 21st, and you will receive a twenty-five percent bonus."

Ali did a quick mental calculation and grunted. That wouldn't leave as much time as he liked for niceties like meals and sleep, but it could be done.

Maybe.

But why?

"So this stuff is being sent to Europe for refurbishment and repair after sitting in the desert for who knows how many years. And now, suddenly, every day counts. Why?" Ali asked suspiciously.

Abdul nodded. "I wondered the same thing. It seems this equipment is just what's needed for a special exploration project with a tight deadline. If it's missed, the project goes to another company."

Ali grunted thoughtfully. Well, that sounded plausible.

Though who knew whether it was true.

"Let's see the cash," Ali growled.

Abdul pulled a satchel out of his vehicle and handed it to Ali.

Without making any additions or subtractions to its contents first.

Ali realized that Abdul had expected him to insist on double the asking price.

If I'm that predictable, I really am getting old, Ali thought.

But he said nothing as he counted the money. To his credit, Abdul also kept his mouth shut until Ali was done.

It was all there.

Now Abdul handed Ali a single sheet of paper.

"Here is the contact information for the shipper in Tangier. Once you make the delivery, he will pay the other half as agreed. And, of course, the bonus if you manage to get there by the 21st. The route is naturally your choice," Abdul said.

Ali nodded. He would have to cross the Tunisian, Algerian and Moroccan borders with suspicious-looking cargo.

Yes. The route would definitely be his choice.

CHAPTER FOUR

Paris, France

Anatoly Grishkov looked out the café's window but saw no one who looked like they might be the courier he was expecting.

He looked down at his now-lukewarm coffee and again thought this was ridiculous. Why these spy games? Grishkov now, reluctantly, worked for French intelligence.

More formally called the Direction générale de la Sécurité extérieure, or DGSE. As it said on the card bearing Grishkov's name and photo that he was now obliged to carry wherever he went.

Along with a Beretta M9 pistol that Grishkov considered a definite downgrade from his familiar Makarov.

Grishkov scowled. He was in Paris.

So why not meet this courier in a nice, secure DGSE office rather than in some anonymous café with nothing particularly to recommend it?

Indeed, not its coffee, Grishkov thought with a scowl. No wonder he was the only customer here, despite the beautiful weather.

Grishkov had asked for a description of the courier. His new boss, Jacques, had just said that Grishkov would "know him when he saw him."

With one of those irritating smiles Grishkov had seen before on the faces of French actors in movies his wife Arisha had forced him to watch.

A smile that said, "I know something important, and soon you will too."

Grishkov didn't want to know soon. He wanted to know now.

But Jacques was Grishkov's boss, not the other way around.

So, Grishkov sat and waited for Jacques' little surprise to reveal itself.

With as much patience as he could muster.

Fortunately, it wasn't tested much longer.

Because against all his expectations, Grishkov immediately recognized the courier.

Who entered the café and walked directly to Grishkov's table. Then sat down across from him and waved away the waiter when he approached.

Grishkov could only stare silently. This was the last person on earth he'd expected to see.

Former FSB Director Smyslov laughed. "A first from my favorite former homicide detective. I've never before seen you at a loss for words. But I must admit, my appearance here comes as a surprise even to me."

Grishkov slowly nodded. "It is good to see you, Director. How have you been?"

Grishkov's expression told Smyslov that his question was not merely a pleasantry.

Smyslov shrugged. "It is public knowledge that I retired for reasons of health. My doctors were certain that I'd be dead by now. Part of my continuing to draw breath is just to spite them."

The wan smile that accompanied Smyslov's statement was matched by Grishkov. But Smyslov could see his heart wasn't in it.

"While you are here, will you see Western doctors? Maybe they could find a treatment not available in Russia," Grishkov said.

Smyslov nodded. "Now that I am a former, not active, high Russian official, I plan to do just that. It's one of the reasons Director Kharlov selected me for this trip. But not the main one."

Grishkov knew better than to ask questions. Smyslov would tell him what he needed to know without prompting.

Smyslov noticed, and smiled. "Very good. If anyone should know when a subject needs no prompting to speak, it should be the former lead homicide detective for the entire Vladivostok district! But before we go to business, I must ask. How are your sons Sasha and Misha and your wife Arisha?"

"They are all well, Director. Thank you for asking. As I'm sure you know, the danger this weapon poses to my sons studying here in Paris is the only reason I agreed to come out of retirement," Grishkov said.

Smyslov nodded. "Yes, and your selection by the DGSE was no accident. They must have foreseen the need for this meeting, though I'm sure they didn't expect me to be on this side of the table."

Grishkov waved his arm towards their surroundings in the empty café.

"I'm sorry, but I don't understand what we're doing here. That waiter could be listening to every word we say and reporting it to the French. Shouldn't we be at our Embassy here in Paris?" Grishkov asked.

Smyslov said nothing, but waved at the waiter, who promptly approached their table.

"Oui, monsieur?" the waiter said.

"Please, Ivan," Smyslov said with a smile. "You can drop the act. Grishkov here thinks this is an ordinary French café, so you've done your job. Now I want him to understand that it's a bit more than that."

"Understood, Director," Ivan said, in Russian. "It is an honor to welcome you here."

"Please get us some real Russian black tea, and take this away." Smyslov said, gesturing towards the tepid cup of coffee in front of Grishkov.

"So, this is an FSB front. That I presume is swept regularly for French listening devices," Grishkov said.

Smyslov nodded. "British and American ones as well. They all maintain surveillance on this café, of course, but not nonstop. The way they do on our Embassy, for example."

"I see," Grishkov said. "So they may spot our meeting anyway, but doing it here will make it harder."

"Correct," Smyslov said. "In this game, we hardly ever deal in absolutes. Making the enemy's task more difficult is often the best we can do."

Now, Grishkov stared at the slim folder he saw Smyslov had placed between them.

"Well, whatever's in there, Kharlov accomplished one thing by sending you. I know that the French weren't lying when they said the threat is real," Grishkov said.

"Oh, yes," Smyslov said. "Very real. But that's not the main reason he chose me for this task. You see, I'm the only one besides Kharlov and the President to know that this file exists."

"The file that details our role in the weapon we're now trying to find before it is used," Grishkov said flatly.

"Just so," Smyslov said, nodding. "Mind you, this was never a decision made by anyone in the Soviet or subsequent Russian governments. We have never knowingly allowed our nuclear weapons or technology to be given or sold to terrorists. In fact, we went to extraordinary lengths to prevent it, like the naukograds."

Grishkov grunted. "Yes, the closed science cities. I've heard of them, though I've never been to one."

"Well, why would you? That was the whole point, keeping out those who had no reason to have contact with the scientists possessing our most closely guarded secrets," Smyslov said.

"Yes, and keeping those same scientists in. I heard the cities were well above-average places to live. But some must have wished to see the world outside, like caged birds wondering what was beyond the nearest window," Grishkov said.

Smyslov arched one eyebrow. "Very poetic. But not wrong. And after the USSR's collapse, the naukograds were no longer such wonderful places to be. The money just wasn't there to maintain the same living standards. Or, unfortunately, the same high levels of security."

Grishkov nodded. "So some scientists slipped out. I heard a few were able to make it out of Russia altogether."

"Yes," Smyslov sighed. "Some of them lived quiet lives as teachers, and those we left alone. Others sought to sell their knowledge of state secrets. Those we tracked down and dealt with."

"But that must have taken time. And meanwhile, some secrets must have been sold," Grishkov said.

"Only a few. But yes, this file details one of the worst security failures. The sale of nuclear technology and materials to Muammar Gaddafi. Not at the same time, of course. It's a complicated story, but I'll summarize," Smyslov said, tapping on the folder.

Grishkov wasn't surprised to see that Smyslov didn't need to open it.

"Dmitri Peshkin was not our best nuclear engineer. Nor was he the worst. Before the USSR's collapse, he was completely unremarkable. For a decade, he reported to work, did his job, and went home to his apartment. Then, one day in December 1991, he was simply gone," Smyslov said.

"We looked for him, of course," Grishkov said.

Smyslov nodded. "But the FSB had just been created from the KGB, which had been purged and disgraced due to its role in the failed August 1991 coup attempt. Maybe no surprise that they failed to find Peshkin, who had been gone for a week before his disappearance was even reported to Moscow."

"So, Peshkin put his services up for sale and was then contacted by Libyan intelligence operatives," Grishkov said.

"No, if he'd done that, even an infant FSB would have found Peshkin first. Peshkin was smart enough to lay low and attract no attention. He was even smarter to flee to Germany. The collapse of the old East German state had left plenty of Russians in its wake who never went home. Peshkin had studied German in high school and university and so had no trouble fitting in," Smyslov said.

"But something must have gone wrong, or we wouldn't be here talking about Peshkin," Grishkov said.

"Yes," Smyslov replied with a smile. "Quite right. German authorities needed time to get around to all the Russians who had claimed refugee status in the early 1990s. But eventually, Peshkin heard that questions were being asked about his background. Naturally, all the details he'd provided on his refugee application were false. So, he made a quick exit to France."

Grishkov nodded. "Another smart choice. No border controls, and no love lost between German and French authorities."

"Correct. But now Peshkin was in a tough spot. Alone in a country where he didn't speak the language, he had to take menial jobs once his limited savings ran out. Finally, he made his way to Paris and an Internet café," Smyslov said.

"The Internet was just getting started then, right?" Grishkov asked.

"For most people, yes. However, the concept of online discussions was already familiar to Peshkin, thanks to message boards restricted to scientists and engineers while he was in the USSR. Peshkin had no trouble reaching those online who were interested in his services. The first to respond were the Libyans," Smyslov said.

"Makes sense," Grishkov said. "As another Mediterranean country, Libya certainly had agents already in France."

"An important advantage," Smyslov replied. "It's why they got Peshkin out of France and on a ship to Libya just hours ahead of the DGSE. French intelligence, of course, monitored online activity relevant to national security."

"But not closely enough, it seems," Grishkov observed.

"No," Smyslov said with a sigh. "But it's hard to criticize since the FSB only learned about Peshkin's travel to Libya from the French. Even when we knew, our leverage with the Libyans was limited."

"Really? I thought we were the only friend Gaddafi had back then," Grishkov said.

"Yes and no," Smyslov replied. "We had up to eleven thousand troops in Libya during the 1970s and early 80s, but the Libyans became more isolationist after Gaddafi visited Moscow in 1985. He didn't re-visit Moscow until 2008, just a few years before his death. Gaddafi was unwilling to pay debts incurred during Soviet days for arms and equipment purchases. So, in the early 90s our protests to Gaddafi fell on deaf ears."

"So what was Peshkin able to do for the Libyans? I thought Gaddafi renounced his weapons programs, both nuclear and chemical, and that Western countries verified Libyan compliance," Grishkov said.

"You're right," Smyslov said. "And so we thought Peshkin's defection to Libya accomplished nothing for Gaddafi. Peshkin died of natural causes in 2009, having remained all that time in Libya. As far as we knew, that was the end of the story."

"So, how did we find out Peshkin was able to produce a working device?" Grishkov asked.

"First, I don't think he did. Not exactly. Gaddafi certainly wanted an atomic bomb. He even hoped a nuclear warhead could be fitted to one of the cruise missiles then under development in Pakistan. Assuming he could get his hands on one. But with the resources and fissionable material Peshkin had available, that wasn't possible," Smyslov said.

Grishkov grunted. "So, a dirty bomb, then."

"Exactly," Smyslov said. "The bomb will scatter radioactive material by conventional explosives over a wide area. Not many immediate casualties. But the extent of contamination will take time to assess. Then, even longer to remove. Finally, even after cleaning is declared complete, many will hesitate to use space that had been irradiated."

Grishkov nodded. "I certainly would. And I would never risk Arisha or my sons by moving to a supposedly decontaminated area."

"So, the value of any property irradiated by a dirty bomb would plummet," Smyslov said. "If that bomb went off in central Paris, the blow to the French economy would be massive. The Paris metropolitan area's production is worth a trillion American dollars annually, or about a third of French gross domestic product."

Grishkov winced. "I see why a dirty bomb would be almost as serious a threat as a fully functional nuclear device. Can the FSB do anything to help me stop it?"

"Maybe," Smyslov said slowly. "Many Russian citizens live in Paris. If you include dual nationals, maybe a few hundred thousand. We have an Embassy there, a rather large one. The Russian government has certain investments in France that would be negatively affected. And even more in other European countries, which could be expected to enter recession along with France if a dirty bomb exploded in Paris."

"I must say I'm surprised," Grishkov said. "I thought our investments in the European Union were either curtailed or frozen after the Ukraine conflict."

Smyslov arched one eyebrow. "I didn't say the investments were openly declared as those owned by the Russian government."

"Ah," Grishkov said, nodding. "Well, I'm the first to admit I'm no expert on financial matters. So, will that all add up to enough reason for the FSB to assist?"

"That decision is no longer up to me," Smyslov said. "But I will recommend to Director Kharlov that we offer to use our only asset that could make a difference. An advanced airborne sensor package capable of detecting radioactive material more effectively than anything available in the West."

"Yes, I remember you explaining how we came to develop that capability in a previous mission," Grishkov said.

Smyslov scowled. "We were generally successful in covering up the string of nuclear accidents we had during Soviet days. Of course, we had total control of the media back then, and there was no Internet. However, we were highly motivated to develop sensors that could detect radioactivity from a substantial distance. Even now, our technology is better than anything available in the West."

"But will the French let us deploy it? To detect a dirty bomb, presumably well-shielded, would require an aerial platform. Is that still the Okhotnik drone?" Grishkov asked.

Smyslov nodded. "Yes, it is. I can only guess whether the French will allow it to fly over their territory. It will depend on how desperate they are to find the bomb before it makes all this much less attractive."

Smyslov waved his arm to take in all they could see from their perch at the café.

Earlier, Grishkov had admired the view on a Paris day with perfect weather. Now, he imagined it as it would be after radioactivity made it too dangerous to approach without a hazmat suit.

Grishkov knew you couldn't see radioactivity. That's one of the things that made it so dangerous.

But Grishkov now saw Paris as gray and lifeless instead of sunny and beautiful.

Not a place where Grishkov would want his sons to live. Not for a minute.

Grishkov turned his attention back to Smyslov.

"Please be sure to tell Kharlov this," Grishkov said. "It is, of course, up to him and the President whether to allow the use of the Okhotnik drone and under what conditions. But as far as I know, the DGSE has no leads on the bomb's location. Without the drone, I fear there is nothing for us to do but prepare to deal with the consequences of a dirty bomb explosion in the middle of Paris."

Smyslov nodded. "I had planned to do just that anyway. In the meantime, I will tell you something that directly contravenes my orders. But I will do it anyway."

Grishkov's eyebrows flew up. He had never heard such words from Smyslov before.

Seeing his astonishment, Smyslov smiled.

"There are certain advantages to knowing you don't have much time left. Losing your fear of official consequences is one of them. You were told to say nothing to your sons for operational security reasons.

Those orders haven't changed. But I am now telling you to ignore them," Smyslov said.

Seeing Grishkov starting to object, Smyslov shook his head.

"I know you are worried that without FSB support, you, your wife, and your sons might no longer be able to live in France. I guarantee that won't be true. I will tell Kharlov and the President that I gave you the order to inform your sons, and that any punishment should fall on me. I will say that after all you and your family have sacrificed, including your mother-in-law's life, I decided it wasn't right to ask for anything further."

Grishkov's face darkened as he remembered his first mission for the FSB. A North Korean agent had indeed killed his mother-in-law and very nearly his wife as well.

"I appreciate that more than I can say," Grishkov said finally. "Of course, I'll make up a reason for them to leave Paris. Probably that they need to help their mother with something."

Smyslov nodded. "A good choice. Your home, not far from the Mediterranean coast, would be well removed from any possible fallout. But I am still hopeful we can avoid the worst."

The two men looked at each other but said nothing.

They both knew that wasn't true. Smyslov thought there was a good chance Kharlov and the President would refuse the drone request.

Otherwise, Smyslov would never have risked defying his orders.

But Grishkov nodded anyway.

"I'm sure you're right, Director," was all Grishkov could think to say.

CHAPTER FIVE

Ras Jedir
Libya-Tunisia Border Crossing

Samir Ali grit his teeth as he saw who was in charge of the Libyan border inspection team. A team that inspected goods both entering and exiting Libya.

Lieutenant Issa.

Ali had been fiercely willing the long line of vehicles waiting for inspection to move faster.

Now, he tried to undo that thought. Issa's shift would end if this took long enough, and a more reasonable officer might replace him.

But no. Ali's father had always said you could be sure of only one thing.

God was always busy.

You would be lucky to have Him answer any of your prayers.

Have a just-sent prayer reversed? Not likely.

And indeed, it looked like God had decided to listen to Ali's prayer.

The first one.

Because no sooner had Ali spotted Issa than the vehicle line seemed to speed up as if by magic.

Much sooner than Ali wished, he found himself face-to-face with Lieutenant Issa.

Ali didn't even bother praying Issa wouldn't recognize him. He'd crossed this border far too many times for that.

"Ah, Ali," Issa said with a wide smile. That Ali thought couldn't possibly have been less sincere.

"I see you have a heavy cargo with you today. Papers, please," Issa continued.

Ali handed them over without saying a word.

Issa examined the papers, at the same time barking orders to his men. In short order, half a dozen soldiers were poking and prodding every corner of the truck's cargo.

It took only a minute for one of them to say to Issa, "Sir, found something!"

Ali worked hard to keep his face impassive. It wasn't easy.

Issa disappeared around the back of the truck to see what the soldier had found.

Ali stayed right where he was.

It didn't take long for Issa to return. This time, his smile wasn't insincere.

No, it was gloating.

"So, your papers say you're carrying oilfield equipment. But the piece that accounts for most of your load looks like nothing my soldiers have seen before. And we get such equipment here every day. Your explanation?" Issa asked.

Ali shrugged. "I'm a driver, not an oilfield technician. If you want to confiscate any of my cargo, you have that authority. But I was told this cargo is vital to opening a new production site near Tripoli. And that the contract has a tight deadline. If anything happens to slow down the repair of this equipment, some in the capital may not be happy."

Now Issa's smile disappeared. "Well, I know you won't be, that's for sure."

Ali nodded. "It's true I've only been paid half of my fee, with the other half due on delivery. But you see from my papers that I'm supposed to go all the way to Tangier. That's a long trip. Frankly, if you decide to take this cargo and send me back with an empty truck, I won't be out that much. But..."

Issa's eyes narrowed. "Yes? But what?"

"I nearly forgot to say that my dispatcher told me to double our normal contribution to the Hero's Fund. Of course, I know that won't affect your decision, but I thought I should mention it," Ali said blandly.

The border post had been attacked by bandits several times, most recently in 2024. That attack had killed two Libyan soldiers and resulted in the post's temporary closure.

The "Hero's Fund" was supposed to be for the families of the dead soldiers. Nobody, including Ali, thought the families would see more than a tiny fraction of the money collected in their name.

However, it was a convenient way to make handing over bribes less obvious for everyone.

Ali could see Issa calculate the variables as he waited silently.

Issa could seize the truck, its cargo, and all the cash Ali had with him. For that matter, he could send Ali to join the other unmarked graves in the low hills nearby.

But Ali could be telling the truth. Maybe someone important in Tripoli wouldn't be happy if the equipment on Ali's truck didn't get repaired and returned.

Maybe someone important enough to do something about it. Like reassign Issa to a much less favorable post.

Or even have Issa occupy one of those nearby unmarked graves himself.

Issa reached his decision quickly, and made a small gesture with his right hand.

"Your contribution will be much appreciated by the families of the soldiers who gave their lives fighting for our country," Issa said.

Ali had the envelope with the cash in Issa's hands seconds later. It disappeared into Issa's uniform jacket even more quickly.

"Let him pass," Issa ordered, and Ali was waved forward.

Now, Ali thought, on to Tunisia.

CHAPTER SIX

Melloula
Tunisian-Algerian Border Crossing Post

It had been quite a while since Samir Ali last crossed the border between Tunisia and Algeria at Melloula. From 2020 to 2022, the entire border was closed because of concerns over the spread of COVID-19.

A year after the border reopened, a wildfire had consumed much of the forest surrounding the town of Melloula. As well as several buildings on the town's outskirts. While dealing with the fire's aftermath, the government closed the Melloula border post and routed all traffic to Babouch, a town about twenty-five kilometers south.

This meant Ali had no idea who he'd be dealing with while trying to cross to Algeria. He only knew it wouldn't be easy.

It was not that there was any particular bad blood between Algeria and Tunisia. On the contrary, their shared opposition to French colonialism and overwhelming Muslim majorities had done much to draw them together.

However, Tunisia's role as the birthplace of the Arab Spring in 2011 led Algerian authorities to start viewing border crossers more closely.

Massive unrest throughout the region led to the overthrow of the rulers of Tunisia, Libya, and Egypt in 2011, and Yemen in 2012.

Algeria's government was able to hold on despite massive protests leading to thousands of arrests, hundreds of injuries, and a hotly disputed number of deaths.

Ali sighed. Enough time had passed that he thought the Algerians should have relaxed their guard.

However, one look at the grim Algerian soldiers manning the border post told Ali he was probably in for a tough time.

The Lieutenant in charge walked up to Ali's truck. The name stitched on his uniform's nametag was "Youssef."

Ali had already lowered the window on his side.

"Papers," Youssef snapped, stretching his right arm forward.

Ali knew better than to keep him waiting, so he handed over his passport and shipping documents without a word.

While Youssef looked over the documents, his men scrambled over everything on the truck's cargo bed.

Accompanied by dogs. No doubt, trained to detect drugs and explosives.

Had Abdul lied to him about what was inside the strange, shiny object?

Well, nothing Ali could do about that now.

"Nothing here, sir," one of the soldiers called out.

Ali breathed an inward sigh of relief. So, it seemed Abdul hadn't been lying after all.

And nobody at this border crossing appeared to be familiar enough with oilfield equipment to know that one item on his truck didn't fit.

Then Ali's heart sank as Youssef said the word he'd dreaded.

"Out," Youssef said, yanking the truck's door open to make it clear he meant right now.

Keeping his face as expressionless as he could, Ali quickly obeyed.

The soldiers who had just searched the truck's cargo now went through every inch of the cab. Ali could do nothing but stand to the side and watch.

"Found something, sir," one of the soldiers said.

Ali thought he knew what it was, but he couldn't see what the soldier was holding from his angle.

In a few moments, though, the small gift-wrapped package was in Youssef's hands.

It was exactly what Ali had hoped.

So was Youssef's reaction.

Gloating, Youssef asked, "Do you object to my opening this so-nicely wrapped box?"

They both knew Youssef would open it no matter what Ali said.

Ali shook his head and said, "Go ahead. I've learned it's outdated and not worth giving, so I stuck it in the glove compartment and forgot about it."

Now frowning, Youssef opened the wrapping to find a new cell phone inside, still in its original packaging.

Ali could see from Youssef's poorly concealed reaction that he knew the value of what he was holding.

When it was released in Algeria two years earlier, this particular Android phone was worth about half the cost of the latest competing Apple device. Ali had been able to buy it from a Libyan reseller at a steep discount, making it a genuine bargain.

Because the Chinese company that made it had left the cell phone business altogether. Instead, it had announced it would invest all its capital in artificial intelligence.

So, the cell phone might have a display as large and nearly as crisp as any on the Algerian market. It might have as much storage and be nearly as fast.

But if anything went wrong, who would service the phone?

Fortunately for Ali, Youssef appeared not to be focused on that issue.

"You may as well keep it. It's useless to me anyway," Ali said in a low voice, pitched so that only Youssef could hear it.

Not the nearby soldiers.

Now, Youssef had a decision to make.

To Ali's relief, Youssef made it quickly.

"I am confiscating this phone for security review. Do you have any objection?" Youssef asked.

Ali shook his head.

Jerking his head toward Ali's truck, Youssef snapped, "You may proceed."

Ali wasted no time climbing back into his truck and putting it in gear.

As he rolled through the checkpoint into Algeria, Ali kept repeating the same thought in his head.

Don't be too pleased with yourself.

Yes, two of the three borders he had to cross might be behind him. But the most difficult was still ahead.

A border between Algeria and Morocco that had been closed for nearly all of the past seventy years.

Between two countries that had fought a war over exactly where that border should be drawn.

CHAPTER SEVEN

Port of Tangier
Morocco

Once again, Ismail Abdul thought it was fortunate that the people funding this project had deep pockets. He'd checked commercially available flights from Libya to Tangier and been horrified by the results.

The best available routing? A flight to Cairo, followed by another to Munich, another to Madrid, and then the last one to Tangier.

It would have taken over two days.

Once Abdul explained the problem, the project organizers provided a small jet. It had two pilots and only one passenger.

Abdul.

The flight took about two hours.

So, here he was in Tangier, in plenty of time to meet Samir Ali. Once Ali had completed the long truck drive from Libya.

But first, Abdul had another person to meet. Saad, the man who would drive the truck and its cargo onto the boat at Tangier to go first to Spain. And then to drive the truck to its final destination in Paris.

Abdul knew nothing about Saad except that the project organizers had instructed him to be used for that single task.

Well, Abdul knew nobody trustworthy in Morocco to ask instead, so he'd been in no position to argue.

However, Abdul was able to obtain full authority to take any measures necessary to ensure that the cargo reached its final destination.

Abdul would shortly be pleased with his foresight in making that request.

"You are Abdul?" the man now approaching Abdul asked.

Before answering, Abdul quickly looked around the train yard he had specified for the meeting and discarded what little was left of his Dunhill cigarette.

Much of the train yard was busy, ferrying goods to the nearby port of Tangiers.

This part, though, had only old, abandoned train cars that had been left to rust.

As Abdul had expected, nobody else was within view.

"I am Abdul," he replied. "Your name?"

"Saad," the man replied curtly.

Abdul nodded. Saad matched the description he'd been given. Short, dark-haired, with a pockmarked face.

"I have your payment here. As agreed, half now, and half on delivery in Paris. Also in the package is a cell phone. I will call with instructions once the truck arrives in Tangiers," Abdul said.

Saad shook his head abruptly. "No. I've been offered another job, so I'll need more to do yours instead."

Abdul nodded as though the request were completely reasonable. "Very well, how much do you want?"

"Double," Saad replied.

Abdul had dealt with greedy men before. Saad had calculated that Abdul had no time to find a replacement, and so would pay more.

That was fine. Abdul had even correctly guessed the amount Saad would demand.

Yes, Abdul even had a second pay packet ready in his left jacket pocket.

But there was still a problem.

The glint in Saad's eye that said double wouldn't be enough. No, Saad wanted even more.

How would he get it?

Offhand, Abdul could think of two possibilities. Delivering the truck and its cargo to someone willing to pay more for them than Abdul. Or tipping off the authorities in return for a reward.

Or some other scheme that hadn't occurred to Abdul.

Abdul didn't have the time or the knowledge of Saad's background necessary to find out for sure.

Abdul's instincts, though, told him that his mission would fail if he had Saad drive the truck after it arrived in Tangier.

Long experience kept all these thoughts off Abdul's face.

Aloud, he said, "Agreed. Here's the packet with the payment. I have to get the extra money from my car."

Then Abdul tossed the packet to Saad. He made sure to throw it a bit short.

Saad lunged forward and nearly caught it. But not quite.

The packet hit the ground at Saad's feet and opened. There wasn't much of a breeze, but a few Moroccan dirham notes still fluttered away.

Cursing, Saad snatched at the currency. Abdul said, "Sorry, let me help you."

Saad's attention was firmly focused on retrieving his money when Abdul took out his knife.

Minutes later, Abdul's mission was back on track.

Saad's body was safely out of sight under one of the nearby abandoned train cars. There had been no witnesses, and Saad hadn't been able to cry out for help.

Abdul had used a knife because it made no sound. Not for the first time, he congratulated himself on that choice.

He would offer the job of getting the truck from Tangier to Paris to Samir Ali. If he refused, then Abdul would drive the truck himself.

That would be a last resort, though. Abdul didn't know what would happen when the truck's cargo reached Paris.

He had no interest in learning the answer to that question.

The money was back in Abdul's jacket. Well, most of it, anyway.

Abdul always carried a small plastic bag wadded up in one of his pant pockets. It often came in handy.

Like now. Blood had stained several of the Moroccan dirham notes.

That was OK. These were dirhams printed recently on a high-quality paper-polymer-paper composite substrate called Durasafe.

The blood would wash right off.

CHAPTER EIGHT

Zouj Beghal
Algerian/Moroccan Border

As his truck idled in the long line of vehicles waiting to cross the border, Samir Ali's thoughts couldn't help but wander.

First, he realized that he remembered the name of this place. Zouj Beghal literally meant "two mules." The story went that two mules had been harnessed and forced to keep moving until they had marked the entire border between Algeria and Morocco.

Ali didn't know much about mules. But keeping a couple of them moving for about two thousand kilometers seemed unlikely.

But who knew? Ali had seen many strange things over his long life, so maybe the story was true.

From the 1960s to the 1990s, Zouj Beghal was closed most of the time after a border conflict between Morocco and Algeria in 1963, which was called the "Sand War."

After years of intermittent closures, Morocco had last sealed the border in 1994. In part because of Algeria's continued support of separatists in the formerly Spanish territory of Western Sahara, that Morocco had seized in 1976. Also, Morocco had blamed Algeria for a bombing in Marrakech in 1994.

After over thirty years, Morocco had finally announced that just one border crossing spot would be reopened.

Zouj Beghal.

It was no coincidence that Zouj Beghal was only about fourteen kilometers from Oujda, a Moroccan city of about 700,000 inhabitants. That made it by far the largest city in the area.

In theory, Algeria's gross domestic product per person was about 4,300 American dollars. That made the average Algerian roughly a thousand dollars per year wealthier than the average Moroccan.

In theory.

But as everyone did in North Africa, Ali knew that the reality was far different.

Whenever the border between Morocco and Algeria opened, far more traffic went westward to Morocco than the reverse. That was because many more consumer goods were available on the Moroccan side at much better prices.

In part, this was because decades before, Morocco had struck deals with several European countries, such as France, to produce goods under license rather than import them. Starting out with items like disposable razors and diapers, over the years, Morocco had moved onto higher-value items such as vehicles.

Now, Morocco exported about fifteen billion dollars' worth of vehicles to Europe annually and several billion dollars' worth of aircraft parts.

All that on top of twelve billion dollars in traditional phosphate, clothing and agricultural exports from Morocco to Europe.

In short, Moroccan goods transported by trucks and ships to Europe exceeded the value of exports from either Algeria or Tunisia.

That was particularly true because much Algerian natural gas was transported by pipeline to Spain.

That meant Madi's company was not interested in shipping from Tunisia or Algeria to Europe but did for the much larger and faster-growing exports from Morocco.

Ali was about to find out why that mattered.

As the Moroccan lieutenant approached his truck, Ali's eyes went automatically to the name stenciled on his uniform. "Berrada."

Before Ali could say anything, Berrada barked, "Papers," and thrust his arm forward.

He looked annoyed and anything but friendly.

Ali silently handed over his transport documents and passport.

Berrada waved at the men in his squad, and in seconds, they swarmed over Ali's cargo. Accompanied by dogs.

Well, Ali thought, dogs had checked his cargo before and found nothing.

Yes, a voice in his head whispered. But maybe dogs trained only in detecting drugs. And for all he knew, these had also been trained to find explosives.

Shut up, Ali told the voice. I've hit plenty of potholes on the hundreds of kilometers I've driven with this cargo.

And I'm still here.

Ali had a story planned and a "gift" to give Berrada but never had a chance to use either one.

Berrada had been looking at a clipboard while his men worked and now looked from it to the documents Ali had just handed over.

Ali could see a flash of recognition cross Berrada's face, and his breath caught in his throat.

Was there an alert for Ali's truck?

Berrada waved again at his men, and a Sergeant trotted up to him in seconds.

"Anything?" Berrada asked.

"No, sir," the Sergeant said.

Berrada nodded and said, "We need to get this line moving, or we're going to spend the night here again."

The Sergeant nodded and smiled. "Now that you mention it, sir, I wouldn't mind seeing my wife."

Berrada handed Ali's papers back to him and jerked his thumb westward. "Get a move on," he said.

"Yes, sir," Ali replied, wasting no time obeying the order.

As he sent a prayer of thanks heavenward.

In truth, it was Madi he had to thank. His company paid officers like Berrada well to expedite particular vehicles.

That didn't mean drugs, explosives, or contraband would be allowed into Morocco. And if any had been detected, officers like Berrada would have quickly stopped accepting payments.

No, their military careers were worth more to them than foreign bribes.

Not to mention the prospect of a highly unpleasant stay in a military prison. From which they were unlikely to emerge alive.

But hurrying through a legitimate shipment? Payment to get things moving more quickly was a bedrock part of Moroccan society and had been for centuries.

Today, it had been a godsend to one Samir Ali.

CHAPTER NINE

Tanger Med Special Agency Headquarters
Tangier, Morocco

Tareq frowned as he looked at the sign for the Port Authority Head-quarters. Then he remembered that in the English he was used to thinking in outside France, the city was called Tangier.

In Morocco, the name was spelled Tanger.

Even more confusing was that the National Ports Authority was headquartered, naturally, in Morocco's largest port, Casablanca, which also happened to be the largest artificial harbor in the world and one of the largest ports on the African continent.

So why was he here? Because the Tanger Med "Special Agency" con-trolled over thirty ports on Morocco's Mediterranean coast. That in-cluded Tangier's Roll-On/Roll-Off (RO/RO) port, which handled over half a million trucks from Morocco to Europe annually. Which was the port where their "special cargo" would be transported.

Or not, depending on Tareq's success with this meeting.

Madi had just learned and passed on to Tareq that a revived European Union project called COSMIC could derail their plans. COSMIC in-volved installing sensors to detect Chemical, Biological, Radiological, Nuclear, and Explosive (CBRNE) weapons passing through EU ports.

COSMIC had run as a pilot project from 2018 to 2021, and the EU had declared it a success. Much to Tareq's annoyance, COSMIC had been directed by an Israeli company. However, he couldn't argue with Madi's observation.

Chemical and explosive weapons had repeatedly targeted Israel. Unsurprisingly, it had developed the best commercially available detection technology.

However, for years after 2021, little was done to follow up on COSMIC until just a few months ago.

Improved detection technology had been installed at many EU ports and at several North African ports, including Tunis, Algiers, and Cairo.

And Tangier.

Fortunately, not all EU ports had the new detection equipment. Madi had identified an EU port without coverage with daily RO/RO ship arrivals from Tangier.

But that still left Tangier itself.

Nassar Alaoui was Deputy Director of the Tanger Med Special Agency. Tareq had objected when Madi scheduled the meeting with Nassar. Why not go straight to the Director?

Madi had smiled and told Tareq, "he'd understand."

Well, now Tareq was being ushered into Nassar's office. Madi always seemed to know what he was doing.

Time to see if that was still true.

"Thank you for taking the time to see me, sir," Tareq said as one of Nassar's assistants brought both the men tea.

Traditional Moroccan tea. A caffeine-heavy gunpowder tea, given sharp flavor by adding fresh mint leaves.

Nobody ever asked if you wanted sugar. You did, and that's all there was to it.

The only difference in this office setting was that Tareq received a medium-sized glass with all the ingredients already present.

No ceremony with the tea being poured into the glass from a height. Which Moroccans would insist improved the flavor.

The message was simple. Nassar wasn't rude. Tareq would get his tea as a welcome visitor.

But Nassar was a busy man. Best Tareq come straight to the point.

"You are most welcome," Nassar replied. "I understand you represent an important French shipping company, one of our best customers. What can I do to help?"

"Actually, sir, I'm here for two reasons," Tareq replied. "The first is a bit embarrassing. We made a mistake in routing a truck shipment to Europe, and so it's behind schedule. The shipment is for one of our oldest clients, and the delay could derail an important project. We would appreciate anything you could do to get it on a RO-RO today."

Nassar frowned and repeated, "Today." Then he paused.

"I don't know if you've heard that we've just started a new screening procedure for all shipments bound for EU ports. I'm afraid it will take too long to make shipment today possible," Nassar said.

"I understand," Tareq said. "All we can ask is that you do your best."

"Of course," Nassar replied. "Please give the details to my assistant, and we'll do all we can to help."

A raised eyebrow told Tareq that Nassar had expected a visitor all the way from France to do more to press the request.

But Nassar wasn't going to question an easy win.

Taking a sip of his tea, Nassar asked casually, "And the second request?"

"This one comes from Director Madi himself," Tareq said. "He would like to offer you a position with the Société Générale de Transport International, with responsibilities similar to the ones you have now. Of course, the salary would be considerably higher than your present compensation, to account for the greater cost of living at our Paris headquarters."

Tareq saw with satisfaction that Nassar nearly choked on his tea but recovered just in time.

"How much higher?" Nassar asked cautiously.

Tareq shrugged. "The pay package would be subject to negotiation.

Of course, your move would be covered. Permanent visas for you, your family, and any domestic employees you wish to accompany you. Full medical coverage. Annual trips to visit family in Morocco. We also have an office to help you identify and purchase suitable housing in Paris. As for the salary, as a starting point, I'd say you should ask for triple what you're getting now. Don't settle for less than double."

Thoughts were racing through Nassar's head at breakneck speed, and Tareq had to bite down hard not to laugh.

Nassar could hardly be blamed for having trouble concealing his glee at this unexpected windfall.

Tareq reached into the slim attaché case he had brought and extracted a folder, which he handed Nassar.

"You will find all the details and contact information for our personnel department here. Please get in touch with them as soon as possible, if you are interested," Tareq said.

"Yes, yes, of course," Nassar said distractedly, his eyes already on the documents.

"Well, then, I won't take any more of your time," Tareq said, and reached one more time into his case, removing a single sheet of paper. "I'll just leave the shipment details with your assistant."

Tareq stood and started walking to the door. One, two, three...

"Wait!" Nassar said.

It took a real effort of will for Tareq to remove the smile from his face before he turned around.

"Yes?" Tareq asked, doing his best to look puzzled.

"Give me the shipment details," Nassar said. "You may tell Director Madi his shipment will be on its way later today."

"I'm sure he will be happy to hear that, sir. I hope to have the pleasure of seeing you soon in Paris," Tariq said.

As he left Nassar's office, Tareq permitted himself a small, rueful smile.

Yes. Once again, Madi had proved that he knew what he was doing.

Tareq was looking forward to returning to Paris but still had trouble believing how that would happen by this evening.

When Tareq had researched flights from Tangier, he hadn't been surprised to find that all three left early in the morning. So, at first, he'd been resigned to spending the night in Tangier.

Then Tareq learned that he could travel the 323-kilometer distance from Tangier to Casablanca in a little over two hours on a high-speed train called Al Boraq, which would get him to Casablanca's Mohamed V Airport in plenty of time for this evening's nonstop flight to Paris.

Which was why a car quickly summoned by Nassar's assistant was now taking Tareq to the train station in Tangier.

Tareq had made the exact same trip by train before, and it had taken nearly five hours, so he took the time to do some research.

Al Boraq started service in 2018 and ran every two hours in both directions, using locomotives and technology provided by...the French.

OK, that made sense. The French had been operating high-speed trains for nearly half a century, and Tareq had used them many times.

But high-speed trains in Africa?

A little more checking on Tareq's phone confirmed that Al Boraq was the first and so far only high-speed train operating in Africa.

Another thought made Tareq smile, and the Internet only took seconds to confirm his guess.

The fastest American train, Acela, reached speeds on their East Coast of up to 241 kilometers per hour.

Al Boraq went 320 kilometers per hour on over half of its route.

The Moroccans had a higher-speed train than the Americans!

Well, Tareq thought with a smile, it looked like the West wasn't always superior after all.

And after the blow Madi was going to direct on Paris, that lesson would be even more clear.

CHAPTER TEN

DGSE Safehouse
Paris, France

"I don't like this," Henri said flatly.

Captain Giraud looked up from the papers he had been reading and asked mildly, "What don't you like, exactly?"

Henri scowled and replied, "I didn't join the DGSE to sit and turn my thumbs around."

At least, that's what Grishkov thought Henri had said. Though his French continued to improve, it still wasn't as good as his English, which was fluent. Since English and French had much more in common than Russian and French, he tended to translate what he heard into English.

Then Grishkov realized that "se tourner les pouces" in French actually meant "twiddle your thumbs" in English. And shook his head.

Expressions. Always the hardest part of learning a foreign language. Grishkov knew he couldn't complain too much since Russian had plenty of them too.

"Well, if you have any ideas for how we could spend our time more constructively, you have my full attention," Giraud said. "Felix here has been promised a lab report on the samples he collected in Libya later today. Once he gets it, it may give us a lead we can follow."

Grishkov had noticed that Felix went out of his way to keep his mouth shut. It was one of several traits he'd seen and approved in the German-born French Foreign Legion Sergeant.

Felix, true to form, said nothing.

But Grishkov was not the only one to guess that Felix was, in fact, thinking about their situation.

"Anything to share, Sergeant?" Giraud asked Felix.

Felix took several moments to consider his response.

Again, Grishkov approved. The four of them represented the best chance to stop whatever attack was being planned on Paris.

Careful thought was warranted.

Finally, Felix said, "The lab report will probably be able to tell us whether we're dealing with a nuclear weapon, and if so, what type. Principally, plutonium or uranium-based. They may also be able to tell us where the radioactive materials originated. But what we really need is help tracking the device. There, I doubt the lab report will do us much good."

Giraud frowned. "Are you sure?" he asked. "I thought our military had instruments capable of detecting radioactivity from a considerable distance."

Felix nodded. "That is true. But we must assume the weapon's shielding would significantly cut its radiation signature. By how much? Impossible to say. But I am not optimistic."

Giraud opened his mouth to speak but was interrupted by an insistent buzz from his secure cell phone.

"Giraud here," he said into the phone.

That was followed by, "Yes, he is here."

Now, Giraud began writing notes on a small pad.

"Évreux-Fauville Air Base. Yes. Understood."

Giraud put his phone back in his pocket and looked at Grishkov.

"You are going to Évreux-Fauville Air Base. Immediately. The car you requested is outside. Good luck," Giraud said.

Moments later, Grishkov was gone.

"What's that all about?" Henri asked incredulously. "I know that base. It has planes for two missions, transport, and intelligence collection. How is it that our new Russian team member is the only one who goes there?"

Giraud looked thoughtful. "I was not told. Which does not mean I am not asking myself the same question. Even more, why was I told specifically to send Grishkov on his own?"

"Something is wrong here!" Henri exclaimed. "First, we're delayed just long enough to miss finding the weapon in Libya and then nearly blown up when we do get there. Now, Grishkov is sent to drive a hundred kilometers by himself. Why?"

Felix looked like he'd just bitten into something unpleasant.

"He's right," Felix said to Giraud, who nodded.

"I agree with you both," Giraud said. "I'd already decided we would be following Grishkov at a discreet distance. If this goes wrong and you're asked, you had no idea I was ordered to send Grishkov without escort."

Henri and Felix nodded, and moments later, they were on the road, heading west after Grishkov.

"How much of a lead does he have?" Henri asked.

Felix tapped the center LCD screen, and a blinking red dot appeared on the display. Henri grunted and answered his own question.

"Some distance," Henri said. "If he's attacked on the way, he'll be alone."

Felix shrugged. "Well, we're in a Peugeot 508 Sport. Maybe we can catch up in time if we push it hard."

Henri frowned. "Yes, I'm familiar with the model. About three hundred fifty horsepower and a hybrid gas/electric powertrain that delivers excellent performance. And large enough to accommodate the whole team and its gear. But what vehicle did Grishkov request? Is it even faster?"

Giraud grinned. "I think we have nothing to worry about there. He asked for a Clio."

For once, Giraud was satisfied to see that Henri was speechless.

CHAPTER ELEVEN

En Route to Évreux-Fauville Air Base
France

Anatoly Grishkov had seen Captain Giraud's surprise when he had requested a Renault Clio as his official car while with the DGSE. What the French called a "supermini," the Clio was the opposite of impressive by any measure.

Yet, for Grishkov, it was the only choice that made sense.

First, Renault had produced over sixteen million Clios since 1990, making them so common they were practically invisible.

Second, it was the only French car Grishkov knew inside and out. Before the Ukraine invasion, Renault had a factory in Russia that made Clios, and it was one of the few cars Grishkov could afford on an - honest - Russian policeman's salary.

Most importantly, though, Grishkov knew any highway opponent would underestimate his Clio.

Indeed, the Clio's engine was unimpressive, delivering under 100 horsepower. But that engine had to move a much smaller and lighter mass than sedans with more muscle.

The Clio's power-to-weight ratio made it surprisingly nimble. Especially if, like Grishkov, you were old enough to know how to drive a car with a manual transmission.

And the Clio was one of a shrinking number of cars to still have a manual transmission available.

When he started the engine, Grishkov's DGSE cell phone automatically paired with the Clio's audio system, which made him smile.

The Clio's body and engine might not have changed much from the one he'd owned in Russia, but the technology inside certainly had. There was even a built-in GPS guidance system and a rear-view camera display.

To Grishkov's surprise, his DGSE cell phone rang, and an unfamiliar voice came over the Clio's audio system.

"This is Agent Grishkov?" the voice asked.

Grishkov thought for a moment and then shrugged.

Who else but the DGSE could have his number?

"Yes," Grishkov replied.

"The route on your vehicle's GPS has been updated. To avoid observation, you are to enter Évreux-Fauville Air Base via the back gate. The guards there will be expecting you. Please confirm that your GPS has received the new route," the voice said.

Grishkov glanced at the GPS screen. Sure enough, it now said to pull off at the next exit rather than continue straight on the N12 highway.

"I have received the new route," Grishkov replied.

"Good," the voice said. "Advise no one that your route has changed for security reasons. Again, the air base guards have been advised to expect you at the rear gate."

Whoever it was hung up.

Well, this was interesting, Grishkov thought.

Three choices.

Continue driving straight down the N12.

Try to reach Captain Giraud and ask him whether to follow the new route.

Obey the new orders.

Here comes the exit. Only seconds to decide.

Grishkov took the exit.

If asked, Grishkov planned to say he had simply been following orders.

But long experience told him this was almost certainly a trap.

Right now, they needed something to work with. Grishkov had believed Felix when he'd said the lab report would probably tell them little.

And aerial surveillance, which Grishkov presumed was why he was headed to an air base?

Grishkov doubted that would work, either.

But if he could get his hands on some of the people behind this attack? With at least one, preferably, still alive and able to talk?

Well, then they might get somewhere.

Grishkov slowed quite a bit as he took the exit since this would be a likely ambush site.

Nothing amiss. But there was a gas station.

Good.

Grishkov eased the Clio next to the air compressor at the back and took stock. Of course, he had his 9mm pistol.

But if the sensor box trap in Libya were any indication, a pistol would do little to save him from what was coming.

The Clio was a hatchback, and its little storage space was at the rear. Grishkov carefully positioned his body to conceal what he expected to find inside.

He was not disappointed. As he had asked Giraud, several cases held everything Grishkov had requested.

First, a FAMAS G2 dating back to the 1990s. Grishkov had used one of the original FAMAS semiautomatic rifles before after it was taken off the body of a dead Chechen terrorist. FAMAS was a bullpup rifle that managed to be short overall by placing the action and magazine behind the trigger. That meant the gun was still relatively compact, even with the long barrel needed for accuracy.

The G2 used NATO standard 30-round magazines holding either the old M193 rounds or what Grishkov had requested.

The newer NATO SS109 armor-piercing rounds.

Two APAV 40s, a 40 mm rifle grenade effective against both personnel and vehicles, were also present. Each weighed less than half a kilogram, even with a tail featuring stabilizing fins.

The APAV 40 was lethal to exposed personnel up to a twelve-meter radius, and its shrapnel was dangerous to anyone within one hundred meters.

Against vehicles, at a direct angle of attack, the APAV 40 could penetrate up to a hundred millimeters of armor.

This was fortunate, since the professionals Grishkov was expecting could be counted on to have vehicles with at least some reinforcement.

Now came the Clio's main disadvantage. It was small. That meant Grishkov had to make some choices since it would be impossible to fit all these armaments in the seat next to him.

It didn't take Grishkov long to decide. The G2, three 30-round magazines, and one APAV 40 went next to him. The rest Grishkov positioned in the back where, he hoped, he could reach them if needed.

Though the truth was, Grishkov thought darkly, that if he needed more, he'd probably be dead already.

The only items Grishkov put in his combat vest pockets were the ones Felix had recommended. Giraud hadn't been particularly pleased to supply them but had to agree they were the best choice for this mission.

The DM51 was a German hand grenade known to Felix from his service in the Bundeswehr before he had joined the French Foreign Legion. It came as a standard fragmentation grenade weighing about half a kilo, and Grishkov thought carrying one wouldn't slow him down much.

But two? Not with everything else he had to carry.

Felix, though, had pointed out that the DM51 offered a solution. The fragmentation body could be easily removed to leave just the explosives and fuse, weighing only one hundred fifty grams.

That, Grishkov could handle.

Then Grishkov shook his head. Positive thinking. Just as important now as when he'd been a soldier in Chechnya fighting terrorists, and a detective in Vladivostok taking on organized crime.

Yes, back then, he'd rarely been alone. Even in the FSB, he'd usually had a partner.

And when you separated from him in Ukraine, you were nearly killed, a stubborn voice inside his head observed.

Grishkov shook his head again. This time, the lives of his two sons were at stake.

That motivation more than compensated for any lack of backup.

As Smyslov had suggested, Grishkov had told his sons to join their mother well out of the danger zone. But of course, he couldn't say why, just that their mother needed them.

To Grishkov's chagrin, Sasha and Mischa had not blindly followed his orders. Instead, they had called their mother Arisha.

Who, of course, said that they should stay right where they were in Paris and complete their studies. And that, no, she didn't need any help.

A voicemail from Sasha told Grishkov all this and asked for "clarification."

Much worse, Grishkov now had several calls to answer from Arisha.

On the whole, Grishkov thought with a wry smile, it may be easier to face this ambush.

Grishkov looked around. No one in sight.

Minutes later, the weapons Grishkov needed were ready to hand, and he resumed the route recommended by the GPS.

Grishkov had to acknowledge that even secondary roads in France were in better shape than many major highways in Russia. Especially after you left major cities and their suburbs.

But though it was well paved and marked, one thing above all marked it as "secondary."

It had little traffic. Grishkov drove several kilometers at a time without encountering any vehicles on the other side of the road.

Grishkov was deliberately going at the speed limit for two reasons. First, he would doubtless face uncomfortable questions from any highway patrolman stopping him for speeding about the items sitting next to him in the Clio.

More importantly, though, Grishkov wanted plenty of time to see what was ahead.

On the N12 highway, Grishkov had driven about ten kilometers an hour over the speed limit. Yet, the other drivers had passed him as though he were standing still.

And several had made gestures while passing that Grishkov took to mean they considered his speed...unacceptable.

Yet not a single driver had passed him on this road. Strangely, with every passing kilometer, it seemed emptier and emptier.

Then Grishkov nodded. This road was supposed to lead directly to the air base's rear gate. One that he imagined usually saw very little use.

Grishkov knew that Western military bases were often sited in rural areas with relatively low populations to avoid collateral damage in the event of war. It seemed that was true here.

But if an ambush were ahead, they would have to strike before he was within sight of the base. Otherwise, the gate guards might hear the attack and report it to the local police.

There!

Grishkov smiled to himself. Bushes on the side of the road mostly concealed the low sedan. Easy to miss.

Unless your life had depended on spotting far better concealment efforts by Chechen terrorists. Over a period of many months.

The Russian soldiers who weren't as good as Grishkov were all dead.

And Grishkov still remembered that hard-earned knowledge.

Grishkov only had seconds to react.

He waited until he was nearly level with the lurking sedan.

Then Grishkov shifted gears, braked, and spun the Clio in a maneuver that a larger car could have never managed.

Even before the Clio had come to a full stop, Grishkov had exited, FAMAS G2 in one hand and rifle grenade in the other.

The sedan's doors had just begun to open, a move Grishkov discouraged by emptying one 30-round clip from the G2.

The doors closed again. Grishkov was disappointed, but not surprised, to see that even armor-piercing rounds had done little damage to the sedan.

Professionals. Or at least professionally equipped.

The revving of the sedan's engine revised Grishkov's opinion of his opponents upwards.

Why risk exiting into the G2's fire, when the sedan itself could be used as a weapon?

Grishkov was totally exposed. There was no time to jump back into the Clio and escape.

The Clio had no hope of outrunning the sedan, and its thin metal walls would also provide little protection.

No. Grishkov had only one option.

But did he have time?

Grishkov had drilled fitting a grenade to a rifle many times with many different weapons. He'd even used them in combat.

But never an APAV 40 attached to a G2.

It didn't matter. In seconds, the grenade was ready to fire.

Which was fortunate because the sedan was starting to move.

Quickly. And right at him.

Grishkov pulled the trigger. He aimed for the sedan's front grill, hoping reinforcement would be low there.

From the result, it appeared that the amount of armor there was nonexistent instead of low.

The grenade exploded as designed about a second after impact.

The sedan's front end disintegrated.

Then, a massive secondary detonation told Grishkov that he hadn't been the only one carrying explosives.

Yet Grishkov's problems weren't over. The sedan's occupants were no longer a danger.

But the sedan certainly was.

Its tumbling, flaming remains were still headed straight for Grishkov.

Snarling a curse, Grishkov darted out of the path of the oncoming wreckage.

Though he could feel the heat from its flames, Grishkov still escaped without injury.

Not that Grishkov was pleased.

Far from it.

The state of the wreckage made it clear there would be no survivors to question.

Grishkov was still in motion, his head swiveling from side to side as he sought cover.

Movement!

Grishkov dove for the questionable safety of several roadside bushes as several rounds spanged off the asphalt nearby.

Whoever it was, they were ahead of where the sedan had been lurking. Probably planning to shoot at Grishkov's car as it passed.

The sedan had been there as a backup in case they missed.

Well, they had indeed missed so far. But the morning was still young, Grishkov thought.

How many were there?

Using a trick Grishkov thought had probably first been invented by someone living in a cave, he lobbed a rock into some bushes about five meters away.

Being careful to keep his throwing arm from view.

Grishkov was rewarded by semiautomatic rifle fire from a single location.

But from two different weapons.

Fortunately, directed at the branches swaying from their encounter with his rock.

Grishkov would know the distinctive sound made by an AK-74 Kalashnikov anywhere. With over seventy million produced, finding one in use here was no surprise.

The other rifle was very bad news. A Heckler & Koch HK417, in much more limited production at a far higher cost. Ordinarily available only to Western militaries, it was normally provided only to the best marksman in a squad.

The fact that he was still breathing suggested to Grishkov that the rifle had been stolen. And that its current user was no marksman.

Plus, their foolish decision to stay together.

Time to act before they realized their mistake.

First, the DM51 without the fragmentation jacket to flush them from cover. The other with the fragmentation jacket would follow if Grishkov saw movement after the first impact.

Have to hurry before they move.

Grishkov had never thrown such a light grenade. Would it have any effect?

Grishkov realized he'd made a foolish error as he felt the explosion in his bones.

It was possible to doubt German competence in certain areas, like fine wine and cuisine.

Not when it came to manufacturing weapons.

A scream told Grishkov he'd scored at least one hit. Movement near the source of the sound gave him hope that the two attackers had stayed together.

The second DM51 was in the air before Grishkov had even finished the thought.

Grishkov hugged the ground. He knew that at this range, fragments might hit him, too.

As several whistled overhead, Grishkov tried to press himself into the earth even harder.

Unbidden, the image came to Grishkov of an American cartoon he'd seen, drawn in the Second World War. In it, a soldier doing exactly what he was had told another, "I can't get any lower. My buttons are in the way."

Silence. Grishkov cautiously took stock.

He appeared to have escaped without injury.

No movement.

Grishkov waited.

Still nothing.

Well, he thought, they might have called for reinforcements. Time to see if there's anyone left to question.

One look at the two bodies told Grishkov the answer was no.

However, unlike the charred remains in the sedan, these men had at least wallets and one cell phone that might contain helpful intelligence.

Of course, if they had been true professionals, their cell phones would have been burners with no GPS and no call history, and their wallets would contain nothing but fake IDs.

But their poor performance told Grishkov there might still be something here.

He certainly hoped so.

It would have been a shame to deliberately walk into an ambush for nothing.

CHAPTER TWELVE

En Route to Évreux-Fauville Air Base
France

Captain Giraud frowned as they approached the scene Grishkov had left behind just minutes before.

"According to his GPS signal Grishkov has already reached the air base. We need to gather any leads we can from whoever tried to stop him," Giraud said as their sedan slowed to a stop.

Felix and Henri nodded, and they all fanned out with weapons in hand.

No movement they could see.

They'd seen the smoke from the still-burning sedan well before they arrived. It took no more than a glance to confirm there was no point to looking through its remains.

The two bodies riddled with grenade shrapnel offered no better prospects.

But two motorcycles hidden behind some bushes not far from the bodies provided more reason for hope.

"Henri! Come help me with these," Felix said as he examined one of them.

Henri bent down and returned, holding a small black plastic item.

"A GPS," Henri said. "It looks like one custom-designed to be used on a motorcycle."

Felix nodded and held up an identical GPS from the second motorcycle.

Giraud walked up to them and said, "Good. Let's hope they're in better shape than their owners. We'd better take them and go before the police arrive. Someone will have reported seeing the smoke."

Moments later, they were headed for the N12 highway, and back on the road to Paris.

"So, we have no idea why Grishkov used this back road to go to the air base?" Henri asked.

"No," Giraud said tersely, his eyes fixed on the road ahead.

"Well, at least he's still alive, so we can ask him when he returns," Henri said.

Giraud frowned but then slowly nodded.

"Yes," he said. "I have many questions that need answers. And I'd better like the ones I hear."

CHAPTER THIRTEEN

Évreux-Fauville Air Base
France

Grishkov looked curiously at the guard standing next to the rear gate. If his memory of French rank badges was accurate, a corporal.

The guard was armed with a Glock 17 pistol and an HK416 F assault rifle. An Austrian pistol and a German rifle, Grishkov mused.

Then he looked past the guard.

An armored personnel carrier idled nearby, which Grishkov recognized as the most recent VCI model. Its turret moved, just slightly, in Grishkov's direction.

As if to say, yes, we are paying attention.

The VCI was French and, in fact, manufactured by a Renault subsidiary. The same company that made the Clio he was now driving.

They could hardly have been more different, Grishkov thought.

The VCI had a 25mm autocannon and a co-axial 7.62 mm machine gun. It was difficult to imagine any terrorists forcing their way onto the base past this beast, Grishkov thought.

I wonder if it's always parked here?

"Papers, please," the guard said pleasantly, stretching his right hand forward.

Grishkov silently handed the guard his DGSE ID and his orders authorizing entry to the base.

Would the guard say anything about the state of his vehicle? Grishkov had seen at least two bullet holes and several pieces of shrapnel embedded in the Clio, though thankfully, the tires had remained unscathed.

The guard scrutinized his ID and orders, comparing the ID photo to the man before him.

Then Grishkov noticed movement in the guard shack behind the corporal. The thick and heavily tinted glass made it difficult to see inside.

No doubt deliberately so, Grishkov thought.

Then he noticed a firing slit in the side of the shack. That now had the barrel of a rifle poking out and aimed directly at Grishkov.

Excellent, Grishkov thought. Whoever's in there isn't trusting the armor commander to keep his fellow soldier safe.

As it should be.

The guard completed his examination of Grishkov's ID and orders and returned them.

Then he cocked one eyebrow and said, "I see you ran into some weather on the way here. Any chance it will come our way?"

Grishkov shook his head and replied, "No, I don't think so."

The guard nodded. "Good. The hangar you want is straight ahead, about a kilometer from here. Another of these will be parked nearby, so you can't miss it."

With that, the guard gestured toward the nearby armored personnel carrier.

Grishkov nodded and put the Clio in gear. As he drove off, Grishkov revised his opinion of French security upward.

At least, their military security.

As the guard had said, another VCI armored personnel carrier stood idling next to the hangar.

When Grishkov exited the Clio, he saw another similarity. Just as before, the APC's turret moved slightly in his direction.

Yes. Occupied and alert.

Grishkov got the message.

This time, there was no guard Grishkov could see. He was confident, though, that the one he had just encountered had radioed ahead Grishkov's description. Both for himself, and for his vehicle.

And if he hadn't, Grishkov was sure his reception at the hangar would have been quite different.

The front of the hangar, which any aircraft inside would use to exit, was firmly shut. But a pedestrian door on the side was hanging slightly ajar.

Grishkov didn't hesitate and walked straight in.

The first thing he saw was exactly what he'd hoped for: an Okhotnik drone. Its twenty-meter wingspan made it hard to miss, Grishkov thought.

The drone had performed well on a previous mission for Grishkov's team, and he had been impressed with its capabilities. A range of up to six thousand kilometers meant it could stay airborne long enough to give them some hope of spotting their target.

Smyslov had come through again, Grishkov thought.

Now, let's hope whoever was sent with the Okhotnik knows their business.

No sooner had Grishkov completed that thought than he saw someone on the other side of the drone. He was bent down, and was examining what Grishkov thought might be the sensor package the Okhotnik would use to detect radiation.

Well, this was the only person Grishkov could see in the hangar. So, it must be who he was here to meet.

Grishkov had only crossed half the distance to the drone when the man stood up and said sternly, "Well, I see that my request for high security has been completely ignored! They're letting anyone wander in!"

Grishkov suddenly stopped as the familiar voice registered, and his eyes focused on the man's face.

Mikhail Vasilyev! His partner on many previous missions for the FSB.

They had saved each other's lives so often that Grishkov had lost count.

But why was he here?

Grishkov crossed the remaining distance in a few strides and shortly had Vasilyev in a tight grip, pounding his back as Grishkov said, "It's good to see you, my friend."

Vasilyev grunted and said, "I see you've lost nothing of your strength despite your advanced years. But I hope you remember how our last mission ended."

Grishkov immediately released him and looked at Vasilyev with concern. "Yes, of course! I heard you were recovering from your injuries, but it would take some time. It's why you were the last person I expected to see here!"

Vasilyev nodded. "I'm recovered enough for desk work or, as you can see, international travel. I'm not yet cleared for active missions abroad, though I hope more physical therapy will make that possible. I'm sure, though, that you're wondering why Director Kharlov chose me for this mission."

"Probably because he knew I'd believe whatever you tell me. Even more than I would from Smyslov," Grishkov said thoughtfully.

"Correct," Vasilyev replied with a smile. "And what I have to tell you will indeed be difficult to believe."

Grishkov frowned. "Really? We both saw this drone in action before. We know it's highly capable of detecting radioactivity from a distance. Doesn't this drone do that?"

"It does," Vasilyev replied. "But it does something else as well."

Then he paused and added solemnly, "It reads minds."

Grishkov's reaction was exactly what Vasilyev had expected.

Well, maybe his language was more colorful than even Vasilyev had foreseen.

Finally, Grishkov collected himself. "OK, so you've had your fun with me. Now, what else does it do, really?"

Vasilyev raised one eyebrow and asked, "Have you heard about research done in many countries about helping those otherwise unable to communicate? By implanting one or more electrodes in their brain?"

Grishkov slowly nodded.

"Good," Vasilyev said. "Now, you probably haven't heard about research done in Australia, first by their military in 2023. They developed the capability to use signals collected from a helmet worn by a soldier to control a robot remotely. That was then able to act as a scout for a combat platoon."

Grishkov snorted. "Sure they did. Well, I can type up any fantasy I like and claim it's true."

"Well, yes," Vasilyev said with a smile. "But they released a video online showing exactly what I just described."

"So what?" Grishkov replied. "Movies have shown all sorts of incredible things over the years. It hardly makes them true."

Vasilyev nodded patiently. "Next, Australian researchers showed that collecting and decoding speech from a person wearing a skullcap was possible. Without implanting an electrode."

"Speech. With what level of accuracy?" Grishkov asked.

"Initially, about forty percent," Vasilyev replied. "But that number has since improved. Kharlov saw the technology's potential and made obtaining it a top FSB priority."

Grishkov slowly nodded. "Yes. I can see its value for interrogating a suspect. But what does any of that have to do with this drone?"

"Well, with any technology, once you've established that something is possible, further advances will come naturally. The first heavier-than-air flight lasted only seconds and covered less than three hundred meters. But it led directly to flights that can now take a person literally anywhere on the planet," Vasilyev said.

"So, the skullcap is outside the brain but very close to it. Are you saying that reading a person's thoughts from a greater distance later proved possible?" Grishkov asked.

"Exactly!" Vasilyev exclaimed, obviously pleased. "We obtained the initial research from the Australians, but since then have been able to take it much farther."

"I presume we stole the technology? Surely, the Australians didn't part with it willingly," Grishkov said.

Vasilyev shrugged. "You might say we stole it. We simply found an Australian researcher willing to accept a substantial sum in return for the technology's key data. All done online, with payment in crypto-currency."

"The researcher didn't have much time to enjoy his newfound wealth, I'm guessing," Grishkov said.

Vasilyev shrugged again. "Australia has its share of traffic accidents, as does every country."

"Fine. I'll believe for now that nobody knows we have this capability," Grishkov said.

"We have gone to quite a bit of trouble to keep its possession secret," Vasilyev said, nodding.

"So, this drone can home in on the target through intercepting thoughts," Grishkov said. "Like, 'I sure hope the shielding on this nuclear bomb holds up long enough for me to deliver it before I start glowing.' Or something equally descriptive and incriminating."

Vasilyev laughed. "Nothing so useful, I'm afraid. No, we can only hope to find much more basic thoughts using a drone in flight. Ones that are nearly universal and don't rely on language."

"Basic thoughts," Grishkov slowly repeated. "Like fear, for example."

"Precisely!" Vasilyev exclaimed. "I must stress, by itself, using this new capability to help locate the target would be impossible. But if the drone detects even the slightest hint of radioactivity, it will focus all its sensors on thought interception. Ones like fear, certainly. Worry. Many other primal thoughts might be present in someone dealing with the transport of a nuclear weapon."

Grishkov nodded. "That makes more sense. And I suppose we have nothing to lose by trying this new technology. One thing puzzles me, though."

Vasilyev just cocked his head and waited. He'd known Grishkov long enough to be sure he'd need no prompting to proceed.

"How could you be sure the French wouldn't discover our new capability was present on this drone? Surely, they insisted on examining it before allowing it to fly over their airspace," Grishkov said.

"It was a risk," Vasilyev acknowledged. "But as long as we only allowed their technicians to do a brief review here in this hangar, not in a lab, we thought discovery unlikely. You see, the drone's basic sensor package is nearly unchanged. It was always designed to pick up radioactivity and other data in the electromagnetic spectrum. Of course, any drone also requires the capability to send and receive such data for communication and flight control."

"Yes," Grishkov said, drawing the word out slowly as he thought. "The really sensitive work would be processing the intercepted data. I imagine that's done in Russia."

"You imagine correctly," Vasilyev said with a smile. "The other factor helping us in this situation is time. The French are aware that this bomb is headed for their country now and that any delay will make finding it before detonation that much less likely."

Grishkov nodded but then frowned. "I'm still surprised to see this drone here. Many in Russia remember the help the French gave Ukraine in the last war and still harbor bitter resentment. Yes, Smyslov told me about our investments in France, the Russians living in Paris, and so on. I still think something else explains the decision to send this drone to France."

Vasilyev's eyebrows rose, and then he raised one finger to his lips. Next, he walked to the hangar's only door and poked his head outside.

When Vasilyev returned to Grishkov's side, he said, "It's good to see you're as skeptical as always. There is indeed more to this drone's mission. It will collect useful intelligence for the FSB, including much that has nothing to do with finding this bomb. It is an opportunity we've never had before, and are unlikely to have again."

Grishkov visibly relaxed. "Good. I'm always happier when I understand what's really going on. Any chance you could join our team once this beast is airborne?"

Vasilyev shook his head. "Kharlov was clear that I am responsible for the Okhotnik's security. And that I have not yet been cleared for active mission duty. As much as I would like to resume our partnership, I cannot."

"Well, you can't blame me for trying," Grishkov replied with a crooked grin. "Anyway, I'm glad to see you again. With luck, next time, it will be in more relaxed circumstances."

Vasilyev laughed. "Yes! Without any of the nuclear weapons nearby that always seem to dog our every step. But, we will be spending some time together, nonetheless."

Grishkov cocked his head, obviously confused, but said nothing.

"Kharlov insisted that you be ready to take over for me if, for any reason, I need to be recalled," Vasilyev said. "Or if, for some reason, I cannot carry out my duties here."

Grishkov's eyes narrowed. "So, your health is still not quite one hundred percent."

"I'm fine," Vasilyev said, clearly annoyed. "But I suppose you don't get to be Director without planning for every contingency."

"I'm no technician," Grishkov said with a frown. "Doesn't Kharlov realize I can be of much more use in the field?"

Vasilyev tried to suppress a smile but failed. "I know little about the DGSE. But surely, they can handle this without you holding their hand."

"I think this isn't what they're used to dealing with, at least this close to Paris," Grishkov said, nodding toward what remained of his Clio.

"Well, for now, at least, they'll have to make do," Vasilyev said flatly. "My orders are for you not to rejoin the DGSE team until I'm satisfied you can supervise the drone's operation. You won't have to fly the drone or operate its systems. We do indeed have technicians for those tasks. However, you must understand the information the drone sends back from flights."

Grishkov sighed. "Including information only you or I are cleared to see."

"Good," Vasilyev said with a smile. "Now, let's begin."

CHAPTER FOURTEEN

Port of Tangier
Morocco

Samir Ali grunted with satisfaction as he moved his truck into the parking space. Abdul had given him a GPS unit with a preselected destination before Ali departed from Libya.

The GPS unit had now just announced in English, "You have arrived at your destination."

Throughout his trip, Ali wondered whether Abdul had been able to use the GPS unit to monitor his progress.

In fact, his particular GPS unit had no such capability.

But the cell phone Abdul had given Ali?

Yes. It could do so as long as it was connected to either a cell phone network or a wireless network connected to the Internet.

Abdul lost contact with the truck many times during Ali's drive because cell phone network coverage in North Africa was far from perfect.

Service was excellent in most of Morocco outside the southern desert regions, though, particularly in and near large cities like Tangier.

Just moments after Ali's arrival, Abdul's sedan pulled up alongside him.

Ali exited his truck when he saw Abdul, who he saw was grinning widely, and waving one of his ever-present Dunhill cigarettes.

"Well done, my friend!" Abdul said. "You are here in plenty of time for your bonus! Congratulations!"

Ali relaxed a fraction. He'd actually arrived with just hours to spare, but Ali certainly didn't plan to argue the point.

All he wanted to do now was collect his money and sleep in a real bed. Preferably after a nice long hot shower.

After getting paid, of course.

Ali eyed the thick brown envelope Abdul was carrying in his free hand. Abdul noticed and laughed as he discarded the remains of his cigarette.

"Of course! What you need is your money, not my thanks. And here it is, just as promised. Please, I insist that you count it," Abdul said.

Ali had planned to anyway. Once he'd finished, the only surprise turned out to be...a pleasant one?

Before Ali could say anything, Abdul said, "I hope you noticed that you've received a small bonus on top of the promised one. I hope that will encourage you to consider my next offer."

"Next offer?" Ali repeated suspiciously.

Abdul lifted both his hands. "I'm sure you're exhausted by your long trip and want nothing more than a comfortable bed. And you will have that rest. At a fine hotel not far from here that I will pay for, regardless of whether you accept my offer."

Ali nodded. He was always reluctant to spend his hard-earned money on any but the cheapest hotels. Ones that were anything but "fine."

OK. He'd at least hear Abdul out. Even though he had no intention of agreeing to whatever Abdul wanted.

It had been a long and nerve-wracking trip from Libya. And Ali didn't believe in pressing his luck.

"Now, I meant what I said about your getting plenty of sleep at a nice hotel," Abdul said. "I'm sure you need it. And by the way, order whatever you want from room service. I'll cover the bill, whatever it is."

Now Ali had trouble believing his ears. He'd only stayed once in his entire life at a hotel offering room service and had dropped the menu as though it were on fire when he saw its prices.

"I need you to take your truck and its cargo a little further, in fact, to Paris," Abdul said.

Before Ali could reply, Abdul hurried on.

"Now, you won't have to go until tomorrow afternoon, so you'll get a full day's rest and food. Plus, I'll give you double what I paid you for the trip you just finished. As you know, this trip will be shorter and will take you over better roads than the one you just made. So, what do you say?" Abdul asked.

Double. Tempting.

But Ali was very tired.

Still....

How far could he push Abdul? He seemed desperate.

Ali shook his head firmly. "I appreciate the hotel. I really do. The only way I'd do this trip, though, is for triple what you just paid me. All up front. And I know there's no way you can do that."

Abdul said nothing but opened the left rear door of his sedan.

When Abdul emerged, he was carrying a slim leather satchel. Still, without a word, he handed it to Ali.

Inside, Ali found travel documents and all the other paperwork he needed to drive his truck from Tangier to Paris.

As well as the entire sum he'd demanded. Plus, a bit more.

Enough that Ali could think about retiring someday.

Not in luxury, perhaps. But on his terms, without having to drive a truck literally until he dropped.

Ali hadn't planned to agree. The prospect of being able to retire at some point, though, was just too tempting.

"Very well," Ali said heavily. Abdul could hardly miss his lack of enthusiasm, but he still smiled.

"Excellent, my friend!" Abdul said. "Leave your truck parked where it is. I will drive you to the hotel and then back tomorrow in time to catch the ship that will take you to Spain."

Ali nodded. Good. He knew Abdul was driving him to ensure he was on time for the ship.

But Ali didn't care. After so many hours on the road, any time at the wheel he could miss was welcome.

Chapter Fifteen

DGSE Headquarters
Paris, France

Captain Giraud had only encountered one person at DGSE Head-quarters before this mission. That was Antoine Bertrand, DGSE Deputy Director for Technical Support and Financial Investigations. A previous joint Army/DGSE mission in Africa that had posed what Antoine had called an "interesting technical challenge."

Portly, with rapidly thinning hair and gold wire-rimmed glasses, Antoine looked nothing like someone you'd expect to find at an intelligence agency.

But Giraud had seen the sharp intelligence behind those glasses at once. As well as a sense of humor and dislike of bureaucracy that almost matched his own.

Giraud's reception as he walked into Antoine's office, closing the door behind him, was everything he'd hoped.

"Ah, good to see you, my friend!" Antoine exclaimed. "Back from Africa, and still in one piece! Not for lack of trying, though, I heard!"

Giraud laughed and sat across from Antoine's desk, which was just as messy as always.

"You are well informed as always, Antoine," Giraud said. "But I wonder whether you have heard about an attack that just happened against one of my team right here in France."

Antoine's smile immediately disappeared. "No, I have not. What happened?"

After Giraud's description, Antoine was silent for a moment. Then he shook his head.

"The call to Grishkov over his secure cell phone, sending him to the ambush. It could only have come from someone within the DGSE. I'm sure you would like to know who that was."

Giraud nodded. "Yes, I would. I'm glad to hear you say so before I had to ask. I've also got another favor to request. Grishkov recovered a cell phone from one of the men who attacked him. It only called one number."

Giraud handed Antoine a slip of paper with the number.

Antoine nodded. "I will let you know who this belongs to before you leave. Tracking down whoever called Grishkov may take a little more time. I'm sure whoever did it made some effort to cover his tracks. Or even make a quick ID come back to someone else."

"Understood," Giraud said. Then he hesitated but finally added, "I would normally have included the Deputy Director for Counterintelligence in something like this, but I've heard there are some questions about him."

Antoine's eyebrows shot up. "Well, now it's my turn to call you well-informed. What have you heard, specifically?"

"Just that he's the only Deputy Director picked personally by the new Director," Giraud replied. "Who is the first DGSE Director to be a politician rather than a former military officer or diplomat."

Antoine chewed his lower lip and was silent for a moment.

Then he said, "That's all true. I've been keeping an eye on both of them. I won't hesitate to tell you if either was involved in the attack on this Grishkov. So far, though, I have no concrete evidence against either one."

"When you say 'keeping an eye on them' does that include tracking the movements of their vehicles and cell phones?" Giraud asked. "I suppose that's possible for you, yes?"

Antoine was silent again.

This time the silence was longer.

Finally, he said, "Let's just say this. If anything I find is relevant to your mission in any way, I will tell you at once. Good enough?"

Giraud stood and stretched out his hand. "That's everything I could ask for. Thank you, Antoine."

Antoine shook Giraud's hand and shrugged. "Of course. In here, my only exercise is jumping to conclusions. All I dodge are meetings and memos. Out there, you and your men have to avoid bombs and bullets."

Then Antoine patted Giraud on the shoulder and grinned. "Just one thing is essential, my friend. Don't forget to duck."

Chapter Sixteen

Centrolio Truck Parking
North of Valladolio, Spain

Samir Ali eased his truck into its reserved spot, one of over four hundred at this massive truck stop. He'd already refueled, so he would be ready to return to the road tomorrow morning.

Ali shook his head. Morning. This truck stop had a hotel on site that he could walk to from his truck, and the room was prepaid. He could eat dinner tonight, and breakfast tomorrow.

Both would be welcome. After the two-hour ferry ride from Tangier to Algeciras, he found that the GPS in his truck had already been programmed for his route to Paris.

To Ali's surprise, he'd been routed well to the west of Madrid. To avoid police? Or just traffic congestion?

Well, he certainly hadn't avoided road construction and accident delays. The route through Seville and past the famous Salamanca Cathedral had been frustratingly slow and had taken over ten hours. Night had long since fallen.

And Ali couldn't shake the feeling that he was being followed. By men working for Abdul?

If he was right, nothing else made sense. If local authorities suspected something about his cargo, they would have just pulled him over.

But while Ali had thought he'd spotted one car or another following him, he'd never been sure. Each time he'd been nearly certain, the vehicle he suspected would exit the highway, and not return.

But before long, he'd start to suspect another sedan.

Was he just being paranoid?

Ali shook his head again. Probably. He was so tired and stressed that he was most likely jumping at shadows.

God willing, a meal and a good night's sleep would help.

CHAPTER SEVENTEEN

Société Générale de Transport International Headquarters
Paris, France

"Roland Dubois says the Russians are going to do more to help the French government find the bomb."

Tareq couldn't help himself and blurted the first thing that came to mind after what Khaled Madi had just said.

"Why in the world would the Russians do so much to help France?"

"I asked Dubois that question," Madi said. "I won't bother telling you his answer because I don't think it matters. Instead, I will answer the more important question you haven't asked. How will the Russians find the bomb?"

Tareq nodded. "You're right, of course. So, what are they doing besides sending the agent already working with the DGSE?"

"They're providing a special drone and a crew to operate it," Madi said. "It's supposed to detect small amounts of radioactivity from a great distance. Do you think the bomb is shielded well enough to avoid being found?"

"I'm not sure it will escape detection when it nears Paris," Tareq said. "But I am positive they won't find it now."

Madi cocked his head, clearly puzzled. "And why not?"

"Because the bomb is not yet in France," Tareq said.

Seeing Madi's reaction, he hastily added, "It will be soon. It's already most of the way through Spain. But for now, the fact that the bomb is not yet in France gives us time to deal with the DGSE team."

Madi nodded. "And you are confident the men you've hired can do the job?"

"Yes," Tareq said. "Dubois has helped me arrange an ambush for the Russian agent, and I expect to hear good news soon. Then, taking care of the other three men on the DGSE team will just be a matter of selecting the right time and place."

Though in fact Tareq was getting worried. He'd expected to hear "good news" by now, but had not.

Would Madi notice?

"Fine," Madi said. "I'll let you get on with it then."

Tareq wasted no time in exiting Madi's office, working hard to suppress a sigh of relief as he did so.

Madi was usually not so easy to fool, Tareq thought.

And then swallowed hard at his next thought.

If eliminating the DGSE team didn't go according to plan, Tareq's misplaced confidence would be the first thing Madi remembered.

Chapter Eighteen

Near the Saint-Lazare Train Station
Paris, France

"This fellow Grishkov makes me nervous," Henri declared. "Six dead bodies. How did he manage that?"

Captain Giraud shrugged but kept his hands on the sedan's steering wheel. "Grishkov believed he was a likely target. I thought he was right after he was ordered to proceed alone to the air base. Fortunately, I had made certain preparations in his favor."

Henri and Felix both looked at Giraud expectantly. Finally, Giraud sighed.

"An F2 and grenades," he added.

Felix said quietly, "An APAV 40, correct?"

Despite himself, Giraud was impressed. "I'm surprised just a glance at the sedan's remains told you that much."

Now it was Felix's turn to shrug. "I've used one before in Africa. One of the best French weapons."

Giraud smiled. "Since you've been kind enough to praise our ordnance, I'll add that I also gave Grishkov a couple of German DM51s."

"I recommended them when he asked. I'm sure they helped him escape combined semiautomatic weapons fire," Felix said with a nod. "Clearly, a man who is no stranger to combat."

Henri scowled. "Yes, but none of that explains what we are doing here," he said, waving at the nearby train station.

"Saint-Lazare is the second busiest train station in Europe, with one hundred million people passing through every year," Giraud replied. "It has helped the 9th arrondissement become one of the most popular locations for office space in Paris. Rents here range from four to five hundred Euros per square meter yearly. Would you like to guess who has an office here?"

Giraud nodded toward an office building a block away from the train station.

"Someone connected to the attack on Grishkov," Henri said thoughtfully.

Then he frowned and added, "Someone with access to more money than a typical terrorist."

"Just so," Giraud replied. "One of the GPS units we recovered led us to this address. Many businesses have offices there. One is a company that provides security services with no questions asked."

Henri grimaced. "Except, how much do you have in the bank?"

"Yes," Giraud said with a smile. "Grishkov sent me a text with the only number called by a cell phone he recovered from one of the attackers. I gave the number to Antoine, the only person I know and trust in the DGSE. He's the Deputy Director of Technical Services. He was able to trace the number to a cell phone Antoine says is presently in that office building."

Henri nodded. "I've heard about Antoine. Everyone says he's a good man. So, we are waiting for that phone's owner to depart and will then follow him," Henri said rather than asked.

"Correct," Giraud replied. "The afternoon is nearly over, so we probably won't have long to wait. Antoine is keeping me updated on the phone's location."

With that, Giraud held up his phone's display so Henri and Felix could see a map with a pulsing red dot at its center.

"Once it moves, so will we. At a discreet distance, of course," Giraud added.

"Do we know how many employees work for this security company?" Henri asked.

"You mean, are we likely to be outnumbered? And is any backup coming to help us?" Giraud replied. "The answers are perhaps and no."

Henri grunted. "Well, since we are only three, even a small outfit will likely have more men. But why not ask the DGSE for help? This is a top priority mission, after all."

"Ordinarily, I would," Giraud said with a nod. "However, I didn't like Grishkov's answer when I asked him why he had chosen back roads to reach the air base. He said it was orders from DGSE HQ, given to him on his secure cell phone."

"What sort of idiot would have given such an order..." Henri's voice trailed off.

Giraud saw with satisfaction that Henri was figuring out the implications for himself about his agency.

Finally, Henri shook his head. "Captain, you are French Army. Felix is Foreign Legion. Grishkov is...well, whatever he is, he's not DGSE. I'm the only career DGSE agent here for a mission that is supposed to be a top priority. I've thought from the beginning that something was wrong here. So, now you believe that the less DGSE HQ knows, the better?"

Giraud shrugged. "We can only accomplish so much on our own. But for now, I think it is safer to rely only on ourselves. That way, at least, we can avoid ambushes of the sort that nearly cost us the services of Monsieur Grishkov."

About half an hour later, Giraud tapped on his phone's display. "They're on the move."

Moments later, a long black sedan emerged from the office building's garage. Felix let out a low whistle.

"An Audi RS7 Performance model. Over six hundred horsepower. Let's hope we don't have to try chasing it on the highway," Felix said.

Giraud smiled. "If I'm doing my job correctly, the Audi's driver should never see me. Whoever is in that car is probably not who we want. With luck, he's headed to someone higher up for new orders. By now, they must know that their attempt to kill or capture Grishkov has failed. But from what we've seen so far, I doubt they will stop trying to interfere with our mission."

The Audi was soon lost to sight in the busy Parisian traffic, but with the aid of the tracking display, their Peugeot had no trouble keeping up the pace. In less than an hour, they were clearly heading away from the capital.

"Do we have any idea where they might be going?" Henri asked.

Giraud nodded, his eyes still firmly fixed on the road ahead. "The security company's owner has his residence in this direction. Situated on a rather large piece of land, and surrounded by farms. Very private."

Henri made a face. "And I'm sure with all the most modern security measures."

Now Giraud did look at him, and then smiled.

"I'm counting on it," he said.

The next half hour passed in silence. The Audi was still ahead and out of sight.

Finally, the dot on the display slowed and then stopped.

"As I thought," Giraud said with satisfaction. "The residence of Raphael Boucher, the company's owner. There is a gas station just a few kilometers past it, which has a small café attached. We will wait there for nightfall."

Minutes later, Henri was scowling into the contents of a chipped white ceramic cup.

Giraud grinned. "The coffee is not to your liking, Henri?"

Henri glanced at the counter, where he saw the bored middle-aged woman behind it, who was giving her phone all her attention.

"Very well, I'll admit it," Henri replied. "Paris has spoiled me. No café that served coffee like this there would stay open long."

Giraud and Felix smiled at each other.

"Those of us who have spent many years in Africa know to be grateful when the liquid poured in our cup is both hot and actually coffee," Giraud said.

Then Felix's smile changed to a frown.

"And only coffee. Once in Senegal I was served what I later learned was called café Touba. An 80/20 mix of coffee and Guinea pepper. Also known as alligator pepper," Felix said darkly.

Now it was Henri's turn to smile. "Not to your liking, then."

"You could say that," Felix replied stiffly, reaching for his cup as if to wipe out the memory.

"I've heard of it," Giraud said. "Did you know that one café Touba variety includes both alligator pepper and cloves?"

Felix spluttered and nearly choked on the coffee he'd just started to drink.

Henri nodded toward the none too clean glass panes that fronted the café. Through them they could all see several gas pumps.

As well as the fact that night had fallen.

"What is our plan?" Henri asked.

"I saw a spot not far from here where we can pull off the road unobserved," Giraud said. "We can go from there to the house and ask Boucher our questions."

"Just like that," Henri said, shaking his head. Lowering his voice, he said, "I think, at best, he'll tell you to talk to his lawyer. At worst, his men will start shooting. Maybe before we even get to the front door."

Giraud nodded. "Let's have the rest of this conversation in the car."

Moments later, they were on the road.

"Felix, you checked the equipment I told you to bring? You're satisfied it's in working order?" Giraud asked.

Felix nodded. "I'll need a few minutes to tap into the wired component of the security system for Boucher's house. With the schematics you provided, I can do the work not far from the road and well out of sight."

Then Felix shook his head. "For what's supposed to be one of France's most expensive security companies, I'm not impressed."

"Well, the equipment you're using is only available to a few within the DGSE. Antoine says few even know we have it. And besides, the company doesn't make its real money from installing security systems," Giraud said.

"Right," Henri said. "Instead, by being willing to kill or kidnap anyone for the right price."

"So it would appear," Giraud replied. "Therefore, we will take no chances."

Giraud cut the sedan's headlights a kilometer before reaching the house and pulled over when Felix nodded.

When he opened the trunk, they saw something from Felix for the first time.

A smile.

"I see you didn't give all the toys to Grishkov," Felix said as he removed the equipment he would need to disable Boucher's security system.

"Certainly not," Giraud replied. "I just hope we won't have to use them."

Seeing the expressions on Felix and Henri's faces, Giraud smiled.

"Not because I think someone like Boucher doesn't deserve to be on the receiving end of grenade and semiautomatic rifle fire. Because I need him alive to answer questions," Giraud said.

Henri frowned. "Yes, but how will we accomplish that? Once Felix has disabled the security system, how will we approach the house?"

"We will call ahead, and once we receive permission, this sedan will drive through the front gate," Giraud said.

Henri started to laugh, but when he saw Giraud's expression stopped.

"You're serious! But then, why bother disabling Boucher's security system?" Henri asked. "Which I'm sure you've noticed includes an electrified fence, extensive lighting, and a massive vehicle gate."

"Because I need to justify what follows to our superiors," Giraud replied. "We have no higher authorization and no arrest or search warrant. But, if I have a conversation recorded on my phone showing that Boucher invited us in, and then we were attacked…"

Henri interrupted. "Yes, I see that. I also understand the need for Felix to prevent Boucher from calling in reinforcements. But don't you expect Boucher's men to attack our car before we even reach the front door?"

"I do," Giraud replied. "Particularly since I will call just after Felix has disabled his security system, thus showing we are a genuine threat. Otherwise, I expect he would try to threaten us with his lawyers. But don't worry. We won't be in the car."

Henri looked confused, but Giraud saw understanding in Felix's eyes.

"An American electric car manufacturer released a feature they called 'Smart Summon' several years ago," Giraud said. "It was designed to allow the car's owner to move it to them in a parking lot or to any location selected using a phone GPS. Certain high-end European vehicles, including our hybrid sedan, now come with a similar feature."

Henri slowly nodded. "The sedan's windows are heavily tinted, and I suppose you'll have the high beams on. So, we'll take up positions around the house once the security system is disabled, and you'll then drive the sedan straight down the driveway using a command from your phone. Have you done this before?"

"No," Giraud said with a shrug. "But I've used drones to track terrorists driving vehicles in Africa several times. By comparison, I think this will be simple."

Henri was unconvinced but wisely decided to say nothing.

It only took Felix a few minutes to look up and say, "Ready. I will cut the security system, power, and landline phones on your command. Electricity to the gate is on a separate circuit because of the power needed to move a metal mass that size. I'll leave it operational so

Boucher can open it. Once you finish the call to Boucher, I'll block all cell phone and radio communication."

"Good," Giraud said. "Cut everything but cell phone and radio communication now."

It took only moments for Giraud and his team to climb the now harmless fence and drop to the other side. In the sudden darkness lit only by a crescent moon, they closed to positions around Boucher's home in just a few moments more.

They could hear confused movement inside the house, but so far, no one had exited.

Giraud placed the call to Boucher. It was picked up immediately.

Then Giraud played the message he had prerecorded demanding entry. And stating that force would be used if he refused.

Giraud heard a long pause as Boucher considered his options.

Finally, Boucher said, "I am opening the gate."

Giraud had already programmed the house's GPS coordinates as the sedan's endpoint. Its self-driving safeguards would stop it on the driveway several meters short of the house.

Now, to see whether anyone inside the house would try to stop it sooner.

Headlights blazing, the sedan moved slowly but steadily toward the house.

Halfway down the drive, still no reaction.

Had Giraud misjudged Boucher?

Glass shattered in many windows as multiple rounds from semiautomatic rifles were fired from inside the house at the sedan.

The sedan's windows were bullet-resistant, and it was armored against anything short of a grenade.

Multiple dents and a few holes appeared in the sedan. One of the headlights shattered.

But it kept coming toward the house.

The front door cracked open. An arm appeared through it and tossed a grenade toward the advancing sedan.

106 · TED HALSTEAD

It bounced once on the driveway and then came to rest directly underneath the sedan.

Giraud had no idea whether the throw's accuracy was due to luck or skill, but either way, had to admit he was impressed.

The front door slammed shut at the exact moment the grenade detonated.

The force of the explosion visibly lifted the sedan, and it came back down heavily.

It slowed but still didn't stop.

Was its continued progress sheer inertia, or was the engine still intact?

Well, Giraud decided, it didn't really matter.

Because the sedan had come to within a few meters of the front door and stopped.

So did the semiautomatic rifle fire.

The silence that followed lasted only seconds but seemed much longer.

Finally, the front door cracked open again.

This time, a head came out, cautiously swiveling from side to side.

As Giraud had ordered, no one on the team fired but remained hidden.

The man at the door gestured at someone behind him. Then, he and two other men emerged.

At first slowly, and then with increasing confidence, the three men walked toward the sedan, weapons in hand.

The first man tried to open one of the sedan's doors.

That was the moment Giraud had ordered his team to open fire with their FN SCAR assault rifles. Equipped with the SureFire SO-COM762 RC2 suppressor, they could shoot without muzzle flash and noise giving away their positions.

All three gunmen around the sedan were hit and fell to the driveway. Even in the illumination from the single remaining headlight, it was easy to see the blood pooling around each body.

Still, Giraud looked at each one carefully for several seconds. No movement.

The front door was still ajar. Doubtless left that way deliberately, in case the gunmen had to beat a hasty retreat.

Giraud's rifle was equipped with the FN40GL Enhanced Grenade Launcher, capable of firing any 40x46mm NATO standard low-velocity grenade.

One was quickly on its way through the gap in the door.

Could the door have withstood an exterior grenade detonation? It looked quite solid, and from what Giraud could see, it appeared to rest on a solid metal frame.

Fortunately, it would not be necessary to answer that question today.

Because the grenade hit the floor just inside the door, blowing it off its frame and into the driveway.

Giraud promptly sent another grenade through the now-empty space at the front of the house. The screams that followed the next explosion told Giraud that, indeed, more gunmen had been waiting inside.

Time to speak to Boucher if he was still alive. That need was all that kept Giraud from sending a third grenade into the house.

He had really liked the Peugeot.

Giraud and his team entered Boucher's home, each scanning their assigned sector for targets. It turned out that Boucher's remaining men had made the mistake of clustering near the front entrance.

Probably ordered there in case the gunmen outside needed reinforcement. And then lacking the courage to follow once the first three out the door were cut down.

All the gunmen inside were down, but two were still moving.

But not for long. Giraud's orders had been clear.

Only Boucher was to be taken alive. There was nothing to be gained by questioning hired guns.

And with a nuclear weapon to stop, they had no time to deal with other prisoners.

Giraud nodded toward the stairs. "Check upstairs. If you find no one, return and report."

Felix and Henri went cautiously up the stairs, half expecting a grenade to come bouncing down toward them.

But nothing happened. A few minutes later, they were standing in front of Giraud again.

"Nobody upstairs," Henri said. "Do you think he went out the back?"

Giraud shrugged. "It's not impossible," he said. "But unlikely. There's nothing for kilometers in any direction but farmland. Plus, can you hear that?"

Henri and Felix both cocked their heads curiously. Giraud's grenades had shattered the glass on the back door, and through it, they could indeed hear something.

Felix recognized the sound first. "Sprinklers," he said.

"Exactly," Giraud replied. "They're often set to turn on in the evening when there will be less water loss through evaporation. Could Boucher have decided to strike out cross-country? Maybe. But through muddy fields at night? I doubt it."

Henri made a face. "So, Boucher was never here at all?"

"Maybe," Giraud said with a smile. "But there is one other possibility. I've thoroughly studied the blueprints for this home filed for construction permits. And the dimensions in that corner don't match. By quite a bit."

Giraud pointed to the most distant corner, where several paintings were hanging askew. There were also a couple of tall potted tropical plants, now each tipped over.

"A panic room," Henri said immediately and then frowned.

"So, do we look for the door?" Henri asked.

"We could," Giraud replied. "But I'm sure that this panic room has an independent battery power source and dedicated cameras and microphones. Perhaps they survived the explosions."

Then Giraud raised his voice.

"Monsieur Boucher! We only wish to talk. After you answer our questions, we will place you under arrest and take you to civil authorities in Paris. If you do not respond, we will use the same grenades that allowed us entry to your home to force our way into your panic room," Giraud said and then paused.

"I'm sure the men who did the installation told you forcing our way inside would be impossible. That may be true. But even if it is, I guarantee that the force of repeated grenade explosions will first rupture your eyes and eardrums and eventually your internal organs. I have no wish to do so unless you leave me with no choice. You have sixty seconds to surrender," Giraud said.

It took about thirty. First, a crack appeared in the wall, and then a door swung silently outward.

Three rifles were trained on Boucher as he emerged.

"Don't shoot!" he cried, his hands over his head. "I'm unarmed. I won't give you any trouble."

"Lower your hands, slowly," Giraud said.

Felix moved toward Boucher, zip tie in hand, but Giraud shook his head.

At the same time, Giraud noticed that while he and Felix had secured their rifles, Henri had kept his steadily aimed at Boucher.

Giraud made a mental note. Not as dumb as he seems, sometimes.

"I think we can believe Monsieur Boucher," Giraud said. "Now, where are your phone and laptop?"

Boucher jerked his head toward the panic room he'd just left, where the door was still ajar.

Felix was on his way before Giraud had to say anything, and a few moments later, he was standing next to him, phone and laptop in hand.

"I presume you need to do something to allow us access to these, correct?" Giraud asked.

Boucher nodded, and Felix handed him the phone and then the laptop. It took Boucher only seconds to open each one.

"I notice that opening each device required a biometric scan but no password, correct?" Giraud asked.

Boucher nodded again.

"Good," Giraud said. "Now, who do you work for?"

"I honestly don't know. I was paid online in cryptocurrency and never met him," Boucher said.

Giraud shrugged and drew his 9mm pistol from his holster.

"Too bad," he said.

"Wait, wait!" Boucher cried, his eyes widening in fear. "I did try to trace the payment source through a hacker I've used before. He said the funds were routed through a company in France before they were transferred to me, but he couldn't find out which one. Before they came to France, he says he thought the ultimate source of the funds was Syria. That scared him."

Giraud nodded. "I'm sure it did. The name and contact information for this hacker are in your laptop? As well as the information he gave you on the payment?"

"Yes," Boucher said tonelessly. "But I don't think you'll find him. I offered double his usual fee to try to get more information. No response."

"Understood," Giraud said. Then, in a single smooth motion, he lifted his pistol and shot Boucher twice in the chest.

Boucher dropped to the floor and didn't move.

Giraud turned to Felix. "Have you changed the settings on the phone and laptop to ensure biometric login is not required after a certain time has passed?"

Felix nodded and jerked his head toward Boucher's body. "Yes. I guessed he wouldn't be around long to reopen them for us."

Henri shook his head. "From the Foreign Legion, this might not surprise me, but a French Army officer? You shot him down in cold blood! Boucher may have been a criminal, but he was still a French citizen with rights!"

"He forfeited those rights once he became involved in a plot to detonate a nuclear device in Paris," Giraud said.

While thinking he had been right the first time about Henri's intelligence.

"Consider this," Giraud continued. "If we had taken Boucher in, he would have immediately hired the best lawyers money could buy. We would have been forced to spend hours writing reports and depositions to justify our actions. In the meantime, do you imagine the terrorists would be sitting idle?"

Henri glared at Giraud, started to open his mouth, and then closed it. And paused.

Good, Giraud thought. Not a complete idiot, after all.

"Speaking of sitting idle, I'd like your permission to request a warrant at once from a magistrate through the DGSE to allow a search of Boucher's offices," Henri said. "Based on Boucher and his men firing on us first, we now have plenty of justification."

Giraud nodded approvingly. "An excellent idea. At this time of night, how long do you think it will take for the warrant to be issued?"

"I will ask for maximum speed," Henri said.

He sounded doubtful, even to himself.

Giraud decided to take pity on him. After all, his heart was in the right place, at least on this matter.

"It's worth a try," Giraud said. "Maybe we can get to Boucher's office before the terrorists do."

"I have relatives in Paris," Henri said stiffly. "Not close ones. My parents are dead, and I have no siblings. But it's the only family I have left. I don't want to lose them. And yes, I don't want to lose any of the other innocent people targeted by these lunatics. But you can't be surprised that this is hard for me to take."

Henri gestured toward Boucher's body and said nothing further.

"Frankly, I'd be worried if you weren't upset," Giraud said, surprising himself.

Not with the words. He'd planned to say them to calm Henri down.

But because Giraud found that once he'd said the words, he meant them.

"Felix and I have both spent years in combat in Africa, where it's usually kill or be killed," Giraud said. "We're not policemen, and we're not intelligence officers. But it's not a coincidence that men like us were put in charge of stopping this weapon. You, though, are making an important contribution to the team, as your idea of a search warrant showed. Unless you want to leave it?"

Henri shook his head decisively. "No. You're right. Stopping the weapon has to come first."

Then he glanced at Boucher's body.

"Let's hope this is the last person who dies because of it," Henri said.

Giraud nodded. "On that, we can all agree."

Chapter Nineteen

Société Générale de Transport International Headquarters
Paris, France

Khaled Madi looked at his security chief, Tareq, with an icy fury Tareq had never seen.

Suddenly, the plush chair across from Madi's ornate wooden desk felt considerably less comfortable.

"They're all dead? All the men you hired to stop the DGSE team? And the DGSE didn't lose anyone? How can that be?" Madi asked.

"You told me that the head of the DGSE, Dubois, had selected a team of misfits and rejects. With a retired Russian FSB agent added at the last minute by Dubois' deputy," Tareq replied. "The security company I used always came through for us in the past. I told their chief, Boucher, that this would be their only job until it was finished. But now I know why it went so wrong."

The look on Madi's face told Tareq to get on with it.

Tareq tapped a set of file folders on his lap. "When I advised you this morning of what happened to Boucher and his men, you sent me these personnel files from Dubois. The answer is there, supplemented by some other information I've obtained. Yes, none of the men Dubois selected are well-regarded by their superiors. But their records show they are the worst possible picks for us."

Madi shook his head. "Explain," he said shortly.

"I'll start with the team leader, Captain Giraud," Tareq replied. "He's due for retirement soon, having been passed over for promotion yet again. By now, an officer who has done so many combat tours should be a Colonel. But repeatedly, he has defied orders from his superiors, leading to poor ratings. If you look more closely at his record, you can see why this happened."

Madi sighed. "Because the situations he faced forced Giraud to ignore his orders. Which is why, after so many years of combat, he's escaped death or serious injury."

Tareq looked up from the file, startled. "But if you knew this..."

"I didn't," Madi said, shaking his head. "I only glanced at the files when Dubois first sent them to me, which is my fault. But if you say these men are bad news for us, it's the only explanation that makes sense."

"The story is similar for the Sergeant seconded from the Foreign Legion," Tareq said. "He recently refused orders to advance into what drone footage later showed was an ambush. The officer ordering the advance had sent this Sergeant to Paris for a disciplinary hearing before the drone footage emerged. The hearing has been put off for weeks, probably to give the officer time to disappear the evidence that would prove the Sergeant right."

Madi made a face. "Next, you'll tell me that the DGSE agent on the team is the best in the agency."

Tareq shook his head. "Not at all. Unlike the other two, he's only had a few years of field experience. In one respect, though, he is similar. Excellent performances overseas but poor reviews by his superiors due to his failure to follow orders. Even when those orders were later shown to be mistaken."

"So Dubois picked three people," Madi said thoughtfully. "Each from a different organization, to make it more likely they'd work together poorly. The Army, Foreign Legion, and the DGSE. All of them had substandard performance reviews because they were unwilling to follow orders. Even if that refusal turned out to be justified. What have you learned about the Russian?"

"There, I'm afraid the news is even worse," Tareq said. "To sum up, the Russians were willing to tell the DGSE very little. But that little is very bad for us. Anatoly Grishkov is a combat soldier with experience in Chechnya at the height of the war there. For many years the lead homicide detective for the Vladivostok region. And he was then put on so-called special tasking for the FSB. Most of these taskings were related to locating and either retrieving or destroying rogue nuclear weapons."

"Exactly the man who should have been kept as far as possible from this mission," Madi shouted.

Then he collected himself.

"Sorry," Madi said. "The mistake was Dubois', not yours."

Tareq shook his head. "No, that selection was not made by Dubois. It was done by Jacques Montand, his deputy. Apparently, Dubois decided it would be too risky to overrule him once Montand made the pick. But Dubois did tell me eliminating Grishkov should be our top priority."

"Fine, as far as that goes. But what did Dubois do about it?" Madi asked.

Tareq shifted uncomfortably in his chair. "Dubois helped me set up an ambush, to which I assigned six heavily armed contractors. Somehow, Grishkov not only survived but killed all six."

"Well, at least there were no survivors left to question. Though I see why you say this man is bad news for us," Madi said.

"Yes," Tareq said. "Though there were no survivors, I suspect that there was evidence of some type collected at the ambush site. Perhaps cell phones. In any case, that's the only way I can imagine the DGSE linking the attack on Grishkov to Boucher."

"And then Captain Giraud and his team attacked Boucher at his home, killing him and all his remaining armed employees," Madi said bitterly. "What sort of evidence do you think they would have been able to retrieve there?"

Tareq tried to keep the worry he felt off his face and out of his voice.

As soon as he heard himself speak, though, he knew he had failed.

"Someone with Boucher's experience should have known to keep any sensitive information locked up at his office," Tareq said. "My men have already been to Boucher's office, removed all laptops and hard drives, and then set fire to what was left. They got out just before the arrival of Giraud's team. They followed my orders not to attack them."

Madi's face was expressionless. "You were right to give those orders. Giraud and his men would have been on high alert, and the priority had to be keeping the evidence they'd just collected out of Giraud's hands. And I'm guessing you sent just a few men for this task."

Tareq nodded but said nothing.

"Still, we cannot know what Boucher may have been careless enough to have on hand at home. Is it possible what they found could connect Boucher to us?" Madi asked quietly.

Well, there's the question I've been asking myself for hours, Tareq thought.

He didn't hesitate with his answer, though.

Tareq knew Madi well enough to know that any delay would just make matters worse.

"I don't think so," Tareq said. "We never met in person, and I paid Boucher in cryptocurrency. I also used our best people to make the funding source as untraceable as possible."

Madi nodded. "But we both know that with the resources of the DGSE behind them, 'untraceable as possible' may not be good enough."

"Maybe not," Tareq said. "But it will be neither quick nor easy. I think our best option is still to take out the source of the problem. Eliminate the DGSE team, and nobody will be left to take effective action in time to stop the plan."

"Do you have another security company in mind?" Madi asked.

Tareq shook his head. "There's no time for that. Now it's up to me and my men to handle this directly."

Madi looked dubious. "We've discussed that approach before. You know, at all costs, we must avoid anyone linking the attack to me or this company. If you or anyone else who works for us is captured, that's exactly what will happen."

"I'm positive I can avoid that," Tareq said. "This won't be a simple frontal assault of the sort that failed against Grishkov. And I guarantee none of us will be captured alive. It's better that you don't know the details. Please, leave it with me."

Madi still looked unconvinced.

"There's something else to be considered," Tareq added. "There is also a risk to leaving the DGSE team alive and free to continue their investigation. Of course, once they're dead, they will be replaced. But that will take time. And time is on our side. If we can eliminate the DGSE team before they make any further progress."

Madi was still unsure but finally nodded.

"I have faith in you," he said. "You've always come through for me before, and I'm sure this time will be no different."

CHAPTER TWENTY

Near the Saint-Lazare Train Station
Paris, France

Captain Giraud put their new sedan into the closest parking space he could find.

Two fire trucks parked outside the office building where Boucher's security company was located made any closer approach impossible.

Henri shook his head with disgust. "Well, we've finally got our warrant. Much good it will do us."

"I've seen the report from the fire brigade," Giraud said. "The men torching Boucher's office did a sloppy job. They splashed some petrol about after, I'm sure, taking all the hard drives and files they could carry. But they weren't there long, and the fire caused no structural damage to the building. I think there's a good chance we'll find something they missed."

Felix, as usual, unless directly addressed, said nothing.

A few minutes later, they had arrived at Boucher's offices. They'd passed what turned out to be the last two firefighters assigned to the incident on their way up.

They ducked under the yellow tape placed across the entrance doors. They were glass and had been shattered by the heat of the fire, leaving only the metal frames behind.

The smell of smoke was strong but bearable. At Giraud's insistence, they were all wearing filter masks.

"I will take Boucher's office," Giraud said, pointing as he continued.

"Henri, you take his secretary's office and those filing cabinets. Felix, you take those cubicles, where I'm guessing the security staff prepared their reports after time in the field. Priority targets are hard drives, cameras, and any other storage medium, such as USB drives or memory cards. Run your hands under drawers and desktops since people often tape small objects there to hide them."

"Very good," Henri said. "Sounds just like the training I got not so long ago at the DGSE."

Giraud and Felix exchanged glances and smiled. "Terrorists and rebels are surprisingly good recordkeepers," Giraud said. "And in Africa, one of the first things you learn is that knowledge is a more powerful weapon than any bullet."

Giraud began to think Henri's skepticism justified as the minutes stretched over an hour.

Until he took a critical look at Boucher's bottom desk drawer. Like all the other drawers, it was completely empty. Still, something about this drawer didn't look quite right.

It's not deep enough, Giraud realized. And that must mean...

Seconds later, Giraud had confirmed his suspicion. A metal-lined false bottom!

Within it, a cell phone.

A quick check, though, showed that it was locked.

Well, technicians back at headquarters would deal with that quickly enough.

"Any luck?" Giraud called out.

"Nothing," came almost simultaneously from both Henri and Felix.

Giraud strode out of Boucher's office, triumphantly holding up the cell phone he'd discovered.

"Well, at least we're not leaving empty-handed," Giraud said. "Between this and what we found at Boucher's home last night, maybe we'll finally get a lead we can use."

CHAPTER TWENTY-ONE

Goussainville-Vieux Pays
20 Kilometers North of Paris

Tareq crouched down to ensure his observation post couldn't be seen by anyone outside.

Nearly half a century ago, Goussainville-Vieux Pays had been abandoned by almost all its residents. Departures from the village began when it was put directly in the flight path of Charles de Gaulle Airport.

The noise was bad enough. Then, in 1973, a plane came down and smashed through fifteen houses and a school, killing six crew members and eight residents. The government gave the surviving villagers the opportunity to relocate. Almost all of them did at once, many leaving behind their possessions in their haste to escape from a place many considered cursed.

Tareq had doubted that part of the story until he'd come to Goussainville-Vieux Pays for the first time. Sure enough, some moldering possessions could still be seen through grimy windows inside the houses today.

The oddity of an abandoned village so close to Paris had even sparked tours for a while. But no longer.

These days, everyone had forgotten about Goussainville-Vieux Pays. Which was perfect for Tareq's purposes.

Would the DGSE team find the cell phone he'd had his men leave behind? Would they then use it to come here?

Logic said maybe. Maybe not.

But Tareq felt in his bones that they would.

And he would be ready.

Tareq had three men in one of the abandoned houses. Hired under a twice-removed contract and disposable.

As long as the DGSE team appeared, no matter what followed, none of those three men would survive.

Tareq had rigged the house with explosives before his men arrived. He had a radio trigger in hand, ready to use as soon as the DGSE team entered the house.

The best part was that Tareq was certain Captain Giraud and his men wouldn't just flatten the house themselves. No, they'd want survivors to question.

How would they do it? Tareq had no idea.

But he was looking forward to the show.

Especially since he would write the ending.

CHAPTER TWENTY-TWO

"I apologize for the delay, Deputy Director," Grishkov said.

Jacques Montand looked at Grishkov sharply. But no. There was no trace of sarcasm in the man's tone or on his face.

"Just Jacques, please. Have a seat," he said, waving to a plain wooden chair in front of his desk.

In contrast to the chair, Jacques's heavy desk was quite ornate and looked like an antique.

That's because it was. Jacques had pulled it from storage when he received the Deputy Director assignment after a career spent almost entirely overseas. A career where he had received numerous awards in recognition of repeatedly risking his life for France.

Jacques still looked much more like the field agent he had been than the headquarters bureaucrat he had become.

Almost as an act of rebellion, Jacques had spent the money budgeted for hiring an assistant on having his desk refinished to its original splendor.

Jacques had thought to himself, if the rest of my career is to be spent on my posterior, then at least it should be splendidly framed.

And I don't need an assistant.

In the process, Jacques had actually saved the French government some money. And in case of future challenge, he also had a written purchase offer from the antique shop that had done the refinishing.

They had offered four times the refinishing cost, for a desk that had initially looked to be useful only as firewood.

In the event, all of Jacques' concerns and precautions were unnecessary. His new boss had turned out to be a political appointee, whose only interest in the DGSE's budget was increasing it.

"It took longer than I expected to familiarize myself with the drone we will use to find the bomb," Grishkov said.

That was quite an understatement. Driven by a nagging feeling that time was running out, Grishkov had operated on little food or sleep over the past day.

Grishkov had pushed Vasilyev hard to complete his minimal training on the drone's capabilities while making it clear he wanted no shortcuts. The more time he spent with Vasilyev, the better Grishkov understood Kharlov's concern that he might have to be recalled to Moscow.

Grishkov would never know how long Vasilyev had stopped breathing at the end of their last mission. He was sure, though, that it was an experience bound to leave a mark.

"But nothing so far," Jacques said rather than asked.

"No," Grishkov replied. Then he tapped the earpiece he was wearing.

"I appreciate your making an exception to allow me to bring this and my personal cell phone to our meeting," Grishkov said sincerely. "Without it, I'd have no way to stay in contact with the technicians operating the drone."

Jacques nodded. "My security people were unhappy. But finding the bomb takes priority over everything else."

The phone on Jacques' desk buzzed, drawing his immediate frown as he picked up the handset. He had left strict orders not to be disturbed.

"Yes?" Jacques snapped. His frown cleared as the voice on the phone explained the purpose of the call.

At the same time, a voice began speaking on Grishkov's earpiece. Jacques noticed.

As he hung up the handset, Jacques gestured toward Grishkov's earpiece and said, "You first."

"A report from the drone's operating team," Grishkov said promptly. "A radioactive signature consistent with a dirty bomb has been detected at a town called..."

Grishkov frowned with concentration as he struggled to remember how to pronounce the unfamiliar name.

"Goussainville-Vieux Pays," he finally said. Slowly.

But it turned out correctly.

"That fits in more than one way," Jacques replied. "First, because the town has been mostly abandoned for decades now. Yet is still not far from Paris. Also, Captain Giraud has advised me that the men who attacked both of you in separate incidents had visited there recently. He and the rest of his team are on their way there now."

"Then I must join them!" Grishkov exclaimed.

Jacques nodded. "Agreed. When you return, there will be plenty of time to review what happened outside the air base. Good luck."

Grishkov nodded and rushed out of Jacques' office.

He felt he'd already used a fair bit of luck by escaping the meeting. Grishkov had expected unhappiness with the amount of firepower he'd used to defeat the ambush. However, in his view, six-to-one odds were all the justification necessary.

Would Jacques have agreed if the meeting had continued?

Grishkov was just as happy not to know.

CHAPTER TWENTY-THREE

Henri frowned as he looked at the object in Felix's hand.

"That's some sort of nano drone, right? It looks like the Black Hornet, but different somehow."

Felix looked up, surprised. "That's correct," he said approvingly. "It is indeed similar to the Black Hornet but more advanced in several respects. Flying time is nearly an hour instead of half an hour. And, it can now carry a payload, though it must be tiny. Yet its weight has stayed unchanged at about eighteen grams."

"A payload? What could it possibly carry in a package so small?" Henri asked.

Felix smiled. "A gas capsule that, once released, should knock out anyone within a ten-meter radius. The only challenge is that the gas can only be deployed once."

"So you'll have to wait until everyone in that house is in the same room," Henri said.

Captain Giraud had been peering through a pair of binoculars at the house across the street but now looked up.

"Ideally," he said. "But if that doesn't happen for some reason we'll use the drone to knock out as many of them as possible. And then use more old-fashioned methods to deal with whoever is left."

Giraud patted the pistol at his belt, just in case his meaning hadn't been clear.

"And how will this little jewel get inside the house?" Henri asked.

Felix pointed to a broken window in the kitchen of the home they were using as an observation post.

"Every home I've seen here so far has many broken windows," Felix said. "Some perhaps caused by weather over the years. More, I suspect, by vandals. I plan to fly this drone in a wide circle around the house once night falls, which will be soon. Our luck will have to be truly poor for there to be no way to enter the home from the back."

Henri nodded. "Won't flying this be a challenge in the dark?" he asked.

"Not at all," Felix said. "The Black Hornet could display infrared video, and the capture quality on this drone is even more advanced. As is its collision avoidance capability."

"Really?" Henri exclaimed incredulously. "You mean if you try to fly it into a wall, it won't let you?"

Giraud grunted. "These things cost over two hundred thousand Euros apiece. For that price, I'd expect it to make coffee, too."

"Coffee, it cannot do," Felix said with a smile. "Collision avoidance isn't absolute, either. I'm sure I could run it into a wall if I wanted to. So far, though, the feedback I've received from the drone's sensors has helped me avoid losing one. As the Captain says, they're expensive. A soldier who loses one through carelessness wouldn't get a replacement quickly, if at all."

"Nor should he," Giraud said irritably. "Are you ready to go with that thing?"

Felix nodded. "I've attached the battery pack. I've also checked all drone systems, and everything is green. Winds in this area are well below the operational maximum of twenty-five knots."

Then Felix seemed for a moment about to continue but instead fell silent, his eyes fixed on the display in front of him.

Giraud shook his head and said quietly, "You still want to do a perimeter sweep with the drone, right?"

Felix looked up hopefully and nodded. "It saved us more than once in Africa. You know as well as I do that nothing is more dangerous than an ambush."

"Except this time, an ambush will be impossible," Giraud said. "We're literally going across the street. If everything goes according to plan, our targets will be unconscious. Of course, the enemy may have a lookout somewhere. But you've seen how many rooftops have a line of sight to this street. The drone could never cover them all before nightfall. And might be spotted in the process."

Felix looked unhappy but finally nodded. "Those are all good points. In about half an hour, I think it will be dark enough to get the drone underway unobserved."

"Good," Giraud said. "We have no way to know when those men may try to move the bomb out if it's indeed in there with them. At least the terrorists were kind enough to pick an abandoned village without working street lights."

The next half hour passed in silence. Then Felix looked up from the drone's control screen and said, "Ready to proceed with mission."

Giraud simply nodded.

Felix held the drone above his head and activated its motor as he opened his hand.

The drone flew steadily to the broken kitchen window, pausing as Felix activated the hover command.

Henri almost commented on how little noise the drone made in flight but caught himself in time.

One look at Felix's total concentration on flying the drone told Henri this would be the wrong time to speak.

Felix used the drone's thermal video feed to look up and down the dark street.

Nothing.

Then he pointed the drone's sensors across the street.

Three thermal signatures. Two were in what Felix thought was probably the living room, and one was in what was perhaps the kitchen.

If the house across the street was the same as the one they were sitting in. Which, from all outward appearances, was very likely.

Most importantly, no heat sources were near the windows with a street view. And they had already seen that the curtains were firmly closed.

Hopefully, safe to proceed.

Felix kept the drone low to avoid standing out against the night sky to a rooftop observer.

There was no sign of one? Maybe not, but Felix's natural pessimism said one was probably up there anyway.

The drone only took a few minutes to circle around to the back of the house.

The thermal view said someone was still in the kitchen. Yes, the drone's flight was quiet.

But the downside of an abandoned village was practically no ambient noise, except when a plane flew overhead. And the only sound inside came from the other two men talking to each other.

Would the man in the kitchen hear the drone just outside?

Just as Felix was about to move the drone further back from the house, his prayers were answered.

First, a plane flew overhead. As both the house he was in and the target house trembled slightly, Felix shook his head.

No wonder the village had been abandoned and, even years after the crash, never reoccupied.

Then, the man in the kitchen walked toward the other two men.

Felix moved the drone closer to the target house.

And saw the broken window he'd been hoping to find.

Then he frowned. The opening seemed to be large enough for the drone.

But not by much.

Should he keep looking?

Movement on the thermal display caught Felix's eye. Could the third man be heading back to the kitchen?

Time to decide.

Felix moved the drone to the broken window, which he could now see would put him in a den to one side of the kitchen.

Anti-collision warnings, both visual and audible over his headset, did their best to distract Felix as he piloted the drone through the tight opening.

Yes, I know, I know, Felix thought with more than a little exasperation.

But seconds later, the drone was inside, and the warnings fell silent.

Felix found a dark corner and set the drone down.

Time to take stock.

All three men were still in the living room.

Should he act at once to release the gas?

Felix frowned at his impatience. That's how you make mistakes, he told himself sternly.

To their credit, Giraud and Henri both sat silently nearby. They understood distracting Felix could lead to the mission ending with failure.

Before charging in, let's see what we've got, Felix decided.

The location he'd picked placed the drone in a pool of darkness that effectively made it invisible to the men in the living room. The only light there came from what looked like a battery-powered lantern.

Felix decided the lantern must have a sliding illumination setting. Set as low as it could go, because the three men were barely visible in the drone's standard video feed.

No wonder they had seen no light through the curtains, Felix thought.

Right. They must have been ordered not to allow any light to be visible from the street.

And how would such an order be enforced?

Felix nodded to himself. He'd been right. There must be someone watching from the rooftops.

He almost said so to Giraud but then stopped himself. Have to focus on what's in front of me.

Then, as one of the men moved, he saw it.

A large metal trunk, resting on a pallet jack. The size you might expect could contain the bomb they were seeking.

Felix looked more closely at the trunk and then frowned. Something about it didn't look right.

What?

He wasn't sure.

Did it matter?

This time, Felix started to open his mouth to say something to Giraud but then closed it again.

"Something about the trunk looks wrong?"

No. It was time to carry out the plan.

Felix commanded the drone off the floor and into hover mode.

Now came the most dangerous part. The drone was small and quiet.

But even in the low light provided by the battery lantern, the three men could hardly miss it once it entered the room.

Felix had to be ready to disperse the gas instantly.

Otherwise, any of the men could shoot the drone with a pistol.

Even grabbing the drone and throwing it against a wall or the floor could work.

Here we go.

Felix moved the drone as close as he could to the men before pressing the "deploy gas" button.

Under other circumstances, the look of astonishment on the men's faces would have been highly amusing.

Now, though, Felix's only reaction was relief. Every second of confusion was time that the drone needed to empty its cargo.

One of the men lifted his arm to grab the drone.

Then, the arm fell back down to the man's side.

His eyes rolled in his head, and he bonelessly fell to the floor.

The other two men looked at each other in evident alarm.

Seconds later, they had joined the first man on the floor.

Were they all still alive? They'd been warned that the effects of the gas were unpredictable without knowing the medical history of each subject.

Felix had the drone hover over each man in turn. He thought he could detect a slight rise and fall of their chests but couldn't be sure.

That each man was at least unconscious, though, was completely clear.

"All three men are down," Felix announced quietly.

At the same moment, Giraud's secure cell phone vibrated.

Felix and Henri both looked at the phone and then at Giraud.

Who made a face, and then picked up the phone and read the text it displayed.

"It seems Monsieur Grishkov has decided to grace us with his presence," Giraud said. "He will be here in the next few minutes."

"Will we wait for him?" Henri asked.

Giraud hesitated. Grishkov had proved his worth in Libya. And a combat veteran who could survive a six-man ambush...definitely an asset.

But the gas would wear off. And they'd been warned that just as the gas might kill rather than render a man unconscious, its effect on some people might not last long.

"Felix, keep a close eye on those men. If any so much as twitches, I want to know about it."

Without waiting for a reply, Giraud turned to Henri. "You and I are going to check our gear one last time. And be quick about it, because I won't wait long."

Henri nodded and began his gear check.

A few minutes later, Giraud tapped his watch. "We're not waiting any longer. I'm in the lead."

Then Giraud started to pull the front door open.

At the same instant, there was a quiet tapping at the back door. Followed by a barely audible voice saying, "Grishkov."

Giraud swung the door nearly closed. Then he strode to the back door and opened it, pistol in hand.

Grishkov. And nobody behind him holding a gun to his head, as Giraud had half-feared.

Giraud waved Grishkov inside, and he immediately walked to the drone's display screen.

"So, all three men are unconscious?" Grishkov asked.

"Yes, but who knows for how long, so we have to hurry," Giraud snapped.

Grishkov looked intently at the screen. "Can you zoom in any closer at that trunk?"

Felix wasted no time doing so. In a strange way, he was almost glad someone else had noticed something too.

Even though Felix could see from Giraud's expression that he'd better be quick about it.

"Look there, do you see it?" Grishkov asked Felix.

Felix's eyes focused on the spot Grishkov's finger was pointing at on the screen.

"Yes...it's a brown patch on the bottom of the trunk. Only a few centimeters square," Felix said.

"So what?" Giraud snapped. "The trunk has some rust. Why does that matter?"

Grishkov shook his head. "That's not rust. The color is wrong. That's the color of cardboard."

"Cardboard?" Giraud said incredulously. "You mean that..."

"Exactly," Grishkov said. "They used cardboard to create a fake trunk, and then used spray paint to make it look like metal."

Grishkov turned back to Felix and asked, "How difficult was it to surprise those men and knock them out?"

"Not difficult at all," Felix said quietly.

"So you're saying this is a trap set by the terrorists, with a fake bomb and a few disposable men," Giraud said.

"Yes," Grishkov said. "The Chechens did this several times. They always killed far more Russians than they sacrificed themselves. There may be no bomb in that fake trunk. But I guarantee there's one in that house somewhere."

Then Grishkov paused.

"Did you do a sweep of the perimeter? Including the rooftops?" Grishkov asked.

"There was no time," Giraud said. "We couldn't risk those men getting away with the bomb so close to Paris."

"I've been looking for some sign of a trigger, especially anything connected to the front door," Grishkov said. "But I see nothing. Of course, if they have a man on a roof nearby, they don't need a trigger inside the house."

"This may all be true," Giraud said. "But what would you have us do? Walk away from these men and whatever is sitting there between them? What if you're wrong?"

Grishkov shrugged. "You are the team leader. It must be your decision. If you say assault that house, I'll lead the way. But I think you know as well as I do that would be a mistake."

Giraud hesitated. What Grishkov was saying made sense. But the risk...

Then Grishkov pointed to the front door, which was still slightly ajar. "Were you about to assault the house when I arrived?"

Giraud nodded.

"Then if there is a lookout, he's only waiting to set off whatever explosives are in that house because he saw me arrive and wants to get me too," Grishkov said firmly. "But he won't wait forever."

"You think even here, we're not safe," Giraud said.

Grishkov gestured toward the walls around them. None too sturdy when they were brand new, after decades of neglect they obviously provided little protection.

"Safer than we'd be across the street, perhaps," Grishkov said. "But I think the danger we're in is limited only by the terrorists' access to explosives. I recommend we head out the back door as quickly as we can."

Giraud nodded sharply and waved toward the back door.

Felix had already closed the case containing the drone's video display and spare batteries. Now, he followed Henri out the back door, followed by Grishkov and Giraud.

Grishkov fought back a sigh of relief as his right foot crossed the back door's threshold.

Just how much explosive had the terrorists packed in the house across the street?

Chapter Twenty-Four

Goussainville-Vieux Pays
20 Kilometers North of Paris

The THALES O-NYX night vision goggles Tareq was wearing hadn't been easy to get. Released to the French military only a few years ago, their availability had been limited by the factory's production capacity.

However, if enough money was offered, nearly every valuable item could become available. Fortunately for Tareq, his employer had deep pockets.

With its fifty-one-degree field of vision, the O-NYX gave Tareq an excellent view of the house occupied by his men from his rooftop vantage point.

And the house across the street where the DGSE team was now preparing for their assault.

Frowning, Tareq looked at his watch again. His men had failed to check in several minutes ago. Should he risk calling or texting them?

No. Tareq would do nothing that could let the DGSE team know that someone was watching nearby.

His men were expendable. He was not.

Tareq's heart leaped as he saw the house's front door open. The DGSE team was taking the bait!

Who was that?

At nearly the same moment, a car drove up to the back of the house. A man quickly exited and came through the back door.

Just as the front door swung closed.

Snarling a curse, Tareq willed himself to calm down and took stock.

He quickly realized this could be a good thing.

This could be the missing fourth man.

Tareq had seen the other three men as they entered in daylight. None had looked Russian to him, and he was sure that one of the men was Captain Giraud, the team leader.

So maybe this latest arrival was the Russian. In that case, fate was smiling on Tareq today.

Tareq looked at his watch again. It seemed like hours had passed since the Russian's arrival.

But his watch told Tareq the truth that he'd suspected. It had only been a few minutes.

Patience. Then, I'll have them all.

Tareq's head swiveled. What was that? Motion at the back door?

What were they...

A wave of anger shook Tareq as he realized what was happening.

They thought they could escape.

Tareq's lips peeled back in a feral snarl.

No. There would be no escape today.

His thumb smashed the radio trigger.

At the same moment, Tareq hugged the rooftop. He thought he was far enough away from the blast.

But he'd had to be sure he could see both houses clearly.

Well, Tareq would know soon enough if he'd chosen well.

Or if he would be off to Paradise a bit earlier than planned.

A tremendous roar was followed almost immediately by the surface he hugged rocking like a small boat on the open ocean.

Tareq gripped the roof tiles even more tightly, and held on for dear life.

The noise and motion seemed to go on endlessly.

Once again his watch told the truth. It had been a matter of seconds.

The motion stopped, and Tareq lifted his head. The night vision goggles still worked.

Glorious!

The house his men had occupied was completely destroyed.

All the homes nearby had fared little better. A few walls were still standing.

But in the clouds of dust that covered over a square block, nothing moved.

Tareq couldn't even see anything recognizable as a body.

He quickly realized that, short of sifting through the rubble, he wouldn't get better confirmation of success than he had right now.

And Tareq could already hear sirens in the distance.

The village might be abandoned. This close to Paris, though, Tareq had expected that someone would hear and report the explosion.

Time to go.

Now, at last, with success to report to his boss.

CHAPTER TWENTY-FIVE

Les Invalides
Paris, France

Anatoly Grishkov opened his eyes and immediately regretted it. The bright light overhead sent a lancing pain through his head.

Concussion. Again.

"Just a second, let me get the lights," a familiar voice said.

Seconds later, blessed darkness coaxed Grishkov to open his eyes again.

Better. Though there was still a throbbing that told Grishkov his head would hurt for some time yet.

"It's a good thing your head is so hard," the voice said. "Even better that you had a helmet on top of it."

It took only a slight movement of Grishkov's head to bring the voice's owner into view so he could confirm his guess.

Yes. It was Vasilyev.

Grishkov winced. He had paid a price for even that slight movement.

"I was told to give you some good news as soon as you were conscious. You are the only one on the team who required hospitalization.

Also, assorted scans and tests show nothing seriously wrong with you. You may be discharged from here as soon as tomorrow," Vasilyev said.

Grishkov grunted. "That brings me to my first question. Where am I?"

"Right, sorry," Vasilyev said with a smile. "I forgot for a second that you've just regained consciousness. This is a French military hospital called Les Invalides, located in Paris."

"Really?" Grishkov said. "I've heard of it but thought it was now just a museum."

Vasilyev nodded. "Me too. In fact, there are several museums in this complex, as well as a military home for the retired and disabled, which is the purpose that gave Les Invalides its name when Louis XIV commissioned it in the 17th century. You are in a small military hospital that now primarily serves for special cases."

"Yes, I see," Grishkov said. "Ones like mine, where civilian doctors might wonder how I came by explosive trauma and ask awkward questions."

"Exactly," Vasilyev replied. "Also, the military doctors here are far more experienced in assessing and treating such injuries. Now, I should give you the other bit of good news."

A nurse walked in with a clear plastic bag filled with a liquid of some type, which she attached to a metal stand next to Grishkov's hospital bed. Looking down, he saw that an IV shunt was already in his right arm.

"Your doctor told me you would be given no pain medication until you regained consciousness," Vasilyev said. "In your case, they believed it might interfere with your natural healing process. Now, though, you are about to get some relief."

The nurse had been busy checking the monitors arrayed around Grishkov's head but now stopped and looked at him critically.

"And how is your pain, Monsieur Grishkov, on a scale of one to ten?" she asked.

Grishkov shrugged. "Let's say three."

The nurse made a sound that Grishkov could only interpret as "skeptical."

"I'm the one who cleaned and stitched your head wound last night, so I doubt that," she said. "But either way, your colleague says you would only accept a non-narcotic painkiller. Is that correct?"

"Yes, it is," Grishkov replied immediately. "I've seen too many good men, ones I respected, fall prey to addiction. So there are no narcotics in that bag?"

The nurse's eyes followed Grishkov's outstretched finger to the IV bag and nodded.

"Yes," she replied. "Non-narcotic and anti-inflammatory. It won't eliminate the pain, but it should give you enough relief to let you sleep. And no, unconsciousness isn't the same as sleep, which you still need. With more rest and sleep, your doctor says you may be eligible for discharge tomorrow."

With that, the nurse made a few more notes on her small tablet and left.

"So, who's been minding the store while you've been waiting for me to wake up?" Grishkov asked.

"I was ordered to stand down drone operations, and come here to see whether you'd be able to resume your role as my backup, if necessary," Vasilyev replied.

"And if I hadn't been, Moscow would have ordered someone else here, I suppose," Grishkov said.

Vasilyev shook his head. "I doubt it. By the time another agent could be selected, briefed, and flown here, I think the bomb will have either been found or exploded."

"You're right," Grishkov said with a frown. "So my guess was correct that the explosion was not from a dirty bomb?"

"Yes and no," Vasilyev replied. "The amount of radioactive materials wasn't enough to pose a real danger to you or the rest of your team as long as you were quickly decontaminated."

Seeing Grishkov's expression Vasilyev hastily added, "Which you were."

Grishkov nodded in relief and Vasilyev continued.

"The DGSE has shared their analysis of the radioactive material with us, and I have used it to review the readings we got from the drone just before you went to the target site. It's now clear it was a fairly large quantity of nuclear waste generated by medical scanning equipment. Controlled, but apparently not strictly enough."

"How did the drone mistake it for a real dirty bomb?" Grishkov asked.

Vasilyev made a face. "Because we had the search settings set on the assumption the bomb would be housed in a well-shielded metal case."

"Yes," Grishkov said. "The sort of case faked by the terrorists in case we got a look at it."

"Exactly," Vasilyev replied. "Now that we have this experience behind us, that trick won't work again. I've reset the search parameters to screen out the radioactive elements commonly generated by medical scanning equipment. For the bomb to pose a real threat, those aren't the elements most likely to be present, anyway."

"How about the drone's...other capability? Did it work?" Grishkov asked quietly.

Vasilyev stood up and opened the door to the hospital room. He then quickly looked up and down the corridor.

Empty.

"I've scanned this room for listening devices," Vasilyev said. "Still, I'm going to keep my answer brief. Yes, we think it did. The level of anxiety and fear detected were perfectly consistent with the men having been told they were guarding a dirty bomb."

"So, the men with the fake bomb were lied to twice," Grishkov said. "First, that they were guarding a dirty bomb. Second, that it would blow up later on in Paris. Not as soon as the DGSE team showed up."

"Correct," Vasilyev replied. "Your Captain Giraud looked in on you a few hours ago. He told me then that it would take time before anything else was known about the men. Even at top priority, a records search based on DNA results isn't instant. Assuming that there are any matching DNA records available. Of course, the condition of the remains doesn't help."

Grishkov just nodded. He knew from his time as a homicide detective that many factors could compromise the accuracy of DNA test results. Such as the chemicals found in explosive residue. And the high heat and pressure from an explosion.

Despite the best efforts of defense attorneys and the scientists in their pay, they had yet to demonstrate that a DNA match found after surmounting such obstacles was false. But Grishkov had seen many cases where a match he'd expected to find turned out to be elusive.

Vasilyev was right, though, Grishkov thought. The real problem would probably be that these terrorists were recent arrivals. And so not in a European DNA database.

"Did Giraud say anything about any other leads to the terrorists or their bomb?" Grishkov asked.

"No," Vasilyev replied. "I don't know the man, but my sense wasn't that he was hiding anything from me. Just that he had nothing to say."

Then Vasilyev paused.

"Anyway, I had the impression that he was here just as much to speak to me as to check on you," Vasilyev continued.

Grishkov nodded. "Makes sense. Once he heard you were here, Giraud wanted to find out whether the drone was searching for the bomb and, if not, how soon it would be back in the air."

"Right," Vasilyev replied. "Giraud asked me quite a few questions. Ones that showed he's relied on drone reports before, including during combat operations. He asked me to let him know as soon as we find anything. I told him we would."

"And now that you've verified my discharge tomorrow, you can report to Moscow that the mission may continue," Grishkov said with a smile.

Vasilyev nodded. "I will. Despite my misgivings about your condition."

Seeing Grishkov's reaction, Vasilyev smiled. "Yes. And despite your misgivings about mine."

Grishkov started to object, but Vasilyev made a shooing motion before he could utter the words.

"We both know I'm not fully recovered," Vasilyev said. "But I'm here for the same reason you are. The lives of your children are at stake. And after all we've been through together, I couldn't abide something happening to them any more than you could."

Before Grishkov could reply, Vasilyev stood up and said, "Good luck, old friend."

And was gone.

Grishkov stared straight ahead at the muted TV, now playing a French commercial for dishwashing soap.

He told himself I should do what that nurse said and try to sleep.

But where will we get another lead if the DNA results come up empty?

Chapter Twenty-Six

Hotel Near Centrolio Truck Parking
North of Valladolid, Spain

Samir Ali had just finished trying to empty his stomach.

Again.

On the bright side, he'd made it to the bathroom the last few times.

Sadly, there hadn't been anything left in his stomach the last time.

Or the two times before that.

But his body had been very efficient in ridding itself of the poor quality food he'd eaten at the truck stop diner.

Now that he was more or less conscious, the first thing that struck him was the smell.

Ali's bleary eyes began to focus on their surroundings.

The source of the smell became quickly apparent.

He had to get out of this room.

What's that ringing in my ears?

Several moments passed before Ali realized the ringing wasn't in his ears.

It was coming from the phone Abdul had given him.

The last thing Ali could remember doing before throwing himself on the bed where he was now was...putting the phone on its charger.

Ali picked up the phone and pressed the green button on the screen.

He was startled to find the screen immediately filled with Abdul's face.

A face that looked very angry.

"Where have you..." Abdul began and then stopped.

Because he had seen Ali's face.

"What happened to you?" Abdul asked in a much more sympathetic tone.

Not that Ali cared. He felt so bad, he truly wasn't worried about Abdul's opinion.

"I think it was the food I ate at the truck stop," Ali said. "I've been sick ever since. I'm going to try to clean myself and go."

Abdul looked at him critically. "Are you sure you can go on, my friend? You know you've been in that hotel room for two days."

That got Ali's attention. "Two days! I had no idea. No wonder I feel so weak. But never mind. I've taken the job. Now I'm going to finish it."

"Good, good," Abdul said with a smile, as he pulled a cigarette out of a Dunhill carton and took a long drag.

Not for the first time, Ali thought one of the uses Abdul had for smoking was to give him time to think before speaking.

Though Ali was sure nicotine addiction had something to do with it too.

After he exhaled a large puff of smoke Abdul finally said, "I'm glad to hear it. Please let me know when you get to the French border. I hope you feel better, my friend."

The screen went dark.

Well, me too, Ali thought.

After showering, brushing his teeth, and putting on the one change of clothes he'd brought to the room, Ali felt...well, better.

After downing a bottle of water from a vending machine in the hotel lobby, Ali mentally upgraded his status to "human."

At least, human enough to climb into the truck.

And to drive the truck to Paris?

Well, Ali thought, I guess we'll see.

CHAPTER TWENTY-SEVEN

Hendaye, France
Spain/France Border Crossing Point

Samir Ali knew all about the Schengen Agreement. First signed in 1985, it has expanded membership many times since then and allows free travel throughout most European Union countries. The exceptions are Ireland, Bulgaria, Croatia, Romania, and Cyprus.

None of those exceptions would concern Ali during this trip.

No, in theory, having crossed into Spain from Morocco, Ali could now travel throughout the "Schengen territory" for up to ninety days. Land borders within Schengen, like the one between Spain and France, had, for all practical purposes, been erased.

In theory.

Practice, Ali had learned, was not quite the same thing.

The first clue was the traffic's glacial pace as Ali's highway approached the French border.

Ali was more than a little annoyed. This was a toll highway! If there was any justification for making its users pay, it should be greater speed.

Not that Ali was paying the tolls. No, those were debited automatically to an account linked to a transponder Abdul had attached to the truck's windshield. He'd done that before Ali had left Morocco for Spain.

As far as Ali was concerned, though, it didn't matter. Someone had paid for the dubious privilege of using this highway. That should buy him the ability to go somewhere near the posted speed limit.

Instead of crawling along at a speed no better than walking pace.

Ali wondered if Abdul had considered sending him along a different route rather than the cursed one he was committed to now.

And he was totally committed. There was no highway exit between where Ali's truck was right now and the French border.

The answer to Ali's question was - yes.

Abdul had looked at alternative routes for crossing the French border. None were appealing.

First, the simple logistics imposed by the Pyrenees mountain range, which extended for about five hundred kilometers. Along nearly the entire border between France and Spain.

The natural border created by the Pyrenees was a major reason for the separate development of France and Spain. Roads crossing it, particularly ones suitable for a truck the size of Ali's, were few and far between.

Next, not all of those roads were open. Starting in 2021, France had unilaterally closed many of the smaller roads leading from Spain. The announced justification had been to reduce illegal immigration.

Spanish localities along the border had objected, pointing out that closure methods such as placing large rocks in the road did nothing to stop immigrants on foot.

The French ignored the protests, and the rocks remained.

Also, in the decades after the Schengen Agreement had been signed, French police and even military units had conducted routine "spot checks" in border regions. Though the claimed focus was preventing terrorism, illegal immigration and criminal activity of all sorts were also targets.

Abdul had finally decided to send Ali through one of the highest-volume land border crossing points for two reasons.

First, Abdul knew the French wouldn't be able to search every truck. Not without effectively closing the border.

Next, Abdul also knew how the French would narrow down the search criteria to find the truck carrying a bomb.

There were several ways to get a bomb from North Africa to France relatively quickly. First and easiest to cover were direct sailings from North African ports across the Mediterranean to France.

All French ports were on high alert, and such direct sailings were not common.

Especially by comparison with shipments from Morocco and other North African countries to Spain.

So, focus on any truck that had been shipped to Spain. Or had a cargo offloaded at a Spanish port. Potentially onto a vehicle that could then be driven to France.

And how would a French customs agent know anything about a shipment that had arrived at a Spanish port?

That's where the Schengen Information System (SIS) came in.

The SIS was the largest international database in the world. Yes, it had information on everyone who entered the Schengen Territory.

And also on every vehicle. And ship. As well as the goods they offloaded.

So, at the Hendaye border crossing point, French officials would be looking for a truck that had arrived from North Africa? Well, the SIS would tell them that Ali's truck had come from...Madrid.

Drilling down further, French officials would find that Ali's truck had been transporting goods regularly from Spain to France for many years.

How? Because Abdul's contacts at the Spanish port of Algeciras, where Ali's truck had arrived, included a Spanish customs agent with SIS access.

A customs agent who the Société Générale de Transport International had paid well for many years.

In fact, their payments amounted to more than his Spanish government salary.

The Société Générale de Transport International was a massive operation, with hundreds of trucks. Including one operating between Spain and France that was a make and model match for Ali's.

"Correcting" the truck's Vehicle Identification Number to match Ali's was a matter of a few keystrokes by someone with SIS access.

The only real challenge had been ensuring that the other truck's physical license plate made it to Algeciras in time for the switch. That had been accomplished with over an hour to spare.

The best part was that this vehicle identity switch covered another key French search criteria.

The French were looking for a truck that was not registered with one of the half-dozen largest companies transporting goods between Spain and France.

Certainly not one registered to the Société Générale de Transport International. The largest of those half-dozen companies.

So yes, Ali would fume for some time yet as he waited to cross the French border.

And his anxiety level would climb every hour and shoot up when he neared the crossing point and saw one truck after another ahead waved over for inspection.

But was there any chance Ali would be stopped and his truck searched?

No. None at all.

CHAPTER TWENTY-EIGHT

Les Invalides
Paris, France

Anatoly Grishkov looked up in surprise as Captain Giraud walked into his hospital room and grinned.

"So, when he left just now, Vasilyev said my ride from the hospital had been arranged. Surely, you are too senior to be my chauffeur!"

Giraud smiled back. "I think I'll let Henri do the driving this time. He and Felix have been guarding your room while you've been here."

Grishkov's eyebrows flew up in astonishment. "Really? I've never seen them."

"Good," Giraud said seriously. "Their job was to guard you, not stand in front of you and chat. I had each guard one of the two corridors providing access to your room. All other patients were moved to other floors. The stairwell doors were locked and bolted, and the elevator will not stop at this floor."

Grishkov nodded thoughtfully. "Unless someone you cleared, like Vasilyev, wished to visit."

"Exactly," Giraud said. "Counting the bomb waiting for us in Libya, the attempt that put you in that bed was the third intended to kill either you alone or the entire team at once."

Then Giraud paused and frowned. "Frankly, I'm starting to take it a bit personally."

"Well, you'll get no argument from me there!" Grishkov exclaimed. "I don't suppose there was enough left of the sacrificial lambs to tell us anything."

Giraud shrugged. "The forensic team managed to salvage some remains for DNA testing. But preliminary results came back with no matches. From what we could see of the men on the micro drone video, I suspect it's because they were recent arrivals in France and are not in any European database."

"Yes, I discussed this matter with Vasilyev, and he thought that might happen. So, do we have any leads to pursue?" Grishkov asked.

"The only one that holds out any real hope is the money trail from Syria to the security company," Giraud replied. "I have a team working on it as the DGSE, but so far, they have come up empty."

Then Giraud paused again, this time for several moments. Finally, he continued.

"I've also contacted an American friend at the Central Intelligence Agency. We worked together in Africa a few years ago. As a favor to me, he's also got analysts working on the money trail," Giraud said.

Grishkov had thought he'd felt astonished before. It took a few moments before he managed to ask, "Did you get anyone's approval to contact the Americans?"

"No," Giraud said. "And I think you know why. Someone at the DGSE is working with the terrorists. Someone in a very high position. There's no other explanation for the traps and obstacles that have been set in our path."

Grishkov nodded vigorously. "I'm glad I don't have to waste time convincing you of that. I'd already reached the same conclusion. Is there anything we can do besides wait for the Americans?"

"Well, yes," Giraud replied. "We can wait for your friend Vasilyev to get us a lead with his drone. And we can wait for your doctor to appear to release you to your superior officer officially."

Grishkov made a face. "Is that really necessary? What would happen if I just got up and left?"

"What would happen in the Russian Army?" Giraud asked with what was obviously genuine curiosity.

"Nothing good," Grishkov said automatically and then shrugged.

"I suppose some things are the same in armies the world over."

Giraud smiled. "I think you're right."

Then Grishkov cocked his head and said, "Since we have a few minutes, like it or not, I'm curious about how you came to be in the French Army. You're not like the officers I remember when I was a Sergeant in the Russian Army, and I mean that in a good way."

"I haven't thought that far back in quite some time," Giraud replied. "It may sound naïve, but I really did want to serve my country. The Soviet Union had already collapsed when I enlisted, but we still faced many threats around the world."

"Really?" Grishkov said. "I know France still has military bases in some of its former colonies in Africa. But where else?"

"First, there are the sovereignty forces, which protect French territory," Giraud replied. Those are in French possessions in the Caribbean, Indian Ocean, Polynesia..."

"Right, right, I'd forgotten that France held on to some islands. But that's it, right?" Grishkov asked.

Giraud shook his head. "No. Our largest detachment of troops is in French Guiana, on the South American mainland."

"Really? Why keep that territory in particular?" Grishkov asked.

"First, because the several hundred thousand people there wish it to remain part of France," Giraud said. "In fact, a few years back, they even voted against a degree of autonomy. Guiana's value to France comes mostly from the European Space Center."

Grishkov nodded. "Right, I remember now. Right on the equator, making it cheaper to launch heavy payloads into orbit."

"Correct," Giraud said. "That's why the Americans had us launch their James Webb Space Telescope from Guiana."

"So, which of your former colonies still host French military bases?" Grishkov asked.

Giraud frowned. "That list changes all the time depending on politics and on the willingness of French politicians to commit funds. We have gone back and forth over the past few years on reopening a base in Madagascar. Right now, though, we have bases in Djibouti, Senegal, Ivory Coast, Gabon, Germany, and the United Arab Emirates. The last two, of course, were never French colonies."

"The UAE? Really!" Grishkov exclaimed. "I'm sure there's a story there, but will leave it since I don't see how it could affect us during this mission. How many French Army troops overseas altogether?"

"About twelve thousand, including Foreign Legion troops," Giraud said. "But of course, that doesn't include sailors on visiting ships of the French Navy. Some islands like St. Pierre and Miquelon, for example, have no French Army presence and rely entirely on the Navy."

"St. Pierre and Miquelon?" Grishkov repeated with a frown. "Never heard of them."

Giraud nodded. "I'm not surprised. The islands are off the coast of Canada and only have about six thousand residents. Fishing and tourism is about all they have going on there."

"No idea that Europe still had any possessions off North America," Grishkov said, shaking his head.

"Not just us. Another European country actually has a land border with North America," Giraud said with a smile.

"My geographic knowledge isn't that good. But now I know you're pulling my leg," Grishkov declared.

"Not at all! You clearly haven't heard the story of the Whisky War," Giraud said.

"I have not," Grishkov said, his eyes narrowing.

"First, you know that Greenland is still under the Danish government for defense and military matters, though it's autonomous in other respects," Giraud said.

Grishkov sighed. "I didn't, but go on."

"For decades, Canada and Denmark had a dispute over Hans Island. Small and uninhabited but still claimed by both countries. Every year or so, a ship from one country or the other would visit. The Danish would leave a bottle of brandy and a flag. The Canadians would leave a bottle of whiskey and a 'Welcome to Canada' sign."

Grishkov laughed. "Now, that's my kind of war! Was it ever resolved?"

"Yes," Giraud replied. "In 2022, Canada and Denmark agreed to split the island in half, creating the only land border between Europe and North America."

"How large is your Navy?" Grishkov asked. "Do I remember correctly that you have a nuclear-powered aircraft carrier?"

"Yes," Giraud said proudly. "The only one outside the U.S. Navy. We have about forty thousand sailors operating nearly two hundred ships and submarines. As well as nearly two hundred naval aircraft. And we are the only Western country outside the U.S. that still makes nuclear submarines entirely on its own, and one of the few to produce its own military jets and helicopters."

"Remarkable," Grishkov said. "But I have to ask, what does France plan to do with all that firepower? I know, for example, there are those in Russia who dream of rebuilding the Soviet Union. China has clear designs to dominate the entire Pacific region. Does France have any such ambitions?"

Giraud shook his head. "No. Our job is to defend France against foreign threats, some of which you've already mentioned. If Russia can conquer territory westward, when would it stop? Can we really rely on the Americans to intervene? And there is only one way French Polynesia is an obstacle to turning the Pacific into a Chinese lake. If we can make Beijing think twice about the price that must be paid to seize it."

"Well, I agree with you there," Grishkov said. "Talk has never stopped an invading Army or Navy. Unless it was backed up by military force."

"Of course, the mission we are on now illustrates even more clearly the need for a capable military," Giraud replied. "The French police are competent. But they seldom face criminals armed with semiautomatic weapons and grenades."

Grishkov nodded. "Or have to search for radioactive bombs with drones."

"Exactly," Giraud replied. "Speaking of that, I encountered your friend Vasilyev on my way to see you. He said the drone will be back in the air later today."

"Good to hear," Grishkov said and then smiled broadly.

Too broadly, Giraud thought.

Giraud turned around and at once saw the reason for Grishkov's pleasure.

The doctor was here at last.

CHAPTER TWENTY-NINE

Hendaye, France
Spain/France Border Crossing Point

Samir Ali had decidedly mixed feelings when he finally reached the end of the long line of vehicles waiting to cross the border from Spain to France.

On the one hand, having the conclusion of this ordeal in sight was a relief.

On the other, Ali had little to do while waiting in line but to think.

None of his thoughts had been comforting.

Ali started by telling himself he couldn't care less about his cargo being discovered and confiscated.

That was absolutely true. As was the fact that Ali had no idea what he was carrying.

Ali had seen movies where suspects were hooked up to a box with many wires, and an expert could determine whether the man was telling the truth.

Well, they could bring it on, Ali thought. I was told I'm carrying oilfield equipment, and I have no reason to doubt that.

In fact, the borders Ali had crossed – including ones with sniffer dogs – had given him more confidence that he wasn't carrying anything illegal.

Like drugs or bombs.

His racing thoughts, though, had come up with another problem.

The large bag of cash Abdul had given Ali at the start of the trip.

Yes, the cash Ali had been given was payment for driving a shipment all the way from Libya to France.

But Ali's documents said his trip had started in Spain.

Even if Ali told the truth, the money in the bag was far too much to drive a legitimate shipment from Libya.

The French police could only come to one conclusion, Ali thought gloomily.

Ali either knew he was driving an illegal shipment.

Or he should have known, if only because he was being paid so much.

Worst case? Ali would be imprisoned indefinitely while the police investigated.

Best case? The police would accept that Ali was merely stupid, not criminal. And they would confiscate his money as part of their investigation.

Ali's chances of ever seeing the money again?

Low. Very low.

Ali did his best to keep these thoughts off his face as he pulled up in front of the uniformed French official.

The man wasn't even looking at him. Instead, his attention was entirely on the tablet he was holding.

Ali guessed correctly that his truck's license number was being checked against a database.

Would the man like what he found?

The man looked up at Ali and impatiently waved him forward.

Forward. Not off to the side for inspection.

Ali could hardly believe his good fortune.

But he had the sense to take "yes" for an answer.

Very quickly, Ali was back on the highway. Thanks to the delay imposed by the inspection point, the way ahead was clear for some distance.

Ali wanted nothing more than to be done with this whole business. The quickest way to accomplish that?

Try to drive straight on to Paris.

Ali knew better, though. He wasn't even close to fully recovered from his encounter with Spanish truck-stop food.

The only hopeful sign was that Ali actually felt hungry. That was quite an improvement from just hours ago when even the thought of food had made him nauseous.

Ali scowled. Anything but truck-stop food.

The hours Ali had spent idling on the highway in front of the border though, had come in handy.

If I can find the sign, there was an area designated for truck parking a short distance ahead.

There it is!

Ali carefully pulled into the spot and heaved a sigh of relief.

Now he felt that he had really reached France!

If Ali had read the map correctly, there was a place to eat a short walk away.

Ali had looked up the meaning of "boulanger" and "pâtissier." Then he'd looked up what customers had written about the place.

His stomach, which had been empty for days, rumbled at the images that accompanied the enthusiastic reviews.

For once, the map was right. It took him under five minutes to reach the bakery.

A sandwich made with fresh-baked bread and a fruit pastry that looked like an artistic creation later, Ali felt like a new man.

But not quite ready to walk to the nearest hotel, about a kilometer away.

The man at the counter had been very pleasant. Would he be willing to help?

It turned out he was. Once he understood what Ali wanted, a taxi appeared at the bakery's door within minutes.

The hotel's reviews were good, and the price was reasonable by European standards, about a hundred Euros.

Would Ali's luck hold?

As he walked into the hotel lobby, Ali's first thought was -yes.

It smelled clean. On the other side of the lobby, sliding glass doors revealed a sparkling blue swimming pool, full of happy children.

Well, Ali was no swimmer. Not since he'd been a child himself, much longer ago than he cared to remember.

But you had to be old indeed, Ali thought, not to have your spirits lifted by children's laughter.

There were two people at the hotel's reception, both busy with other guests when Ali approached. A man who looked ex-military. And a woman who from her appearance Ali guessed was North African.

Ali sent a prayer heavenwards, since he was sure which would be better for him.

God was apparently busy with more important matters. Ali got the man.

He turned out, though, to be just as agreeable as the man at the bakery.

Minutes later, Ali was facing a bed in a room just as clean as the lobby.

The truck stop was now just a bad memory.

Had Ali been forced to spend more money?

Yes.

Had it been worth it?

Absolutely.

As he closed his eyes, Ali's last thought was that he would finally finish this delivery tomorrow.

And could use the cash from Abdul to finally retire.

CHAPTER THIRTY

Near Orléans, France

Samir Ali had been pushing hard since leaving Hendaye, stopping only once for gas and a quick bite.

His reward was that Paris was now only about two hours away.

He should be happy.

But Ali was not.

Because the people who had been following him were back.

Or, Ali realized, maybe they'd never left. In the gridlock approaching the French border, perhaps he simply hadn't been able to spot them.

In any case, Ali was now confident they weren't police. No, they would have stopped and arrested him by now.

In fact, the border would have been the perfect opportunity. His truck at a dead stop, and heavily armed police in every direction.

So if not the police, then who?

Only one possibility made sense to Ali. Men working for Abdul.

Or people working for the same organization as Abdul.

Whatever that might be.

They might have been told to follow him to be sure Ali reached his destination.

Or, a voice in his head said coldly, get rid of him once he arrived and was no longer needed.

Ali tried to ignore the voice. But it kept talking.

And that big bag of cash Ali had in the truck. Certainly large enough to pay one or two people to follow and kill him.

It didn't matter how many times Ali told the voice to shut up.

It kept saying that if Ali kept driving, he would be dead in two hours.

As soon as he reached his destination in Paris.

What could he do?

Almost as if it were a sign from God, the answer appeared.

Ali did not speak French.

But to understand the next highway exit sign, no French was necessary. Along with some words in French, it had a symbol Ali recognized at once.

Train.

At the last possible moment, Ali wrenched the wheel right.

No turn signal.

A chorus of horns behind him said Ali's fellow drivers were not amused.

But when Ali looked in the rearview mirror behind him, for the first time since he'd started driving this morning, he saw...nothing.

For the moment, at least, the people following him didn't know where he was.

Then Ali started kicking himself. Hard.

The phone Abdul had given him. Had made a point of saying must never leave Ali's side.

Ali was no genius when it came to technology. But he knew that a cell phone could be used to track someone.

It went out the window, and Ali was gratified to see it shatter to pieces when it struck the road.

The GPS! Abdul had given him that too!

Could it be used to track him?

Who knew?

Out the window it went and broke up just as nicely.

Ali looked behind him. Still nobody.

OK.

Ali shook his head at his stupidity. He needed to find the train station.

And had just thrown away his only GPS.

Then, as if in answer to his prayers, Ali saw a sign marked "Gare des Aubrais."

That name meant nothing to Ali. But the train symbol next to the name did.

Ali sent thanks heavenward, thinking that God must have a special place in his heart for fools.

Two signs later, Ali had reached the train station. Even better, though traffic had appeared behind Ali as he drew closer to the station, no cars followed him.

It had been easy to confirm this.

Ali had gone exactly the speed limit and hugged the right lane. Every vehicle that had appeared behind him had wasted no time passing his truck. Two had made gestures Ali had never seen before.

But Ali had correctly guessed their intent.

Ali sighed with relief as he parked his truck and thought how happy he would be never to see it again.

His hand reached for the door handle and then froze.

Oh, no!

There was a line of people stretching outside the station entrance! They must all be buying tickets!

Ali knew immediately that whoever had been following him would find him with little effort if he stood in that line.

What can I do?

His phone!

Ali had his personal cell phone, which he hadn't used since Abdul had given him one. After all, Ali knew from experience that international roaming charges were no joke.

But this was no time to worry about such details.

Would it even work in France?

Yes!

Now, what train station is this?

Though Ali had seen the name on several signs, he still didn't remember it since it was foreign.

Fortunately, the station's name was there on its front, in giant letters.

Ali keyed the station's name into his phone's web browser and then "trains south."

A list of several websites appeared, all selling train tickets. Ali first tried one marked "SNCF," which said it was "official."

His reward was a twirling circle that...just kept spinning.

Right. The people in that line have phones too. There's an outage of some kind.

In desperation, Ali tried one site after another.

Finally, one worked! It claimed to have a ticket available on a train that would reach Toulouse in just six hours.

That would get him most of the way to Spain!

Ali had one personal credit card that he had only used twice before. He kept it in reserve for genuine emergencies, because it always gave him a terrible exchange rate, and charged him fees for each transaction on top of that.

Never mind, Ali thought with a sigh. I can't spend my money if I'm dead.

Once Ali had put in his credit card details, he was supposed to get his ticket via email.

Would he, or was this some sort of scam?

Ali checked his email, and sure enough. There was the ticket with a bar code that was supposed to be scannable at the train station.

My papers, my cash...I have to be sure not to forget anything.

Because no matter what, I'm not coming back. I'll barely make this train as it is.

Ali walked past the line of people, ignoring the muttering that followed him. Finally, a scowling man in uniform stopped Ali and said something Ali didn't understand.

Ali showed him the bar code. The man cocked his head in surprise and then reached for the scanner clipped to his belt.

When the scan was complete, there was a chime on a tablet the man held in his left hand. He looked at it, and gestured toward a train just steps away.

Ali wasted no time hurrying towards it. He repeated the procedure with another man next to the train, who at least wasn't scowling.

In fact, after he scanned Ali's bar code, he actually smiled. And showed him to his seat.

It turned out that Ali had bought the very last ticket available. In first class.

As Ali settled into his seat, he thought to himself that now he was home free.

Then he stirred uneasily.

No. Not quite.

Ali thought the train would likely go faster to Toulouse than his pursuers could drive.

But how could he be sure there weren't other men they could call on in southern France? Ali had no idea how large the organization was behind the truck and its cargo, but he already knew that they had real money.

It was time for Ali to take the initiative. But how?

Inspiration hit him like a lightning bolt.

Ali knew, though, that he had to act immediately.

Fortunately, the lavatory designated for first-class passengers was steps away and unoccupied.

Once he'd locked the door, Ali pulled out his cell phone and dialed 112. He already knew that was the number for emergencies because he'd considered calling the police earlier on his pursuers.

But Ali had discarded the idea because he'd seen no way to avoid being stopped and questioned himself.

Now, though, he slowly and carefully reported a suspicious truck. That he thought might be carrying drugs or explosives.

Or maybe both.

The operator's English had been quite limited. But Ali was confident she had understood the two key words "drugs" and "explosives."

Ali had no way of knowing, but he was helped by the fact that about sixty percent of English vocabulary came from French, dating back to the Norman conquest of England in the 11th century.

So, one of the many French terms for drugs was "la drogue."

The French term for explosive was...the same word.

Ali had given a complete description of the truck and its license plate number. And the fact that the truck's journey had started in Libya.

When the operator said something that Ali knew was something like, "Please give me your contact information," he switched the phone off.

Of course, Ali knew emergency services could trace a call back to a location. In fact, he was counting on it.

Ali was sure that the trace would point to the train station. But he thought, correctly, that zeroing in on the train he now occupied would be impossible.

As long as he removed the cell phone's battery and SIM card before the train started to move.

Ali did that with several minutes to spare.

As Ali opened the lavatory door, he glanced at the nearest passengers. He'd done his best to keep his voice low but audible.

Had anyone overheard his call to the police?

Nearly everyone's attention was consumed by a cell phone or tablet. The few exceptions were older passengers holding a printed newspaper or magazine.

Even better, at least two-thirds of the people Ali could see had wireless earpieces, shutting out the world around them.

Nobody paid him the slightest bit of attention.

It was one of the few times Ali could think of when he'd been happy to see modern technology widely used.

Ali regained his seat just as the train started to move.

Yes. Maybe now I've improved my chances.

CHAPTER THIRTY-ONE

Just Past Hendaye, France
Spain/France Border Crossing Point

Abdul had hoped he could remain in Morocco, learn that Ali had made the delivery, and then disappear to enjoy the money he had earned.

But when Ali fell ill and delayed delivery by two days, Abdul decided he had to follow up in person after all.

Yes, he had hired two men to follow Ali, each in a different car. Their job was to tie up the loose end Ali represented once he had reached the delivery point.

The men who had hired Abdul had made it clear that was one of the services Abdul had been paid to provide.

Abdul had used these two men on other jobs, and just like Ali, they had never failed him.

The sum of cash Ali had with him was more than enough motivation for the two men to complete their mission.

When Ali had stopped for first one day and then two in Spain, Abdul's first thought was either alcohol or drugs had caused the delay.

However, Abdul quickly discarded that idea based on what he knew of Ali. No, the man wasn't religious.

But Ali was careful. Nobody would have survived driving a truck around Libya as long as Ali had without a well-developed sense of caution.

Besides, while alcohol and drugs were expensive and difficult to obtain in Libya, it could be done.

Algeria and Morocco not only allowed the sale of alcohol but also produced wine for their domestic market and export.

Morocco was the principal European market source of both marijuana and its derivative hashish, with plenty left over for domestic consumption.

No, if Ali wanted to indulge himself with the money Abdul had provided, he would have done it before reaching Spain.

Abdul had almost ordered the men to break into Ali's hotel room in Spain. But Abdul had held back because once Ali knew for sure he was being followed, he would have been certain to flee.

Though it was good Ali had answered when he did. The patience of the people paying Abdul was...limited.

In fact, when Abdul contacted them to advise that Ali was again on his way, the response had been three simple words.

No more delays.

They didn't have to add, "or else."

Abdul knew the threat was there. It was more potent for being unspoken.

Now, Abdul had just started to regret his decision to follow Ali so he could deal with any other problems in person. Traveling by boat from Morocco to Spain hadn't been so expensive.

A new set of false papers and rental of a decent car for an unknown period in Europe?

Well, it would have cost Abdul nothing if he'd gone to his employers for help. But Abdul had reluctantly decided that would be a bad idea.

The little he'd discovered about them suggested they were very serious people. Who could be counted on to reward excellent performance.

And savagely punish failure.

Abdul had received dire warnings from one source on that point, and he'd nearly turned down the money.

But it was so much money.

And Dunhill cigarettes weren't cheap.

Now, though, he'd been forced to give Ali a significant part of that bounty.

Was Abdul still ahead financially, even after the additional money he's decided to spend following Ali?

Sure.

Was it worth the risks Abdul was running?

Maybe, if Ali delivered the shipment soon in Paris. And if Abdul then received the additional payment he'd been promised.

All those calculations, though, had just gone out the window.

Because one of the men Adbul had following Ali had called. Fortunately, when Abdul had just pulled into a parking lot next to the restaurant where he'd planned to eat his first meal in many, many hours.

It was fortunate because Abdul was neither driving nor visible to anyone else when he received the news.

Ali had abandoned his truck at a train station a couple of hours away from Paris, and they had found it in a nearby parking lot.

At least, one of the men had the wit to bribe a station employee to find out Ali's destination.

Toulouse.

The other man deserved credit as well. While one had been in the train station, the other had been listening to a police scanner.

An alert had been issued for Ali's truck. Police were on their way to the train station.

The question for Abdul had been: What should we do now?

Try to follow Ali?

Drive the truck away from the station?

Have one man each do both?

Of course, to do anything the men demanded additional payment, for two reasons.

First, now the French police were involved.

Second, there was no Ali nearby holding a large bag of cash. And even if they tried to follow him, with Ali's head start, there was an excellent chance they'd never find him.

Abdul didn't have to think long.

If French police found the truck, it would mean two things.

Abdul would never see any more money.

And the shadowy organization that had paid him so far would never rest until Abdul was found and punished.

There was no point in having one or both men follow Ali by car. With Ali on a high-speed train headed south, they'd never catch him.

Abdul told both men to drive the truck toward Paris as quickly as possible. He also promised to send them untraceable cryptocurrency before they arrived.

Thankfully, they agreed.

Abdul ended the conversation, and realized he now had a choice of his own to make.

Follow the shipment to Paris in case of further problems.

Or pursue Ali.

Abdul looked at a map of France on his phone and reluctantly decided there was no point in driving toward Paris. He'd never arrive in time to make a difference either way.

Toulouse was no better. Abdul had no chance of making it there before Ali's train.

Abdul pounded his steering wheel in frustration but then regained control.

He would accomplish nothing that way but injuring his hands.

Focus.

Abdul's eyes widened as he realized he had another option. Don't drive to Toulouse, where he knew Ali would have already left.

Figure out where Ali would go next after Toulouse.

Ok. Ali has no vehicle. He could try to rent one.

Or, more likely, get on another train taking him further south. That would be...a train to Barcelona.

A trip that would take Ali less than four hours.

Abdul smiled, though, as he discovered that the train's next departure was scheduled for ten minutes before the arrival of Ali's train from Orleans.

Would Ali sit around waiting for the next train? Or would he try something else?

Like a bus?

Abdul checked the bus schedules from Toulouse and quickly got his answer.

The first bus south from Toulouse left fifteen minutes after Ali's train arrived. To someplace Abdul had never heard of before, called "Andorra."

Was this Andorra in France or Spain?

It turned out neither.

Andorra was in the Pyrenees Mountains, with France to the north and Spain to the south.

And, incredibly, it was an independent country. One entirely unknown to Abdul.

How could that be?

Well, Abdul would worry about that later.

Ironically, if Ali had waited for the next train to Barcelona, Abdul would never have been able to catch him by car.

And Abdul was sure that Ali would no more risk airport security than he would.

But if he did what Abdul expected, he could just barely make it to Andorra before Ali's arrival.

As he set his GPS for Andorra, Abdul nodded.

He would find Ali. Kill him. And take back the money Ali, after all, had failed to earn.

Without a trace of irony, Abdul thought- I know I will succeed.

Because I'm in the right.

CHAPTER THIRTY-TWO

DGSE Safehouse
Paris, France

Captain Giraud signed off on his cell phone and turned to the rest of the team.

Anatoly Grishkov thought the best description of Giraud's expression would be "grim satisfaction."

"At last we have a lead to follow," Giraud said. "A tip was called into local police in Orleans about a suspicious truck at a train station. A truck that might be carrying drugs or explosives."

Henri nodded. "But you say a lead, not the end of our mission. So that means by the time Orleans police got off their backsides, the truck was gone."

Giraud was clearly neither amused nor appreciative of the interruption.

But finally, he nodded.

"That's exactly what it means. But by then, Antoine at DGSE Technical Services had followed my instructions. Which were to pass on any credible lead to our friends operating the Russian drone. It is on its way to the reported location, and should be there any minute," Giraud said.

Felix looked thoughtful. "Since it will arrive from the north and the truck is probably approaching Paris from the south, there is a good chance their paths will cross."

"That's just what I'm hoping," Giraud said. "So, we're going to get on the road to Orleans and hope for a report from the Russian drone before the truck reaches Paris."

They all stood and made their way to a Peugeot 508 Sport nearly identical to the one destroyed in the blast that had sent Grishkov to the hospital.

It was close enough that when Grishkov arrived at the safe house, he asked how the vehicle had survived. Everyone laughed.

Then Henri explained that whenever possible, French government offices bought French vehicles. Only a few, like the Peugeot 508 Sport, met the requirements for DGSE operations.

Also, the government received a discount for volume purchases of the same make and model.

They had been on the highway to Orleans for less than an hour when Giraud's cell phone vibrated.

Giraud read the text and then turned to Henri.

Pointing to the GPS, he said, "Drive to the coordinates that Antoine has just uploaded at the best speed you can safely manage. He's also had a Code 24 sent to all police on our route."

Henri nodded and gradually increased their speed. Watching from the back seat, Grishkov saw the GPS' calculation of their arrival time rapidly improve.

As in most countries, many French highway patrol cars were unmarked. But due to tell-tales like extra antennas were often easy to spot.

After passing two of them at high speed with no reaction, Grishkov asked, "Does Code 24 tell police that we are an official vehicle and should not be stopped?"

Giraud nodded. "Yes. Henri has received special training in high-speed driving, so is allowed to exceed speed limits without a siren to warn other drivers. Code 24 requires special authorization given only for national security emergencies. We don't want to warn whoever is driving the vehicle carrying the bomb or any potential accomplices of our approach."

"Accomplices," Grishkov repeated with a frown. "You are right. Though we are still nowhere close to the target vehicle, others involved in the attack could be coming to meet it from Paris. Just like us."

"Correct," Giraud said. "And if they heard a siren, warn them. I hope we'll be written off as German if we are noticed."

Grishkov had yet to hear a laugh from Felix. He still wasn't sure that he had.

But the brief snort from Felix had sounded more amused than anything else.

Giraud, though, wasn't smiling. He had a new text.

"Target vehicle has stopped," he reported, looking at Henri.

Giraud didn't have to say anything. They had already been flying down the highway.

Now, they were going at the Peugeot's top speed.

Nobody said a word for the next ten minutes, until they finally reached the highway exit marked by the GPS.

Which said they still had another five minutes to go.

"Have local police been notified?" Grishkov asked.

Giraud nodded. "Yes. But the vehicle is in an abandoned industrial area far from the nearest town. We will get there before any local police. It's just as well, though."

"Agreed," Grishkov said. "Considering the firepower we've encountered, I doubt police could stop them. Though they will be useful as a backup for us."

Giraud looked at him sharply, and Grishkov could guess his thoughts as a fellow soldier.

Giraud wondered whether Grishkov thought the main utility of local police would be as a distraction. Put even more crudely, as targets the terrorists might aim at rather than his team.

Did Grishkov think in those terms?

No. Because Grishkov had been a policeman himself. He knew they were people with real value, not to mention the families who counted on them.

But Giraud was right that Grishkov thought local police would be unlikely to stop the terrorists on their own. They simply weren't trained or equipped for that job.

Another text on Giraud's cell phone.

Giraud frowned and said, "Update from Antoine. The Russian drone is now within visual range of the target. The vehicle isn't moving, and nobody is visible nearby."

Felix shook his head. "It sounds like we may be too late."

"Yes, but let's not assume anything," Giraud replied. "As soon as we've secured the truck, use your equipment to check it for traces of radiation. We need to be sure that it's the vehicle used to move the bomb to Paris."

Felix nodded. They all remained silent until the truck came into view just a few minutes later.

Just as they'd been told, nobody was in sight. A factory with a few small auxiliary buildings nearby had been abandoned years ago. The truck was parked in the center of a crumbling asphalt parking lot scattered with trash and debris.

Henri parked a respectful distance from the truck. They all exited the sedan but remained next to it, with the sedan's body between them and the truck.

Felix removed two devices from their cases.

Grishkov recognized the first one immediately. It was a signal dampener of a design similar to that used by the Russian Army.

A good idea, Grishkov thought. We already know these terrorists aren't shy about using explosives.

Then, he added to himself that one hospital stay per mission is quite enough.

The other device was much newer, and had multiple digital readouts. Grishkov guessed correctly that it was the equipment Felix would use to confirm that the truck in front of them had been used to transport the dirty bomb to Paris.

The signal dampener's operation was straightforward. Felix pressed a switch, and after a few seconds, the device's light changed from red to green.

Grishkov heartily approved. Especially when dealing with explosives, the simpler, the better.

The radiation detector was more complicated, but not by much. It had several digital readouts, which Grishkov thought would probably provide information on different types of radioactive particles.

He was right again.

The numbers on each readout fluctuated for several seconds but then settled to a series of numbers that made Felix frown.

"Radioactive material was definitely transported in that truck," Felix said. "But either the quantity was small, or the shielding was excellent. I'm surprised the Russian drone could detect it from the air."

Grishkov resisted the urge to boast about the capabilities of the Okhotnik drone.

He was helped by the fact that those capabilities were hard-won. Multiple nuclear thefts and accidents in Russia had driven the need for aerial detection of radioactivity at levels much lower than other countries could manage.

Russian scientists had put the first satellite and the first man into orbit. They had also made nuclear missiles, nuclear-powered submarines, and the first mass-produced jet fighters.

Given the resources and direction necessary, Russian scientists could make almost anything, Grishkov thought proudly.

Then, he sighed as he thought about how few technological wonders those scientists had produced had truly helped the average Russian citizen.

Like Grishkov.

However, Grishkov was quickly refocused on the task at hand by the scowl on Giraud's face.

"Can you tell if the bomb is still there?" Giraud asked.

Felix shook his head. "No. Something radioactive was definitely in that truck, and for more than a few minutes. But it could have been removed. As I said, the readings are quite low."

"And there is no way to know from here if the truck has been booby-trapped using a method your jammer won't stop," Giraud said rather than asked.

Felix answered anyway. "A tripwire of some sort could easily be attached to any handle and be invisible from the outside. I see only one way to deal with the possibility."

Giraud looked even less happy.

"You mean the same way you did on our last mission together in Mali," Giraud said.

Felix nodded.

Giraud hesitated but finally said, "Very well. Good luck."

The device Felix now had in his hand was unlike any Grishkov had seen. Small, with what looked like a tiny amount of explosive attached to an even smaller detonator.

The detonator, in turn, was attached to a circuit board the size of his thumbnail. A wire was attached to the detonator about as long as Grishkov's index finger.

The entire device nestled into a piece of what Grishkov could now see was double-sided tape.

Only then did Grishkov understand what Felix was about to do.

Felix walked toward the truck quickly but without haste. Henri started to follow him, but Giraud shook his head.

"We could do nothing to help if this doesn't work," Giraud said. "And some must survive to complete the mission."

Henri started to object, but when he saw Giraud's expression, he wisely closed his mouth and crouched beside Grishkov.

All three of them watched as Felix reached the back of the truck.

Still, nothing moved.

Felix peeled off the back of the tape and gently pressed the device against the handle providing access to the truck's cargo section.

Nothing happened.

Felix walked back to join the rest of the team at the same pace he had approached the truck.

Grishkov admired his nerve. He was sure he would have run as fast as he could.

Moments later, Felix was back beside them.

First, he pulled out the signal dampener and flipped its sole switch.

Its light changed from green, to red.

Then, Felix pulled out a small plastic box with a retractable antenna, and a single large red button.

They were all crouching down already. But, a gesture from Felix told them they were not low enough.

Once they were all squatting below the sedan's windows, Felix pulled out the antenna, and pushed the button.

Grishkov heard a small "pop" and correctly guessed that Felix's device had just removed the truck's cargo door handle.

The "pop" was immediately followed by a much larger explosion.

Fortunately, they turned out to be far enough away to escape injury this time.

After a few moments, they stood up and looked at the remains of the burning truck.

Giraud said something quickly in French that Grishkov didn't understand.

But he was sure he understood Giraud's meaning. There would be little to learn from what the explosion had left behind.

Then Grishkov turned to Giraud and asked, "I know our drone came within visual range only after the truck had stopped. So, most likely, too late to see who removed the dirty bomb and which way it went. But surely there are French aerial assets that could be used as well."

"Yes," Giraud said with a slow nod. "I was told to tell none of you this for security reasons, but I will now disobey those orders. An Aarok drone equipped with an advanced surveillance package has been shadowing the Okhotnik. Antoine is already reviewing the video images it collected and will text me if a vehicle was detected leaving this parking lot."

"An Aarok!" Grishkov exclaimed. "I didn't know any were yet operational. I saw the prototype displayed at the Paris Air Show in 2023, and it looked like it was about the same size as the Okhotnik."

"A little larger, actually," Giraud replied. "The Russian drone has a wingspan of twenty meters, the Aarok twenty-two. And it's not a surprise you hadn't known any were flying. This is one of the few Aaroks in service so far, and its capabilities are highly classified."

Henri made a face and said, "Let's hope they're good enough to tell us which way the terrorists went. So far, they've stayed one step ahead, and if we can't change that, we will lose this race."

CHAPTER THIRTY-THREE

Estació Nacional d'Autobusos del Principat d'Andorra
Andorra

Samir Ali had been worried about whether his passport would be checked once he arrived in Andorra. Especially after he overheard a conversation between two passengers sitting near him on the bus south from Toulouse.

Andorra, it turned out, was a country with about a hundred thousand people that had been independent for centuries. Its economy was primarily based on tourism, bolstered by summer and winter resorts and duty-free shopping.

Though not a member of the European Union, Andorra enjoyed tariff-free privileges for its manufactured exports and used the Euro as its currency. Ali was happy to hear that since it meant he wouldn't have to bother exchanging money once he arrived.

Ali was especially impressed to hear that the unemployment rate in Andorra was only about 1.5%, one of the lowest in the world.

But at the same time concerned. Surely, there must be safeguards to keep out foreigners looking for work?

And customs checks, since Andorra was not a European Union member. Ali had just one bag, containing two items.

One change of clothes. And cash.

A very suspiciously large amount of cash.

Ali's heart was in his throat when he exited the bus to find he was next to a station marked "Estació Nacional d'Autobusos del Principat d'Andorra."

However, no scowling men with rifles were waiting to shepherd Ali and the other passengers into the station. In fact, no one paid the slightest attention to Ali.

He could hardly believe his luck.

Now, Ali's innate caution came back in a rush. What if the men following him in France had somehow managed to beat him here?

One of the men on the bus had mentioned that Andorra had an airport with flights to many countries. He had almost decided to take a flight himself.

What if his pursuers had guessed Andorra would be Ali's next stop?

For a moment, Ali stood rooted in front of the bus station, unable to decide his next move.

Then he shook himself. Hesitation killed in the desert.

Ali doubted it was any different here.

He walked up to the bus station counter and explained in slow English that he wanted to take the next bus to Spain.

It took a while, and the man had to call over another employee whose English was at least slightly better.

But finally, it turned out that a bus to Spain was still available later that evening. It would be the last one today.

Ali would need to walk about half a kilometer to the Estación de Autobuses de Andorra to get on that bus. However, they could sell him the ticket right now.

Ali thought it shouldn't be too bad as he handed over the money. He had no intention of walking any distance with his bag full of cash.

Surely, though, there were taxis.

Perhaps so. But in front of this bus station, only one taxi was dropping off a passenger. Ali waved and shouted, but the cab sped off.

At the same time, the lit "Taxi" sign on its roof went dark.

Right, Ali thought.

Dinner time.

Fine. They said walking to the other bus station should take me less than ten minutes.

I may as well get it over with.

A few minutes later, Ali could already see the lit sign for the other bus station ahead. Then he frowned.

Just ahead there was a pedestrian underpass. Yes, it was also lit.

But not well. In particular, Ali couldn't see through to the other end of the underpass.

Were some of the lights out?

If Ali was a mugger, he knew this was the sort of place he'd pick.

Was there another way around it?

To the right was a broad river, which Ali remembered was called "La Valira."

He didn't feel like a swim. Besides, the bus station was on this side of the river.

Swing around to the left? Maybe, but he'd probably miss the last bus tonight to Spain.

Ali really didn't want to spend the night here, especially since he had no idea where the nearest hotel might be and no longer had a phone.

OK. Bull straight ahead, but keep my eyes open.

As soon as he entered the underpass Ali knew his instincts had been right. The lights at the other end were out.

Though he could see or hear no one.

But what was that smell?

It was strangely familiar.

A few minutes later, Ali had the answer to that question, as he looked down at Abdul's body.

Ali's knife was sticking out of Abdul's chest. Ali quickly pulled the body into deeper shadow, and pulled a set of keys from his right pocket.

And his knife from Abdul's chest.

Who knew whether there might be other pursuers? Ali had certainly not expected Abdul to make the trip.

Moments later, La Viera took care of any questions Abdul's body might raise.

Pressing on the plastic fob attached to Abdul's keys revealed his car's location, as its lights obligingly flashed.

Under the right front seat Ali found what he'd hoped. All the cash Abdul had brought with him.

It was even more than Ali already had. Now, he could retire in style.

Ali checked his watch and nodded. Still ten minutes to go before the bus would depart.

Good. Ali was in no mood to drive in the dark over unfamiliar roads.

Besides, who knew who might be looking for Abdul's car?

Ali thought back to Abdul's clumsy attack. Did the fool think he was the first man to come at Ali with a knife?

Well, to be fair he'd probably counted on surprise. One that had been spoiled by Abdul's foolish habit.

Ali's father had told him so many times, and once again, he'd been proved right.

Sooner or later, smoking would kill you.

CHAPTER THIRTY-FOUR

En Route to Société Générale de Transport
International Headquarters
Paris, France

"So, good news?" Henri asked as he drove their sedan back to Paris.

Captain Giraud shrugged. "Good and bad. The Aarok did get images of the truck that almost certainly picked up the bomb. As we expected, it headed north toward Paris. But there was an underpass where two major highways intersect not far north."

"Where the truck spotted by the Aarok disappeared," Grishkov said flatly. "It's an old trick used by Russian smugglers fearing aerial surveillance."

"Right," Giraud said. "The truck we'd spotted was found abandoned by the local police Antoine dispatched once he'd reviewed the footage. Antoine also released alerts for all trucks that went through that underpass during the next hour."

Henri shook his head. "Surely, it took some time to transfer the bomb from one truck to another. Didn't anyone call in suspicious activity?"

"I had the same thought," Giraud said. "But apparently not. The average French driver seems to pay little attention to anything that doesn't slow him down."

Grishkov frowned. "Henri is right, though, that the transfer must have taken time. Can Antoine focus on finding a truck that went into the underpass and emerged sometime later?"

"He is already doing that and expects to find it soon," Giraud said. "The initial alerts were just quicker to generate."

"Yes, that makes sense," Grishkov replied. "As it is, they've probably had enough time to make yet another transfer."

"But Antoine has already given us another lead to follow," Giraud said. "Even before the most recent blast, I had noticed these terrorists seemed uncommonly well-stocked with explosives. I asked Antoine to analyze the ones used each time to see if he could find a common source. He did. So we're going to talk to the security chief at the headquarters of the Société Générale de Transport International in Paris, a fellow named Tareq."

Henri looked surprised.

"SGTI? They're one of the biggest transport companies in France. Maybe even the largest. What have they got to do with explosives?"

"A good question, Henri," Giraud replied. "It's probably the first one I'll ask."

They were halfway to Paris with Henri at the wheel when Giraud received another update from Antoine.

Everyone else could see without asking that it wasn't good news.

Seeing their reactions, Giraud finally said, "The lead we hoped to receive from drone visuals has turned out to be a dead end. Antoine could identify the truck based on a more thorough video review, but it had already been found in a parking garage by local police based on his initial list. Empty, of course."

"Was the parking garage far from where we are now?" Grishkov asked.

"No," Giraud said. "It is in Étampes."

Henri drew in his breath with a sharp hiss. "That's only an hour's drive from central Paris! Couldn't Antoine develop some leads from additional video review? There must be closed circuit camera coverage of the garage exits."

"Antoine is working on that as we speak," Giraud replied. "But the terrorists planned well. The garage they picked is one of the few in Étampes' center, so it is quite busy. It also has exits on three different streets."

Grishkov shook his head. "I'm the outsider here, but I have to ask. Why is Antoine working alone? For that matter, why are we the only DGSE team in the field looking for this bomb?"

"Outsider or not, you're asking good questions," Giraud said. "The proof is that I've posed them to the DGSE Director not once but twice. Most recently today."

Henri stared at Giraud incredulously. "And what was his answer?"

"That we must keep knowledge of the threat restricted to only a few people," Giraud replied. "Because if word got out, there could be a panic that killed more people than the bomb. When we weren't sure how real the threat was, that made at least some sense. Now, though, after we confirmed radioactivity in the truck blown up two hours' drive outside Paris?"

Giraud shook his head. "The Director is a politician. Could that account for his caution? Maybe. But my gut tells me something is wrong."

"My gut agrees with yours," Grishkov said.

Henri and Felix both nodded.

Now Felix spoke for the first time.

"Captain, what can we do to get more help finding the bomb?" he asked.

"I've been giving that much thought," Giraud replied. "I don't have a good answer yet. I will keep thinking while we continue to this man Tareq at SGTI."

"Any more word from the Russian drone operators?" Grishkov asked.

Giraud shook his head. "No. They've made repeated passes through the area and found nothing so far. Maybe the last two trucks they've used have better shielding than the one that brought the bomb from Libya to France."

They passed the rest of the drive to Paris in silence.

As they approached SGTI headquarters, Henri let out a low whistle.

"This place had to cost quite a bit to build," Henri said. "I've seen pictures, but they don't do it justice."

It was true. The mammoth glass and steel edifice before them practically screamed money.

And power.

The building was not based on traditional French architecture. It would have been just as much at home in any capital city on any continent.

No wonder it stood here on the outskirts of Paris, barely inside the city limits, Henri thought.

Tareq was waiting for them in the headquarters lobby.

"Welcome," Tareq said, shaking each team member's hand in turn.

Giraud introduced each of them, but Grishkov would have bet a week's pay that Tareq listened only for the name of the man in charge.

Tareq ushered them into a conference room steps away from the lobby.

Grishkov, with a policeman's innate suspicion, thought immediately he knew the reason.

Outsiders should be allowed to see as little as possible.

"Please, all of you have a seat," Tareq said. "The requested documents have been retrieved from our files and will be here soon. In the meantime, I have ordered coffee and will answer all your questions to the best of my knowledge."

Giraud nodded, and they all sat. Moments later, a steaming cup of café au lait and a small plate of assorted pastries were in front of each member of the DGSE team.

Giraud took a sip of the coffee and then nodded.

It was excellent. And why not? SGTI obviously had the money to do things right.

So why not do the same with securing explosives?

Giraud decided it was probably best not to make the comparison so bluntly.

"I have read the report from the Paris police on the theft of explosives from your construction division," Giraud said. "But it lacked much detail. I was overseas then, but I'm still surprised I heard nothing about the incident in the press."

Tareq nodded and looked uncomfortable. "Look, I'm going to be honest with you. I've been with SGTI since it was founded, and this was my greatest failure. I offered my resignation after it happened, but our company president refused to accept it. He said my men had done all they could. I think this video from a security camera that recorded the theft will explain what happened more clearly than I could."

Before Giraud could say anything, Tareq had touched a control that turned off the lights and activated an overhead video projector.

The footage started with the exterior door swinging open, followed by two bright flashes from stun grenades.

By the time the video image cleared, a four-man team was already inside. They were wearing black clothing and black combat masks, with nothing visible but lips and eyes.

All armed with silenced semiautomatic weapons.

The three security guards never had a chance.

One managed to get off a shot, and Grishkov saw one attacker stagger.

But he'd been hit in his ballistic vest and didn't even fall.

One of his teammates finished off the guard who had fired with a quick burst.

In seconds, the guards were all lying on the ground, unmoving.

Then, one of the attackers noticed the security camera and swung his rifle toward it.

That was the end of the footage.

"Did any of your men survive?" Giraud asked quietly.

Tareq shook his head. "No. We gave a copy of this video to the police, and you may have it as well."

The conference room door opened, and a man entered, holding a folder and a USB drive.

Tareq nodded his thanks and quickly leafed through the folder. Then he handed it and the USB drive to Giraud.

"Everything we know is here," Tareq said. "We asked the police to keep the incident quiet for obvious reasons. We thought three armed security guards and a steel-reinforced door would be sufficient security for our explosives stockpile. Now we know we were wrong."

Giraud nodded and said, "I'm sorry for the loss of your men. What have you done since then to increase security?"

Tareq looked grim. "Our construction division was one of the first established by SGTI and a key reason for our success. We didn't leave the construction of our facilities to others, but did everything ourselves. Depots, warehouses, everything. But after this, our company president ordered that any demolition required for construction would be contracted out. We no longer keep any explosives in house."

"I see," Giraud said, gesturing toward the file folder before him. "Can you think of anything not in here that would help us?"

Tareq shook his head. "No. But if you find there is something I can do to assist, please let me know. Those were good men with families. It remains my great shame that their killers have not been brought to justice."

Moments later, Henri was back at the wheel of their sedan to drive them to DGSE headquarters.

Giraud was looking over the contents of the folder Tareq had provided. Then he shook his head.

"There's nothing here that wasn't already in the police record."

"I'm not surprised," Grishkov said. "That man wasn't telling you everything he knows."

Giraud looked in the rearview mirror and saw Grishkov looking back at him.

After a moment, Giraud grunted. "Agreed. But his boss is one of the richest men in France. I can't just grab Tareq and throw him into a DGSE interrogation room. No matter how much I might like to, considering we've now hit another dead end."

"Maybe not," Henri said. "I suggest you give that USB drive with the video file of the robbery to Antoine. Ask him to compare that video with footage of the men captured by the security cameras at Boucher's house."

Giraud frowned. "The security contractor? What will that accomplish? The men who robbed SGTI were all wearing masks."

"Gait analysis," Henri said confidently. "Antoine will know how to do it."

Grishkov nodded slowly. "Yes, I've heard of this, though it came after my time in the police. You analyze how a man walks, using a computer to render how he moves into a mathematical expression. Each person's gait is supposed to be as individual as a fingerprint."

"Right," Giraud said thoughtfully. "I have to get back to the finance team working on tracing the money paid to Boucher's company. They said the ultimate source was here in France but would need more time to narrow it down."

"I'm starting to wonder whether that source could have been SGTI," Grishkov said.

Giraud looked startled. "What makes you think that? Those three security guards certainly weren't in on it!"

"Agreed," Grishkov said. "But they might have been a necessary sacrifice to draw attention away from SGTI's role in the attack. Consider this: the explosives storage area door wasn't forced open. What does the police report say?"

"That the lock was picked by an expert who left no marks on the door's exterior," Giraud said slowly.

Grishkov nodded. "Maybe. Or maybe someone gave them a key. Someone like Tareq."

"Even if you're right, we have only guesses so far," Giraud replied.

"I'm going to need more than that before I can ask my boss to bring Tareq in for questioning."

"Too bad," Grishkov said with a sigh. "It might be true that Russia is a police state. But sometimes, that turned out to be useful for..."

Giraud looked in the rearview mirror again and gave Grishkov a wry smile as he finished his sentence for him.

"The police."

Grishkov laughed and said, "Yes, just so."

"Well, the rules and laws are there for a reason," Giraud said. "But that doesn't mean we give up. We just have to keep searching until we uncover the answers. At least now I have some idea of where to look."

Chapter Thirty-Five

Société Générale de Transport International Headquarters
Paris, France

Khaled Madi smiled at the news Tareq had just delivered.

"So, at last, the bomb is in our hands near Paris and will soon be ready for detonation," Madi repeated.

Tareq nodded. "That's right. The explosives experts I hired are working on it now."

"Have you confirmed that the detonation site is still available?" Madi asked.

"Yes, earlier this morning. The top deck of a parking garage close to the Champs-Élysées. It's just across from the Cabaret Lido 2 Paris," Tareq replied.

"Just the sort of decadent entertainment ISIS would be likely to target," Madi said. "Though, as I told you, for me, proximity to another landmark was far more important."

"I remember," Tareq said. "Within sight of the Arc de Triomphe, built to celebrate Napoleon's victories. The ones that helped propel French ambitions to build a global empire."

"That's right," Madi replied. "It's time for the French to learn, finally, that there's a price to be paid for meddling in the affairs of others."

Tareq silently nodded his understanding.

In truth, though, Tareq had always believed that even if the French had refused to participate, Gaddafi would still be dead.

Tareq had looked up the figures. Under NATO direction over 26,000 combat missions were flown over Libya in 2011. If France hadn't joined, the British, Canadians, and other NATO members would have flown the sorties instead.

Of course, Tareq understood how Madi felt. Gaddafi had been his father.

As the leader of Libya the entire time Tareq had been alive, he had been upset and angered by Gaddafi's death, too. But not to the same extent as Madi.

Certainly not enough to risk his life on this dirty bomb plot.

Instead, Tareq had been far more motivated by the treatment he had received from the French since his arrival.

Hardly a day went by that Tareq didn't overhear a comment about him along the lines of, "I wish they'd all go back home," "They'll never fit in here," or worse.

Sometimes, it wasn't just overheard comments. Some people were bold enough to say them to his face. A few had refused to deal with him at all.

Only a couple had been foolish enough to try to lay hands on him. They'd been breathing when Tareq had left them where they fell.

At least, he thought they had.

Some seemed to hate him because of his religion. Others because he was Arab. Or because he spoke French with what they considered a strange and uncouth accent. Still more because they thought he might carry out a terrorist attack.

Many, Tareq thought, for all those reasons.

Well, Tareq had said to himself many times that if he were to be automatically tagged as a terrorist based on his appearance- who could complain if he proved them correct?

Never mind that far more French people ignored Tareq altogether. Or that a few had gone out of their way to be pleasant.

As if they were consciously or unconsciously trying to make up for the bigots Tareq encountered almost every day.

No, those people didn't matter.

Only one thing did. Paying back the people who had made Tareq feel less than human for all the years he'd lived in France.

Madi had stopped talking and was looking at Tareq strangely.

"Sorry," Tareq said. "Lost in my thoughts again."

Madi nodded. "I understand. It happens to me, too. Now, let's get back to the plan for detonation. Are you sure no one else could carry out what you call overwatch? And is it really necessary?"

Tareq had to fight back a sigh. They'd already had this discussion. Several times.

"The primary method will be a simple wired switch. The Tunisian man I picked has terminal cancer, and has been promised a substantial payment to his family," Tareq said.

Madi nodded impatiently. "Yes, and like just about all immigrants from North Africa, he has good reason to hate the French. But you have a backup detonator via cell phone in case, for any reason, he fails to hit the switch when he gets to the top of the parking garage."

"But the DGSE team can dampen cell phone signals, which could make that method useless. That's why we must have a sniper on over-watch," Tareq replied.

"Fine, but why must it be you? I told you to hire someone else," Madi said, clearly annoyed.

"I tried," Tareq replied. "As I'm sure you can imagine, experienced snipers we could trust with a job like this aren't easy to find. But the more I thought about it, the more I realized we'd be creating another problem. One that might be too hard to solve."

"What's that? Something we haven't already discussed?" Madi asked.

Good. Madi's curiosity was finally overcoming his annoyance.

"Let's say that, one way or another, we detonate the bomb once it's in place," Tareq said. "Whether the sniper we hired turned out to be needed or not, he'd be another loose end we'd need to tie off. No matter how careful I'd been in hiring him."

Madi chewed his lower lip for a moment and then nodded. "You're right. But are you sure you can survive the detonation?"

"Sure is maybe too strong a word," Tareq said with a crooked smile. "I have done everything possible to prepare. I have pre-dosed myself with chemicals that should minimize my body's absorption of radioactive particles. I'll wear a filter mask over my mouth and nose when I shoot. And as soon as the bomb explodes, I will put on goggles and a portable respirator. But the site I've picked as my perch is the most important precaution of all."

Madi nodded. "A good distance away from the bomb, I hope?"

"Yes," Tareq replied. "But with a direct line of sight to the target. The building has been cleared after the discovery of asbestos. The contractors removing it will not start work until next month so that I will have no interference entering or exiting. Best of all, it's steps away from a subway stop. So, once I reach the street, I'll discard the respirator and goggles and put on the mask that some Parisians still wear after COVID. Within minutes, I'll be far away from the explosion and underground where the risk of exposure will be greatly reduced."

"With luck, before anyone understands what's happened," Madi said. "A good plan."

Then Madi looked Tareq in the eye and said, "All that's left is to say I admire your courage and wish you the very best of luck."

Tareq stood and smiled. As he turned to leave, he looked back and said, "To us all."

CHAPTER THIRTY-SIX

DGSE Headquarters
Paris, France

Antoine Bertrand had a cup of coffee to his lips when Captain Giraud strode into his office. And closed the door behind him.

"Welcome, Captain," Antoine said. "May I pour you a cup?"

Giraud shook his head. "I'm going to come right to the point because I don't think we have much time. Your team hasn't been able to identify the funding source I asked you to track, or you would have notified me, yes?"

Antoine put down his cup and nodded. "Yes, of course. Even with our resources, narrowing down the possibilities will take time, as I warned you."

"What if I asked you to check one particular company? Would that make this go any faster?" Giraud asked.

Antoine's eyebrows flew upward. "Certainly! Which company are we talking about?"

"Société Générale de Transport International," Giraud replied.

"I see why you decided to see me in person," Antoine said. "Surely, we are talking about someone using the company's financial system

198 · TED HALSTEAD

without the knowledge of their executives. SGTI is one of the largest French companies, after all."

Giraud shrugged. "I am no expert in these matters. However, remember the sums we discussed. They were quite large. Would an ordinary employee have the access required to move such large amounts?"

Antoine paused and sat for a moment in thought. "No, you're quite right. Unless such an employee obtained an executive's log-on information..."

Then Antoine shook his head. "That's not it. A company as large as SGTI would have basic financial safeguards in place. Such as tying computer terminals authorized to execute large transactions to a particular log-on. Terminals that would be inside a locked office. With the terminals rendered inactive and unavailable for use once the executive swiped his access badge upon leaving the building for any reason."

"Any idea how many executives would be authorized to carry out large financial transfers of the sort we discussed?" Giraud asked.

"Even at a company as large as SGTI, I'd be surprised if the number exceeded a dozen or so. If we do confirm SGTI is the source of the transfers, their internal records should identify whoever is responsible very quickly," Antoine said.

Giraud nodded. "Good. How long will it take your team to determine whether SGTI is or is not the source of the transfers?"

"I'll take this to the finance team leader right now," Antoine said. "If you'll take me up on my offer of some really rather good coffee, I think we'll have an answer before you finish your second cup."

"Excellent," Giraud replied with a smile. "Please go ahead to your team. I'll pour the cup myself."

Antoine was as good as his word. Giraud had just poured a second cup when he returned.

"You were right," Antoine said. "The suspect transactions did originate at SGTI. I know that you asked me to inform no one but you. However, I must point out that protocol says for a matter this serious, I must inform the Director despite my misgivings about him."

Giraud shook his head. "I see now that I must inform you in more detail of my suspicions. There have been multiple leaks of information about my team's current mission that could have only come from within DGSE. Those leaks have led to attacks that have already put one of my team in hospital. I've checked and only two men had the necessary access to that information. Jacques Montand and the Director."

"If that is so, then you must tell Jacques immediately," Antoine said. "He is the only man I trust completely within the DGSE."

"He's my next stop," Giraud said.

"Very well," Antoine said with a sigh. "In the meantime, I will inform no one. I'm sure Jacques will let me know what he plans to do once he's had a chance to consider all the implications."

Giraud nodded and stood to leave.

Antoine shook his head. "I knew no good would come of having a politician as Director."

"There, we are in complete agreement," Giraud said and left.

All the Deputy Directors had offices in the same corridor, so it was a short walk.

"Any progress to report, Captain?" Jacques asked as Giraud sat in the chair before his desk.

Direct and to the point. One of the things Giraud liked best about dealing with Jacques.

"Antoine just confirmed my suspicion that SGTI was the funding source used to pay the security contractor who attacked Grishkov near Évreux-Fauville Air Base. SGTI was also the source of the explosives that sent him to the hospital," Giraud said.

"Who else knows about this?" Jacques asked.

"So far, only you and Antoine," Giraud replied.

"Good. Keep it that way. I am concerned about the Director as the possible source of the leaks that have endangered your team," Jacques said.

"I am relieved to hear you say so," Giraud said. "I already had such concerns, but I thought it might be difficult to convince you to share them."

"After our first conversation, I decided to follow the Director when he left headquarters during the day. Would you like to guess one of his destinations?" Jacques asked.

"SGTI headquarters?" Giraud replied. His tone made it clear even he had trouble believing it.

Jacques nodded. "The Director insisted on replacing just one Deputy Director when he was appointed. The one responsible for counterintelligence."

Giraud scowled. "Exactly the man who should have kept this from happening."

"Just so," Jacques replied. "It seems that from the beginning, the Director has been looking for opportunities to cash in on his position. Now it is up to you, me and Antoine to make sure he fails."

"I felt I could only push Antoine so far on my authority, especially since I'm asking him to risk his career by not informing the Director of our actions," Giraud said. "Can I ask for your support in pressing him to take on more tasks?"

"Of course," Jacques replied. "What do you need?"

"The bomb will definitely be moved to another vehicle," Giraud said. "I think it will most likely be one reported stolen by SGTI. Once it's identified, I want a team under Antoine to monitor all surveillance cameras in central Paris for that vehicle. I'd like a separate team to research two buildings in central Paris. The first would almost certainly be a garage, with parking on an exposed top floor."

Jacques grunted. "I think I can answer your first building question right now. I've lived in Paris my whole life, and only one garage meets that criteria. A greedy developer added that top floor, and many suspected he bribed city officials to get the necessary permits. So far, though, no one has been able to prove it."

"Do you know where it is?" Giraud asked.

"I remember it was near the Avenue des Champs-Élysées," Jacques replied. "One reason it was such a scandal. Now, let me check a map..."

A few moments later, Jacques pointed at his monitor. "Right here," he said. "Close to a cabaret called Lido 2 Paris."

Giraud scowled. "And also near the Arc de Triomphe."

"Yes," Jacques said thoughtfully. "Just the sort of location terrorists would pick. Reporters would have no trouble explaining where the incident occurred to their viewers. The Champs-Élysées and the Arc de Triomphe are known around the world."

"Right," Giraud said. "Now, if I were managing this operation for the terrorists, I would arrange to overwatch. The ideal location would be a vacant room, or better yet, an entire floor."

Jacques nodded. "Or, best yet, an entire building. I see why you need my help. To get the answers you need quickly, these tasks will take everyone on Antoine's staff."

Seeing Giraud's reaction, Jacques raised his right hand and smiled. "Don't worry. We've confirmed the bomb is within striking distance of Paris. That merits all our resources, and I'm sure I can get Antoine to put whatever else he's doing on hold."

"I appreciate it," Giraud said. "There is, however, one more request I need to make. A civilian helicopter."

Jacques' smile disappeared. "Civilian. So, not armed in any way."

Giraud nodded.

"I understand the need," Jacques said. "You can hardly afford to have your team stuck in central Paris traffic. But a helicopter will make DGSE involvement in this business that much harder to conceal."

"You told me you've already tried to get the Director to have us co-ordinate with Paris police, and he refused," Giraud said. "Supposedly because of the risk of leaks and widespread panic."

"Yes," Jacques replied with a sigh. "Well, now we know better. I will make one available. As I recall, the Sergeant on your team has a current helicopter pilot's license."

"Correct," Giraud said.

"I'll let you know how we'll deal with the matter of the Director and the leaks that have plagued your team," Jacques said. "Probably once it's done. In any case, leave it in my hands."

"Understood," Giraud said and left.

Jacques took a moment to consider the implications of the Director's treason before seeing Antoine.

No betrayal had happened at such a high level since the attempted revolt led by several retired Generals against giving Algeria independence. The Algiers putsch had happened...

Jacques had to look up the date on his computer to be sure.

1961. Before Jacques had even been born.

Yes. The Director's treason would have to be dealt with firmly.

But how?

CHAPTER THIRTY-SEVEN

Bagneux, France

Tareq had been forced to spend more time than he would have liked briefing the truck driver, Omar.

From Tareq's perspective, Omar's job was simple. Transport the bomb to the rooftop level of the parking garage in central Paris, at the location stored in the truck's GPS. Once there, press the switch to detonate the bomb.

To be fair, Omar did have one reasonable question. What should I do if the police stop me before I reach the detonation site?

Tareq thought the answer was obvious but quickly realized to Omar it might not be.

So he told Omar the answer: detonate the bomb immediately.

The rest of their exchange could be summed up as Omar wanting reassurance that his sacrifice would be worthwhile.

And that, as promised, Omar's family would be cared for after he was dead.

Tareq had been waiting for a better question, one that he thought should be asked by all suicide bombers.

If this is such a great and glorious mission, with Paradise guaranteed once I'm dead, why aren't you doing it?

A bit rude, sure. But facing imminent death, surely courtesy would take a back seat.

But no. The question hadn't come.

Tareq almost regretted that. Because he actually had a good answer ready.

If someone managed to kill Omar before he could trigger the bomb, Tareq had to be alive to set it off himself. Or if that wasn't possible, shoot anyone who tried to approach the bomb before its timer elapsed.

As it was, Tareq could honestly say that the bomb's explosion would be a historic blow against the French in particular and the West in general.

Tareq had to lie about Omar's family, of course. DNA testing would undoubtedly reveal the man's identity soon after the bomb exploded. Omar's wife and children might talk. They might not know much.

But Tareq agreed with Madi's orders. They would not leave any leads for investigators to follow, no matter how small.

So Omar's family was already dead.

If Omar's belief in Paradise was accurate, Tareq thought coldly, he would soon join them there.

Tareq had ensured Omar didn't have a cell phone to make any last-minute attempts to call his family. He'd explained that a cell phone would be dangerous to the mission because it might be tracked.

True, as far as it went.

Instead, Omar now had a walkie-talkie with excellent range tuned to the same frequency as the one Tareq carried.

Two men from his security team now watched Omar while Tareq left to take up his overwatch position. He had to be sure nothing would interfere with that before Omar could proceed.

Anyway, the delay wouldn't be long. In this Paris suburb, they were only about half an hour from the parking garage, even allowing for Paris traffic.

Even more importantly, his boss, Madi, wanted the bomb to go off at lunchtime. When the maximum number of people would be out and about.

So that as many as possible would risk exposure to the radioactive particles released by the bomb's explosion.

It almost didn't matter how many were actually affected. Fear of contamination would be nearly as powerful a factor in spreading panic and chaos as the thousands who would need treatment.

Tareq nodded. As usual, Madi was right. After all the effort, money, and lives this project had cost so far, it was important to extract the maximum benefit from the explosion.

He'd left himself a little extra time in case of unexpectedly heavy traffic. Or someone showing up at what was supposed to be a building closed to everyone for asbestos removal.

Tareq sighed with relief as he practically glided through traffic to the building he'd selected as his sniper perch. Even the traffic lights seemed to cooperate. One green light after another!

Surely, this was a good sign.

Central Paris had plenty of parking garages, all charging ridiculous prices.

Today, Tareq didn't mind paying. Especially for the one he parked at today, which would give him only a block to walk. He pulled out the case containing his equipment and the disassembled sniper rifle and exited to the street.

Tareq had used his knife the previous evening to put a slit in the heavy plastic sheeting that now encased the entire building he would use for overwatch. He'd picked a spot in the back of the building, where at night, the traffic had been very light.

Now that it was late morning, traffic was heavier, though still much lighter than on the building's other sides. At least there were no pedestrians.

Tareq looked up the street. A traffic signal was about a block away. If he waited for it to change...

Yes. It would only give Tareq seconds to slip in unobserved through the cut he'd made last night.

But seconds were all Tareq needed.

Once he was inside the building, Tareq stood still and listened.

Had anyone observed his entrance to the building and perhaps followed to see what he was doing?

Was there anyone else already inside?

Could his information be wrong, and work on removing asbestos have already started?

The longer Tareq listened, the more confident he became. Outside, there was only the infrequent passage of a vehicle.

No approaching sirens. No voices near the slit in the plastic sheeting where he'd entered.

Inside, the silence was absolute. No mechanical noises suggesting the elevator was in use. No voices, none of the drilling or hammering that would say asbestos removal work had started early.

The only light was what entered through the building's windows.

Tareq sighed as he remembered the stairwell climb to the building's top floor. The downside to using a building with no electricity.

Well, everything seemed safe. Time to get going.

By the time he reached the top floor, Tareq was panting and sweating. His dry run hadn't included lugging equipment and a disassembled sniper rifle.

After unzipping his equipment bag, Tareq pulled out the thick gloves that rested on top of all the other items. After what he'd do here today, Tareq certainly didn't want to leave any fingerprints.

He'd also need to wear them for his next task.

The door to the office suite he'd picked on his last visit was mercifully still unlocked. Even with his tools and experience, unlocking it last time hadn't been so easy. Tareq had decided to take the risk of discovery involved in leaving it unlocked when he left.

Now he was glad he had. The fact that it was still unlocked told

Tareq that nobody was checking the building. Or, anyway, not as thoroughly as he would have if he'd been in charge.

Plus, as tired as he was now, the extra task of unlocking the door might have put him behind schedule.

As it was, Tareq still had several tasks to complete before he could call the driver forward to deliver the bomb.

First things first, Tareq thought as he opened the door and set down his burdens.

Sit down and rest for a few moments. The chair for whoever had been the boss here was easy to identify.

It was behind the biggest desk in the office suite, and it was the only one with more than the thinnest cushions.

Tareq sank into it with a sigh. Within moments, he could feel his heart rate starting to slow and his breathing steady.

This wasn't just a matter of comfort. One of the first lessons Tareq had learned as a sniper was that there was a direct correlation between heart rate and performance.

The lower the heart rate, the more accurate the shot.

Fortunately the distance to target today, while not short, would be far from the greatest challenge Tareq had faced.

OK. Enough rest.

Tareq opened the equipment case and got to work.

The first task, create an opening in one of the office windows to allow him to shoot. Naturally, as in nearly every modern office building the windows weren't designed to open. Particularly ones on a high floor like this.

Tareq could understand the reasons behind this decision. Birds could fly in, which would undoubtedly be a nuisance.

At heights like this, wind gusts could enter and wreak havoc.

And, of course, offering a quick escape to depressed and overworked employees might have unpleasant consequences.

No, better to seal up the workspace as tightly as possible.

But Tareq had come prepared.

The glass circle cutter in Tareq's hands had seen use several times before, over a span of many years. He had last used it to prepare to eliminate one of Madi's business rivals while he was on vacation in Tunisia.

Madi had insisted that each time he'd ordered an assassination, Tareq would have to wait until the person targeted was outside France.

Tareq agreed with Madi's reasons. Most important was that the French police were quite competent and had the latest technology for their investigations.

It also made sense to avoid a string of sniper killings in France that would inevitably be viewed as the work of a serial killer. That would bring down the weight of the entire French law enforcement establishment, not just local police.

Tareq first attached the glass cutter's suction cup to the selected window and began turning its six-wheel turret.

Good. Tareq could feel the glass give way but stay firmly within the suction cup's grip. He carefully pulled the newly created glass disc inside and gently pulled it off the suction cup. As he did, he gave thanks for the quality of his gloves.

Tareq had learned the hard way that the edges of a freshly cut glass disk were razor-sharp.

The wind blew in through the small hole Tareq had just cut. He'd decided to keep the hole's size small to make it less visible. Though he doubted it would matter, it was always better to err on the side of caution.

Tareq frowned as another thought hit him. His ability to move the rifle in different directions depended on the hole's size.

Had he made it too small?

Tareq hesitated but finally shook his head. No. It was fine for what he needed to do. He'd be gone before he'd have to aim at anything but the garage rooftop he could see with his naked eye.

Next, it was time to check the impact of outside air conditions on his rifle's aim. At this range, it shouldn't be much of a factor.

But it never hurt to be sure.

Tareq used a highly accurate device with a barometer to measure the wind most precisely. It measured current wind speed, average wind speed, maximum gust, temperature, local barometric pressure, and altitude.

Everything was shown on a digital display. Pressing a single button produced a reading.

Yes, working for a boss with deep pockets certainly had its advantages.

Tareq removed the thick gloves he'd been wearing, which would have hindered his next steps.

Assembling the rifle, a task he'd accomplished more times than he could count, took only a few minutes.

Calibrating the scope and making sure he'd done the job correctly? Yes, that took a bit longer.

Finally, though, he was ready to shoot.

Well, almost, he thought ruefully.

After taking the shot this time, he would have to follow steps he had never had to take on any previous job.

Tareq removed the mask, respirator, and goggles from his equipment case. To begin with, he'd only wear the mask. That would be difficult enough while using the rifle.

He'd actually tried to talk himself out of using a mask but failed.

How many radioactive particles, he'd thought, could really travel the distance from the explosion to where he was now before he had time to don the respirator and goggles?

Then Tareq had looked at some videos of rescue workers at Chernobyl undergoing treatment once their task was complete.

He had not only decided to wear a mask but also to use one thicker and with a higher protection rating than he'd originally planned.

Annoying, yes. But Tareq had checked, and he could still use the rifle successfully even while wearing the mask.

Tareq pulled out his cell phone and called one of the men he had watching Omar.

And told him it was time.

Time at last to end this.

CHAPTER THIRTY-EIGHT

DGSE Safehouse
Paris, France

Captain Giraud looked around the room at the rest of the team.

"Are we all clear on the plan?" he asked.

Felix looked up from the tablet in front of him. "In most respects the Airbus H145 D3 provided for this mission is excellent. Avionics, top speed, and particularly its ability to hover for extended periods will all be useful."

Giraud sighed. "But..."

"Have you seen the paint scheme for these helicopters? Bright red and yellow?" Felix asked.

"I'm aware," Giraud said with a shrug. "We're getting this one courtesy of the Sécurité Civile. It's ordinarily used for mountain rescue, where you want a helicopter visible for many kilometers. It was undergoing maintenance here in Paris, which was expedited so we could fly it."

"But you say you expect the terrorists to have a sniper on overwatch," Felix said with a frown. "This helicopter has no armor. We will be forced to hover for Grishkov to have any hope of shooting the truck's driver before he can detonate the bomb. We will be hard to miss with our bright red and yellow colors."

"At that moment, you will be vulnerable," Giraud said, nodding. "I agree. The only solution I see is for Monsieur Grishkov to waste no time lining up his shot."

Henri shook his head. "Why not have Grishkov waiting at ground level near the parking garage entrance? Plenty of time to aim with no need to worry about a potential sniper."

"No, I considered that," Giraud replied. "Traffic on that street is always busy. We try to shoot the driver there, and a stray round could easily hit someone else."

Grishkov nodded. "Even if it's a clean hit, the round could pass through and still hit an innocent civilian."

"I also considered trying to shoot the driver inside the parking structure," Giraud said. "Logistically, I see no way to do it safely without closing it to everyone but the target vehicle. And if we do that, the terrorists may find out and change their plans."

Henri frowned. "You say that keeping the visibility of this operation low is a high priority. Who decided that?"

Giraud was silent for a moment. Then he said, "The President."

"Right," Henri said with disgust. "So we're taking a chance of failure to keep this out of sight. Not only because of worry about civilian casualties. And I suppose that's why Grishkov has to use a silenced rifle."

"These are the realities of working in France, where none of us are supposed to be carrying out such a mission," Giraud replied. "Not the French Army, not the DGSE, not the Foreign Legion, and most certainly not the FSB."

"Retired," Grishkov added with a smile.

Henri was not smiling.

"So, you and I are going to the parking garage while Grishkov and Felix go to the heliport?" Henri asked.

"That's right," Giraud replied. "You'll operate the cell phone jammer while I stand ready to check the bomb inside the truck once Monsieur Grishkov has dealt with the driver."

"And I activate the cell phone jammer only once we confirm that the truck has entered the garage structure," Henri said.

"Correct," Giraud said. "We have to assume the sniper has access to a backup way to detonate the bomb if something happens to the driver. And that he'll be checking to make sure it still works."

"I can think of a thousand ways this could go wrong," Henri said flatly.

"Well, so can I," Giraud said. "France is counting on us to find the one way it could go right."

CHAPTER THIRTY-NINE

Aerodrome Héliport Paris
Paris, France

"I'm surprised to see a heliport this large inside the city limits," Grishkov said.

Felix nodded. "A bit under eight hectares. It used to be much larger. Part of the reason the heliport is still here is its history."

"Really?" Grishkov said. "What makes it so special?"

"Well, as far back as 1905, French aviation pioneers like Louis Blériot and Henri Farman were taking off from here in some of the first aircraft flying anywhere," Felix said. "And in those early experimental planes, they risked their lives with every flight. My adopted country deserves criticism in many regards. But respect for history? There, I have to say the French do quite well."

Grishkov nodded. "Do I see military helicopters here?"

"Good eye," Felix said. "I wish we could have obtained one of those. But armed helicopters are forbidden to fly over Paris. Any taking off from here must fly directly out of the city."

"Then why allow them here at all?" Grishkov asked.

"Because many are transporting soldiers to duty within Paris," Felix said. "I suppose that some high officials also wish armed helicopters to be nearby in case of an emergency."

"Like, a dirty bomb about to explode in the center of Paris," Grishkov said.

Felix laughed. "You're preaching to the converted, my friend. But knowing the French as I do, I'm not surprised we're in this," he said, jerking his thumb toward the red and yellow helicopter being fueled a short distance away.

The crewman carrying out the fueling operation saw and misunderstood Felix's motion.

"Finished soon," he shouted.

Felix nodded his understanding.

It was only a few more minutes before Felix and Grishkov stood in front of the brightly-painted helicopter.

"Now, I suggest we prepare this way," Felix said. "Climb on board and assemble the rifle you're carrying in that case. I'll start the preflight check. Call me back when you're done, and I'll help you get strapped in."

"Good," Grishkov replied. "I'll need the help. I have to be lying prone to have any hope of making this shot from the air on a moving target. Will the straps on this helicopter let me do that?"

"Yes," Felix said. "As a mountain rescue chopper, its straps are placed for maximum flexibility. I'm sure you never know where somebody will manage to wedge themselves or at which angle you'll have to approach."

Grishkov shook his head. "I've seen videos of such rescues. Brave men."

Then he paused. "Have we heard anything about where an enemy sniper might be waiting for us? I'm hoping we'll know before we fly into his sights."

"No, not yet," Felix replied. "But Giraud has this helicopter's frequency and will call as soon as he knows. In any case, no sniper will be able to see us for a while."

"And why not?" Grishkov asked.

"Because regulations require us to fly at a minimum altitude of two thousand meters over Paris," Felix said. "A helicopter this size won't be easy to spot at that height, let alone target."

"So once the truck approaches the garage..." Grishkov said.

"Yes," Felix replied with a smile. "We must lose altitude rapidly for you to take your shot. I'm afraid I'll have to cinch your straps in quite tightly for safety. It may not be very comfortable."

"Don't worry about my comfort," Grishkov said. "If I go flying out of the back of this thing, the mission will be over."

Felix nodded. "Understood."

Then Grishkov rummaged in his equipment bag and finally pulled out two items.

A large-scale map of central Paris, and a roll of clear plastic packing tape.

"Since you know where you'll be strapping me in, I need your help in taping this map to the floor where I can see it," Grishkov said.

"Let me guess," Felix said with a grin. "Russian GPS."

Grishkov shrugged. "At least I don't have to worry about equipment failure."

Then Grishkov paused, and his eyes narrowed.

"But I do have one serious question for you. Do you know Paris well enough to recognize the name of a street when I call it out? Even if I mangle the pronunciation?"

"Absolutely," Felix said.

"Are you sure?" Grishkov asked, clearly unconvinced.

Felix nodded emphatically. "Where we're posted overseas, women often don't look so kindly on Legionnaires. But my luck in Paris has been far better. So Paris is where I spend every minute of my leave since I have no family still alive in Germany."

"Fine," Grishkov said. "You take the top of the map, and I'll take the bottom. Don't be shy with the tape. If the map goes flying, I won't be able to tell you how to approach. Remember, if that sniper sees us coming, he might not be able to see you. But he'll know where the pilot is in a helicopter, so he'll still be able to kill you."

Felix nodded. "Don't worry. I've flown many combat missions in Africa, some in helicopters that also lacked armor. I know the importance of a proper approach."

"Good," Grishkov replied. "I'm going to have the sling attached to this rifle pass under my body when you strap me in. Make sure the strap includes it as well as me."

The map was in place minutes later, and Grishkov strapped in with his sniper rifle secured.

Felix also put a helmet with a built-in headset on Grishkov's head.

"I'm about to start the helicopter's engines," he said. "Can you hear me?"

Grishkov nodded but then realized Felix needed to be sure he could hear Grishkov as well.

"Yes, I can hear you," Grishkov said.

"Good," Felix replied. "We'll be underway in a moment."

"The truck hasn't been spotted yet, and we don't know where the sniper may be," Grishkov said. "So, we'll likely be in the air for a while. Won't air traffic control wonder what we're doing?"

"I've filed a training flight plan," Felix replied. "In it, I explained that I'm transitioning from mountain rescue to urban emergency medical response. That tracks with this helicopter type, because the first ones were purchased and deployed for missions in the French Alps. But now that more are entering the civilian helicopter fleet, some are being used for medical transport in large cities."

Grishkov nodded. That all made sense.

The more time he spent with Felix, the more Grishkov realized that he really did know what he was doing.

A comforting thought to have about the man at the flight controls, Grishkov thought wryly.

Moments later, they were climbing and then headed in a bright blue sky to central Paris. It didn't take long before Grishkov could see the Eiffel Tower dead ahead.

As planned, Felix began to circle slowly around central Paris. Grishkov used the time to compare what he saw below with the map taped next to his head. It helped a lot that prominent landmarks like the Eiffel Tower and the Arc de Triomphe were visible even from this height.

"How will you explain to air traffic control what we're doing when we drop to deal with the bomber?" Grishkov asked.

"Mechanical problems," Felix replied. "I'll ask them to identify the nearest safe space where I can set down and directions to reach that location. That should keep them from sending a police helicopter to investigate. At least, not right away."

"So, that will buy us a little time, but not much," Grishkov said. "Probably sooner rather than later, we'll have company."

"Yes," Felix said. "Armed company. And if they get a look at you and your sniper rifle, they won't hesitate to use their weapons."

"Right," Grishkov said, still looking at the ground below and comparing it to his map. "Also, the longer we're at low level, the better the chance that someone on a high office floor will see me and call police. 'Armed man in a helicopter' is likely to get a pretty rapid response."

"I think that all means we can't risk moving down until we have both things," Felix said. "Confirmation that the bomber is on his way. And the sniper's most likely location."

The slow circling continued for what seemed like forever, though Grishkov knew it had been well under an hour.

Well, on the bright side I think I can call out the streets well enough now to guide Felix in the correct approach.

If, Grishkov thought, we don't run out of gas before the bomber shows up.

CHAPTER FORTY

Parking Garage
Central Paris

For the hundredth time, Captain Giraud told himself shooting the bomber as soon as his truck appeared wasn't the right option.

The heavy traffic moving past the parking garage on all sides never stopped. It might slow down sometime in the evening, but not before then.

As long as it was this busy, trying to shoot the bomber before he entered the parking garage would risk hitting innocent motorists.

And if the bomber, even if mortally wounded, managed to reach the switch for the bomb while the truck was in the street? In this traffic?

The resulting carnage would be a disaster.

Never mind the release of radioactivity that would almost certainly follow.

No, Giraud thought decisively. Stick with the plan.

Henri looked at Giraud and smiled.

"Trying not to give in to those second thoughts. Right?"

Giraud nodded. "Yes. Our plan is the best choice out of many bad options. At least I've confirmed that Felix and Grishkov are now overhead."

"Any word from headquarters?" Henri asked.

No sooner were the words out of his mouth than a buzz sounded from Giraud's secure cell phone. Giraud read the text and nodded.

"The answer to your question is now yes," Giraud said. "They have identified a building near here vacated for asbestos removal as a sniper's most likely overwatch location. They have also found a likely match for the truck the bomber will use. A small white grocery delivery truck was reported stolen by SGTI this morning. This information has already been forwarded to Felix and Grishkov."

"But still no sign of the truck," Henri said.

"Correct," Giraud replied. "We have to be patient. In the meantime, are you sure that thing is working properly?"

Giraud gestured toward the black plastic box Henri was carrying. Its sole feature was a large switch with no label.

"I tested it this morning, and it worked perfectly. I'm ready to trigger it when the truck enters the parking garage. As Antoine promised, our secure radios are unaffected," Henri said.

Giraud nodded. "We have to wait until then. If that bomber's cell phone goes out, I'm sure he's been ordered to trigger the bomb wherever he might be in Paris."

Then he paused and looked directly at Henri. "This signal jammer will also work on a walkie-talkie, correct?"

Henri nodded emphatically. "Yes. I had the same thought and tested it for walkie-talkie use as well. Just as effective."

"Good man," Giraud said with evident relief. "Now, all we can do is wait."

The minutes dragged on, and Giraud started to hope something had happened to make the terrorists postpone their attack.

But no.

Giraud's cell phone buzzed again.

"The stolen truck has been spotted about twenty minutes away and is headed straight for us. Felix and Grishkov have also been informed," Giraud said.

Henri nodded.

Giraud received several updates over the next twenty minutes, which all amounted to the same thing.

The bomber is still headed right for you.

Finally, they could see the truck as it rounded a corner. Just as they'd been told, pictures of fruits and vegetables were painted on its sides.

Henri thought, somehow, that made the truck's actual contents even more revolting.

Giraud headed for the parking garage elevator. Several dry runs had confirmed that it would deposit him on the floor below the roof in seconds. From there, just a few steps would be needed to reach the roof.

Why not go there earlier? Giraud had considered it, but was worried about being spotted by a lookout stationed earlier by the terrorists.

Who knew how far ahead one of them might have been planted? Perhaps even out of view inside a parked car.

Yes, Giraud thought, maybe I'm overthinking this.

But as the elevator doors slid open and he saw nobody, Giraud thought he'd made the right call.

"Truck is entering the garage," came over Giraud's radio. "Activating signal dampener and coming to join you now."

Yes, Giraud knew that Felix and Grishkov were on the same frequency.

So far, though, he could neither see nor hear any helicopter.

Well, Giraud thought uneasily, that was the plan.

If I can't detect them, the bomber and the sniper can't either.

Giraud could hear the truck now as it climbed the access ramp inside the parking garage. He opened the door to the short set of stairs connecting the deck where he was now and the roof and stepped inside.

Then Giraud climbed the stairs to the door that would open onto the roof.

Still no truck, but he could hear it approaching.

The plan was to wait until he'd heard from Grishkov that he'd dealt with both the bomber and the sniper before going to the truck.

Giraud was sorely tempted to abandon all his complex preparations. And once the truck appeared on the roof, away from any innocent civilians, jump out of the door and put multiple bullets through its windshield.

But Giraud would be moving. So would the truck.

Could Giraud be sure he'd kill the driver, not just wound him, before he had time to press the detonation switch?

No. He couldn't.

Would a high-velocity sniper bullet do the job?

Yes. It would.

Giraud willed himself to patience.

But why could he still neither see nor hear a helicopter?

CHAPTER FORTY-ONE

Above Central Paris

"You heard that?" Felix asked.

Grishkov nodded at first. Then he remembered Felix couldn't see that gesture, being rightly focused on flying the helicopter.

"Wait thirty seconds," Grishkov said. "Then drop to the first location I told you earlier. As soon as I take the shot, wheel around the target building to our left so I can deal with the sniper. Be sure to stay a dozen meters above the building's roof."

"Right," Felix replied.

He left unvoiced his many concerns.

How could Grishkov be sure he'd kill the bomber with a single shot?

Could Grishkov find and kill the sniper before the unarmored helicopter became a large and easy target?

Either Grishkov would succeed, or he wouldn't. All Felix could do was fly the helicopter.

And pray.

Thirty seconds.

Felix put the helicopter into a steep dive, hoping Grishkov's straps were up to the stress.

This wasn't really what they were designed to deal with, but...

Felix leveled the helicopter parallel to the parking garage but still some distance away.

Good, Felix thought with some satisfaction as he saw the target building to their left.

There's no way any sniper there will be able to see us.

Felix barely heard the sound of the silenced sniper rifle over the helicopter's engine.

He did, though, hear "Target one down. Proceeding to second target."

That was Felix's cue to wheel around and just above the target building. It took only seconds.

Chapter Forty-Two

Evacuated Office Building
Central Paris

Tareq saw the small white delivery truck emerge on top of the roof and felt a thrill of triumph.

So much work and effort, but it was finally paying off!

Tareq reached for his walkie-talkie to give the detonation order.

Then, several things happened at once.

He could hear a sound. Was it...a helicopter?

But he saw nothing.

Tareq looked through his scope at the truck. Why had it stopped moving as soon as it came onto the roof?

Omar was supposed to drive to the roof's center. Was he having second thoughts?

No. Now Tareq could see a hole had been drilled through the truck's windshield.

Omar was slumped forward over the steering wheel.

I told Omar to wear his seat belt because, otherwise, the police might stop him and give him a ticket.

He's obviously not wearing one.

These thoughts flashed through Tareq's head while another much louder voice was shouting, "There's another sniper out there!"

Tareq mashed the remote detonation button.

Nothing.

They have a signal dampener!

Tareq willed himself to calm down. The bomb is on a timer. All I have to do is shoot anyone who tries to disarm it.

That sound is definitely a helicopter!

Confirmation came as a red and yellow helicopter appeared about ten meters above Tareq's position.

Its door was open.

There was a man inside with a rifle. The other sniper!

The helicopter banked slightly so that now the rifle was pointed directly at Tareq.

Who realized that the circle he'd cut in the window wouldn't allow him to point his rifle anywhere near the helicopter above.

Or rise from his prone position in time to escape.

Or

Chapter Forty-Three

Parking Garage
Central Paris

"Target two is down."

Grishkov's voice over Giraud's walkie-talkie was an incredible relief. Could this be over?

Unless their guess turned out to be correct, and the bomb was also on a backup timer.

Giraud was already on the roof by the time he'd completed the thought.

The truck was just steps away. It took no more than a glance at its unmoving driver to confirm he was dead.

Is the back locked?

Giraud had tools in case that was true, but he didn't need them. The truck's back door slid up without much effort.

Yes, there was the bomb.

It nearly filled the cargo space inside the small truck.

The bomb was half a metal cylinder with a flat bottom. The metal was shiny.

Not steel.

Bricks of construction-grade explosives were attached to it on all sides. Wire leads ran from each brick to a single destination.

A timer. With a digital clock counting down second by second.

Just as they'd guessed.

Giraud had considered involving the Paris bomb squad in the mission but finally rejected the idea. First, he had no confidence that they or their bosses could keep a lid on the situation, as the President had demanded.

More importantly, he doubted they would have the time to defuse an unfamiliar device successfully.

Giraud's planning had included the nearest location where the bomb could be allowed to detonate without catastrophic results, as well as a time estimate for driving the truck there.

He had never thought there would be enough time if the truck had a backup timer.

Giraud realized he'd been right on both counts as the remaining time ticked down.

There wasn't enough time to defuse the bomb.

Nor was there enough time to drive the truck somewhere safe.

All that left was Plan C.

Giraud really hated Plan C.

Henri came bursting through the door to the roof.

"Pull the driver out of the truck and move to the passenger side!" Giraud shouted.

Without hesitating, Henri changed course from running to Giraud to heading for the truck's cab.

Giraud closed and secured the truck's cargo door.

By the time he reached the front of the truck, the driver's body was lying on the roof, and Henri was in the passenger seat.

Giraud jumped into the driver's seat and saw with relief that the keys were still in the ignition.

"Backup timer?" Henri asked.

Giraud nodded as he started the truck.

"How much time?" Henri asked.

"It's going to be close," Giraud said as he put the truck into gear.

No matter how much Giraud wanted to speed up, the ramp circled downward, making rapid progress impossible. In fact, even though the truck was relatively small, it barely fit on the ramp.

Like most in central Paris, the parking garage had three subterranean levels.

They were headed to the level furthest down.

The DGSE had several engineers on its staff. All had looked at its blueprints and come to the same conclusion.

A sufficient explosive charge on the bottom level would knock out the supports anchoring the structure.

Causing the entire parking garage to implode and pancake.

What amount of explosives would be "sufficient?"

The answer to that was the one Giraud had expected.

The classic Gallic shrug. How could they know?

The engineers thought there would be no significant damage to the surrounding buildings.

Cars driving on adjoining streets?

Debris could certainly strike them, but most of those inside would be sufficiently shielded by the cars' structural steel and airbags.

Probably.

Anyone inside the garage would undoubtedly be killed.

However, nearly all drivers used this garage to park their car at the beginning of the workday and then pick it up late afternoon or early evening for the drive home.

Giraud hadn't seen or heard anyone in the garage. Giraud still saw no one as the truck made its stubbornly slow way down.

For the sake of those innocent drivers, Giraud hoped that stayed true.

Yes, it had seemed like forever. But Giraud knew driving from the roof to the garage's deepest level had only taken a few minutes.

How much time was left? Giraud could have set the timer on his watch and known the answer exactly.

Instead, he'd decided to skip that step and leave the parking structure as quickly as possible.

Or as quickly as he could climb three flights of stairs.

He certainly wasn't going to push the elevator button and wait for it to arrive.

The engineers had said that to have the best chance of "pancaking" the garage, the truck should be parked as close to its center as possible when the bomb inside exploded.

Otherwise, the structure could tip over onto one of the nearby buildings. With disastrous results.

Giraud had immediately recognized the downside of those instructions.

No parking close to an exit.

Well, nobody ever said military service would be easy.

Every space on the bottom level was occupied.

Not a problem.

Giraud parked the small truck right at what he thought was dead center.

Was he blocking several cars from exiting?

Today that wouldn't matter.

Giraud and Henri had both brought masks for a situation like this.

Should they take the time to put them on?

Giraud bolted from the truck and ran toward the nearest "Exit" sign.

Out of the corner of his eye, Giraud could see that Henri was coming up fast behind him.

Like Giraud, no mask.

He's made the same calculation I did.

Radioactive particles might kill me eventually.

Staying in a building about to collapse will kill me right now.

Giraud bounded up the steps two at a time.

He'd passed his last military physical without difficulty. But to his annoyance, the doctor had commented that Giraud should increase his time on cardio exercises.

This, Giraud thought, should count.

One floor.

Two floors.

Just one more to go.

The exit door!

Giraud could hear that Henri was right behind him.

He was out on the street!

Cars were whizzing past Giraud in both directions.

Giraud instantly decided to take his chances, and didn't slow down as he plunged into the busy city traffic.

A chorus of horns signaled strong disapproval of Giraud's choice.

Fortunately, every driver in Paris had experience dealing with careless pedestrians.

Did they swerve out of human decency?

Well, maybe a few.

But no driver wanted to risk damaging his car.

So, all the drivers managed to avoid hitting him.

Giraud had just reached the opposite sidewalk when he heard Henri come up behind him and start to say something.

Then, a huge hand pushed him forward, and Giraud fell into darkness.

CHAPTER FORTY-FOUR

Les Invalides
Paris, France

Captain Giraud heard sounds that, at first, he couldn't quite place. Though somehow, they were familiar.

He cautiously opened his eyes.

Yes, he knew where he was.

A hospital.

The sounds were coming from the electronic monitoring equipment collecting data on his condition. Familiar, because it was far from the first time he'd been wounded.

Giraud looked down. Still, two arms and two legs. Good.

Then he carefully moved each appendage. A little.

Good.

Now, fingers and toes.

Check.

Giraud knew better than to read too much into the absence of pain. He felt a wooliness that was familiar.

Prescription-strength painkillers. And plenty of them.

He peeled back his thin blanket and peeked under his hospital gown.

A mass of bruises.

But there were no casts on him anywhere.

It took a few moments to get his eyes to focus on the equipment readouts next to his bed.

Giraud was no doctor. But he knew enough to see that all the numbers in front of him were within normal range.

The door swung open to admit Grishkov.

"Ah, you're awake!" he exclaimed. "How are you feeling?"

"Like a building fell on me," Giraud said with a wan smile.

The smile quickly disappeared as he asked, "Henri?"

Grishkov nodded. "He'll be OK. In the room next door, in about the same shape as you. Lots of bruises."

"Civilian casualties?" Giraud asked.

"Incredibly, they were minor," Grishkov replied. "A dozen cars on adjoining streets were damaged, but only a few drivers had to be hospitalized. I've seen them, and they all look better than you."

"So they brought them here?" Giraud asked.

"Yes," Grishkov said. "Jacques thought it best to keep everyone involved together."

Giraud nodded. "And the official version of what happened?"

"A gas main leaked, causing an explosion," Grishkov replied. "The parking garage structure, weakened by adding an extra floor, collapsed. The surrounding two-block radius has been evacuated as a precaution while searches continue for other suspected leaks."

"And in reality?" Giraud asked.

"The parking garage collapsed in on itself just like the engineers said it would," Grishkov replied. "That had the effect of sealing whatever radioactivity was in the bomb under tons of debris. Tests of the air around the site showed increased radioactivity, but nothing dangerous enough to warrant evacuation past the two-block radius."

"Good," Giraud said. "Has Henri been tested for radiation exposure?"

"Of course," Grishkov said with a smile. "You were as well. Both of you went through decontamination while you were still unconscious as a precaution. However, there is no indication that either of you received a significant radiation dose."

"The bodies of the bomber and the sniper?" Giraud asked.

"Already recovered by a DGSE team, posing as disaster recovery experts," Grishkov replied. "Regular police have been ordered to stay away because of the supposed risk of further gas explosions. The evacuated building where they found the sniper's body was, of course, within the two-block evacuation radius."

Giraud nodded. "A good time, I think, to commend both you and Felix on your performance. Did anyone in the office buildings nearby notice your brightly painted helicopter?"

"So far, it looks like nobody was quick enough to capture us on video," Grishkov replied. "Probably helped that the whole business took only a minute or so. Felix had our helicopter back at two thousand meters fast enough that anyone who did notice us would have had little time to record it."

"I'm sure Jacques will make sure removal of the garage's debris is carried out by suitably trained and equipped experts," Giraud said tiredly. "Still, I'll have to speak with him about that."

Grishkov nodded, but Giraud could see he was skeptical.

"Captain, it may not be my place, but as the previous occupant of this very hospital bed, let me give you some advice. Your current mission is recovery. Jacques strikes me as quite capable. I think you can trust him to do his job."

Giraud smiled. "Advice from one old soldier to another is always welcome. Now I'll give you some. Go and get some rest yourself. I promise my eyes will be closed again by the time you've left."

Grishkov nodded and wasted no time leaving.

But a moment later, he could hear Grishkov starting to speak to Henri and shook his head.

Giraud had meant what he said. His eyes were already closing.

But two questions kept circling through his head as he drifted off, this time to sleep rather than unconsciousness.

Would Jacques be able to do anything about whoever at SGTI was behind the attack?

And what about the DGSE Director? Would he be brought to account?

Grishkov is right. I have to trust Jacques to do his job.

Or maybe even more than that.

CHAPTER FORTY-FIVE

Palais de l'Élysée
Paris, France

Jacques Montand had never imagined he would set foot in the official residence and offices of the French President. As the DGSE Deputy Director for Operations, he was just too low-ranking to be here.

Let alone to be meeting President Allard himself.

But, here he was. Time to use this opportunity.

Not for himself. But for his country.

Jacques wasn't even aware that others would have found his way of thinking hopelessly naïve.

It's simply who he was.

Secretary-General Blanchet owed Jacques a favor long before he reached his current position, which would have been called "Chief of Staff" in most other countries. To his credit, he had taken Jacques' call and then agreed to see him in person.

To his even greater credit, Blanchet believed Jacques and agreed that action had to be taken against DGSE Director Dubois.

Yes, Jacques had convincing documentary evidence.

But they both knew it would have been easy for Blanchet to order Jacques to destroy the evidence in the name of "national security."

And then arrange an expedited retirement for Jacques. He had certainly served long enough to qualify.

Jacques thought he knew Blanchet well enough to be sure that wouldn't happen.

However, Jacques hadn't seen Blanchet for years. And he knew time and power could change a man.

Happily, not in this case.

Jacques was ushered into the Salon Angle, a former dining room that had served as the Secretary-General's office since 2007.

Blanchet waved Jacques to a low sofa and took the chair opposite.

Like everything in the Palais de l'Élysée, the furniture had two things in common with the rest of the furnishings.

Everything was an antique. The Palais de l'Élysée dated from 1722 and no expense was spared to maintain its interior at its original high standard.

And everything was designed to impress. Foreign visitors, French politicians, wealthy businessmen- it didn't matter who it might be.

Nobody could enter the Palais de l'Élysée without feeling the weight of centuries of history.

That very much included one Jacques Montand.

"I've briefed the President, who agrees that Dubois must go. But he doesn't want a trial and the scandal accompanying it," Blanchet said.

"And does he understand the alternative?" Jacques asked, eyebrows raised.

"Yes," Blanchet replied. "I think that's why the President insisted he speak with you in person. Before I take you to see him, though, I have to ask you about Khaled Madi, the former President of the Société Générale de Transport International. And one of the richest men in France. I understand from your last report that he abruptly retired and flew in his private plane to Turkey."

"Correct," Jacques said. "We have just received information that he may have gone on to Dubai, but nothing is confirmed yet."

Blanchet nodded. "Your report says you suspect his involvement in the attack but don't yet have proof besides Madi's contacts with Dubois."

Seeing Jacques' raised eyebrows, Blanchet had to smile. "And the co-incidental timing of his retirement and flight abroad, that is."

"That's right," Jacques said. "But our investigation continues. Quietly, as you requested."

"And do you plan to take any action against Madi, in the meantime?" Blanchet asked.

Jacques shook his head. "Madi is a French citizen. Without clear proof, we will do nothing."

"Good," Blanchet said. "I will take you to the President now."

A short walk later, down a flight of stairs, they were at the door in a part of the building Jacques had never seen on television.

"Good luck," Blanchet said and left.

Standing before the closed door, Jacques was initially unsure what to do.

Finally, he shrugged and knocked.

"Enter," a familiar voice said.

Familiar, that is, from many speeches and press conferences.

Jacques entered and did his best to conceal his shock.

The President's public appearances had been limited since the death of his wife from cancer the previous year. That had come less than a year after his election.

Now Jacques understood why President Allard had rarely been seen in public since. Grief had taken a visible toll on him.

Jacques couldn't help but think that here was a man who might never smile again.

"Please, have a seat," Allard said. This time, they were in facing chairs.

"This is the Salon Bleu. For many years, it has served as the office of the First Lady of France. I come here sometimes to remember my wife. I feel that her presence is still here, somehow," Allard said.

"Mr. President..." Jacques began.

Waving his hands, Allard shook his head at the condolences they both knew Jacques was about to offer.

"I'm sorry. I should have come straight to the point. We're meeting here because this is the one place nobody will dare to enter. And for this discussion, there can be no witnesses."

"I understand, sir," Jacques said.

"Good," Allard said. "First, I must congratulate you and the men who work for you on their performance. You prevented a disaster that could have killed many, and crippled our economy for years. All that, and so far, no one but us seems to know what really happened. That may not last, but the longer it does, the more difficult it will be for any-one to reveal the truth."

Jacques nodded but said nothing. The flip side, that covering up the truth would be far more explosive if it were finally revealed, didn't seem to bother Allard.

So why should it worry Jacques?

"Blanchet has already given me a full report, and I agree that Dubois cannot remain as Director of the DGSE," Allard said. "It is true that I do not want to accept the scandal of a public trial. But Blanchet doesn't know why I am willing, in this one case, to sanction the only alternative."

Allard paused and looked at Jacques directly.

"I am far from the only person to lose a loved one to cancer," Allard said. "I know this. It doesn't make me special. But it does give me a spe-cial appreciation for the sort of monster who would condemn his fel-low countrymen to that long, lingering, horrible death for the basest of motives. Money."

That last word, Allard spit out like a curse.

Jacques had never expected to find himself completely agreeing with a politician.

Any politician.

"I assume you can make Dubois' death appear to be an accident," Allard said.

Jacques nodded. He didn't have a plan yet. But he knew it could be done.

Allard had even saved Jacques the burden of bringing up the need for Dubois' death if a trial was out of the question.

But the relief he felt quickly disappeared.

"Once Dubois is gone, I plan to appoint you as his replacement," Allard said.

"Me?" Jacques said, genuinely astonished. "I don't want the job!"

Allard said nothing but instead stared at Jacques intently.

Long enough that Jacques began to feel more than a little uncomfortable.

Finally, Allard shook his head.

"Blanchet said that would be your reaction, but I had trouble believing it. I thought, in fact, ambition might be the reason you kept such a close eye on Dubois. I can see, though, that's not the case. So, you really don't want the job?"

"That's right, sir, I really don't," Jacques said. This time, his relief was even more sincere than his earlier astonishment.

But his relief was just as short-lived as before.

"That's too bad," Allard said. "I'm not giving you a choice. I need a man I can trust in that position, and now I've seen what happens when we put a politician in charge. France needs you. Can I count on you to do your duty?"

Put that way, Jacques could only give one response.

"Of course, Mr. President."

"Good," Allard said. "Please tell Blanchet on your way out that he was right. That will let him know to prepare the appointment paperwork for when you take over."

"Yes, sir," Jacques said, wasting no time leaving.

As he closed the door behind him, he saw Allard still sitting there, looking at something or someone nobody else could see.

No doubt, his dead wife, Jacques thought sadly.

He still has over five years to go as President. I wonder if he'll make it?

CHAPTER FORTY-SIX

DGSE Headquarters
Paris, France

Jacques Montand rubbed his temples tiredly. He couldn't remember the last time he'd had a decent night's sleep.

It didn't help that his cold, dark Paris apartment had Jacques as its only occupant. Since his spouse had left him five years before, declaring that Jacques' real wife was the DGSE.

And now, Jacques could stop pretending and devote his full attention to her.

Jacques sighed and sipped from the bitter dregs left in the bottom of his cup.

And grimaced. Even for office coffee, this was terrible.

Jacques' office door swung open to admit the last person he'd expected. Antoine Bertrand.

The rules of office politics were the same at the DGSE as everywhere else. If you wanted something, you went to the person who could do it for you.

As Deputy Director for Technical Support and Financial Investigations, Antoine could often help other DGSE offices like Operations.

On the other hand, what could Antoine possibly need from Jacques?

Well, Jacques supposed he'd find out soon enough. But first...

Yes. First, let's be sure Antoine closed the door behind him. It wouldn't do for anyone to hear this conversation.

Jacques craned his head to see around Antoine, who had already taken a seat across from Jacques' desk.

Closed. Good.

"Welcome, my friend," Jacques said. "I was sorry to hear about the heart attack that claimed the life of our mutual friend."

Antoine gave Jacques a small smile and shook his head. "Please. I personally swept your office for listening devices just before you came in. We can speak freely."

"Very well," Jacques replied. "Your investigation confirmed that the Deputy Director for Counterintelligence installed by Dubois was the man who made the call sending Grishkov to the ambush outside Évreux-Fauville Air Base. Are you sure the poison you administered won't show up in an autopsy?"

"No chance," Antoine said, shaking his head. "That's assuming the coroner even bothers to order a full tox screen. The man was in his fifties, on medication for high blood pressure and cholesterol, and was seeing a cardiologist. His death could hardly be less suspicious."

Jacques nodded. "Good. But I'm sure you're not here to accept my praise for a job well done."

"No," Antoine said with a sigh. "I'm afraid we may have underestimated Dubois. He's on the run."

"What?" Jacques said with alarm. "I thought you had him under surveillance!"

"We did," Antoine replied. "Cell phone and car. Both said he'd gone to spend the night with his mistress, which was perfectly routine for him."

"Mistress," Jacques repeated, shaking his head. "A traitor to his wife as well as to France."

Antoine raised an eyebrow. "Well, thank goodness the two don't always go together, or we'd all be speaking Russian. I'm sure it's not news to you that having a mistress is hardly unknown among French politicians."

"Yes, yes," Jacques said irritably. "But didn't you check that Dubois was actually at his mistress' apartment?"

"Of course," Antoine said. "I had one of my best men there, and he saw Dubois go in. With the tracker we had on both his car and phone, it didn't seem necessary to keep my man standing outside the apartment all night."

Jacques rubbed his temples again. Not just tired this time. He felt a real beauty of a headache coming on.

"Understood," Jacques replied. "So, do we know how long Dubois has been gone?"

"Yes. Not very long," Antoine said. "Alerts were already out for all airports and train stations, so those options are closed to him. He took his mistress' car and is headed east to Switzerland."

Jacques nodded thoughtfully. "As you say, smarter than we thought. From there, he could fly anywhere in the world. And the Swiss won't act quickly enough to stop him, even if we ask."

"And I'm sure you don't want to tell the Swiss why we want the DGSE Director to be detained," Antoine said.

"No, I do not," Jacques said with a sigh.

"I'm afraid all I can do is give you access to his current location," Antoine said. "His mistress' SUV is very nice, late model, and comes with a theft-prevention tracker we were able to hack."

"Any chance she will report it stolen?" Jacques asked.

Antoine shook his head. "She hasn't so far. And I doubt she will since Dubois is listed as a joint owner on the SUV's registration. He did pay for it, after all."

"Of course he did," Jacques said with disgust. "Very well. I will deal with it from here. Thanks for letting me know."

Once Jacques was alone again, his mind raced furiously to find a solution.

The DGSE had no offices in France outside Paris. Dubois was well on his way to the Swiss border.

How could Jacques do anything in time to stop him?

CHAPTER FORTY-SEVEN

Above the French Alps

"Will we be able to get ahead of Dubois before he reaches the border?" Jacques asked.

Felix nodded, pointing at the blip on the helicopter's GPS display that showed the position of Dubois' SUV.

"But we're only going to get one chance to stop him," Felix said. "And, as we agreed, I'm only going to try if there's no traffic in either direction for at least a kilometer."

"Agreed," Jacques said at once. "Dubois has already cost many people their lives. I won't add innocent civilians to the total."

So far, though, it looked promising. For whatever reason, Dubois had picked a secondary road to enter Switzerland.

Maybe he thought an alert would be less likely to reach a border post in this remote section of the French Alps?

Well, whatever the reason, vehicles on the road below them were few and far between.

A few minutes later, Felix pointed at the dark clouds before them and shook his head.

"Snow," he said. "Just as they said in the forecast."

Jacques cursed. Just when he'd thought they could pull this off.

"Any chance we can intercept Dubois before we reach the storm?" Jacques asked.

Felix looked dubiously at the GPS display.

"I'm already going as fast as I believe is safe. But I can try to squeeze a little more out of this bird. I'll warn you, the ride may get a bit rough," Felix said.

"Do whatever is necessary," Jacques said. "We have to stop Dubois."

Felix nodded and pitched the helicopter's nose forward.

Jacques wasn't just worried about punishing Dubois for his treason.

Dubois had also had access to all the most highly classified information possessed by the DGSE.

Would Dubois hesitate for a second to sell those secrets to the highest bidder?

Jacques was sure he would not.

Felix hadn't been joking. Jacques' stomach protested the helicopter's bucking and lurching in no uncertain terms.

Jacques swallowed dryly and focused on the GPS screen. Where the distance to the pulsing dot ahead was beginning to close rapidly.

"He's not to the snow yet, but the road ahead has to be getting icy," Felix said. "He's slowing down."

Jacques nodded. Good. Maybe this would work after all.

"I think most people in the area know a storm is coming," Felix said. "That's probably why there's so little traffic."

"That makes sense," Jacques replied. "I haven't seen another vehicle on the road for the past several kilometers."

"Yes," Felix said absently, his attention focused on the view ahead.

"When I do our descent, it will be faster than you've ever experienced. Just hold on tight and try not to do or say anything that might distract me," Felix said.

"Understood," Jacques replied.

Jacques had already discussed the plan with Felix, who had immediately pointed out that it could kill both them and Dubois.

Or instead of Dubois.

The first option was unappealing to Jacques.

The second, even less so.

But, after some discussion, Felix had finally agreed there was no better option.

Trying to fire at Dubois from a moving helicopter was unlikely to be as easy as it seemed in the movies.

And, even if successful, it would leave evidence behind that Dubois' death was no ordinary traffic accident.

No, Jacques' plan was the only one offering any chance to stop Dubois before he reached the Swiss border.

But would it work?

CHAPTER FORTY-EIGHT

Near The Swiss Border

DGSE Director Roland Dubois couldn't believe how badly wrong it had all gone.

He thought he'd anticipated anything that could go awry. Even after Dubois learned Khaled Madi had "retired" and fled the country, he'd still thought he was safe.

After all, Dubois had gone to great lengths to cover his tracks. All the money Madi had given him had been in cryptocurrency, which he was sure nobody could trace.

But somehow, he'd been found out.

A friend from his political days who worked in the Palais de l'Élysée had sent him a brief text because he recognized Jacques Montand.

He'd wondered what Dubois' deputy was doing in the Palais de l'Élysée without his boss.

Dubois.

There could be only one answer. Someone at the very highest levels had decided to replace Dubois with Jacques Montand.

Before or after a trial had been Dubois' first thought.

His second was that nobody in the Palais de l'Élysée would want the scandal that would result from trying the DGSE Director for treason.

The alternative? The average French citizen might believe his government would never carry out an extrajudicial killing.

But Dubois had been a politician long enough to know that exceptions might be made in very rare cases.

Treason? Supporting a terrorist attack on Paris?

Yes. Dubois thought those crimes might very well qualify.

Then Dubois heard about the heart attack suffered by the Deputy Director for Counterintelligence. The man he'd appointed to watch his back.

The immediately fatal heart attack.

Dubois' first thought had been to head straight for the airport, but a moment's reflection stopped him.

Airports and train stations in France had certainly been alerted. His car was doubtless being tracked. And his cell phone.

Renting a car would require identification and a credit card, so Dubois was sure an alert would go out immediately.

But the SUV he'd just bought for his mistress? They might know about it.

Then again, they might not.

Dubois went to see her. And then waited until she fell asleep.

When he bought his mistress the SUV, the dealer gave Dubois two sets of keys. Dubois kept one when he gave her the SUV.

Dubois congratulated himself on his foresight. He wouldn't even have to rummage through the woman's purse.

After a moment's thought, Dubois scribbled out a note, telling her that he'd borrowed the SUV. The note said an urgent matter had come up – true – and his car had failed to start.

Well, that wasn't true.

But as lies went, it was probably the smallest Dubois had told in some time.

Dubois had only driven the SUV once, when he'd taken it for a test drive. He was impressed and purchased it on the spot.

The SUV had many features his old sedan did not: heated seats, automatic headlights, and rain-sensing windshield wipers, which even to a man as indolent as Dubois seemed a bit lazy.

But the one feature that did impress him as useful was part of the sound system. There were built-in sensors that could detect the noise level inside the vehicle, and the system would then adjust the music's volume automatically to compensate.

Very clever, Dubois thought.

Of much more immediate interest, though, was the SUV's powerful engine and excellent all-weather tires.

Switzerland. With luck, I'll be there before anyone realizes I'm gone.

And once I'm there, I can fly somewhere safe.

Where the information I have with me can be sold for...well, what it's worth.

Which will be enough to let me live in luxury until I'm old and gray.

There had been two methods by which Dubois had been able to collect information worth selling.

The first was straightforward. As the DGSE Director, he was regularly briefed on a wide range of topics. Dubois had insisted that those briefings be printed.

Yes, his underlings had protested. Said that the days of printed briefs were dead and buried and paper a security risk.

Dubois had suppressed a smile only with difficulty. If they only knew how right they were!

I am old and set in my ways, Dubois had announced. And I am the Director, he'd added.

Dubois had been smart enough, though, to request a shredder.

But not a safe.

No, Dubois said, I will keep nothing classified in my office. Once I read it, everything goes in the shredder.

It had helped Dubois escape detection that nearly every piece of paper did, in fact, go in the shredder. Yes, Dubois thought wryly; shredding probably accounted for the only real work I did in that job.

Nearly all of the information presented to Dubois was of little value. That is, resale value to governments with money.

As a politician, Dubois had a keen sense of what was worth keeping. Not much, but the papers that were? Worth their weight in gold.

Actually, Dubois thought with a smile, quite a bit more than that.

Once Dubois had closed his office door, those documents went in his locked briefcase.

Of course, there was a security inspection for every employee at the DGSE Headquarters exit. Run by the Office of Counterintelligence.

Dubois had been careful in picking the Deputy Director in charge.

One of the first changes the new Deputy Director announced was that Director Dubois, naturally, would not be subject to exit checks.

Dubois had been disappointed to find that there was no computer in his office. Ideally, one with a USB slot he could use to insert a thumb drive. And then download whatever he wished.

Yes, Dubois remembered reading that a U.S. soldier had used that method to download 250,000 diplomatic cables and then give copies to a reporter on another thumb drive.

Instead, there was just a network relay box with nothing on it but a power button. And connections for a mouse, speakers and monitor.

But no USB port.

Like all the monitors in DGSE headquarters, the one in Dubois' office had a filter screen attached. Nobody explained its purpose to Dubois.

Dubois quickly discovered its function the first time he locked his office door and tried to take a picture of the information on the screen with his cell phone.

It was black. Somehow, the human eye could see through the filter mesh to the screen below. But the lens on his cell phone could not.

Dubois had then been forced to think. Did he need to buy a better camera?

No. If I forget and leave it on my desk, how would I explain it?

Besides, it might not work anyway.

Then another thought made Dubois immediately delete the photo on his cell phone, showing the black screen.

Accessing his personal cell phone through the DGSE wireless network might be possible. Who knew what those nosy technicians could be up to?

Right. What Dubois needed was a burner phone with a good-quality lens. That he would not activate with any cell phone service provider. And keep permanently on "airplane mode" to prevent any wireless snooping.

OK. But what about the filter screen? How can I deal with that?

The solution was so obvious Dubois nearly laughed aloud.

He called the man he'd appointed as Deputy Director for Counterintelligence. And demanded he send someone to Dubois' office with a monitor that didn't have "one of those cursed filter screens that was giving him a headache."

Ten minutes later, the problem had been solved.

Dubois had realized, though, that he would have to be more cautious from then on.

So, he had not gone scrolling through the DGSE database looking for the most valuable information he might be able to sell.

Nothing so obvious.

No. Instead, Dubois limited his searches to two categories.

Information directly related to briefings he had just received.

And crises and world events at the top of the news. Ones that a DGSE Director would be expected to be interested in to do his job more effectively.

Dubois was surprised at how much information fell within those two categories as the days and weeks passed.

Including information worth selling.

Months later, Dubois's burner phone was packed full of photos of highly classified material he was certain he could sell for an excellent price. Likewise for the papers in his briefcase, which had become...quite heavy.

Dubois had seen little traffic on the road so far. At first, he'd thought that was a good thing. Nothing to slow down his progress to the Swiss border.

As the road became more icy and dark clouds gathered ahead, though, Dubois began to wish he'd checked the weather before setting out.

Well, it wouldn't have mattered, he decided finally. He'd had no better options.

And besides, the Swiss border was just ahead. Once he was across, Dubois could pull over at the first rest stop and wait out the storm.

He'd still be on a plane soon.

Dubois slowed down a bit. After having come so far, it would be stupid to have an accident this close to success.

As the road climbed up the Alps, it became more narrow and winding. Towering peaks to his right. A single lane going in the other direction to his left.

That lane was bordered by a guardrail that looked like it might hold back a motorcycle. Or a Clio.

Certainly nothing as heavy as his SUV.

Beyond the guardrail? A drop that continued down a considerable distance. To the tops of some trees.

Dubois slowed down a bit more.

Music. That would help the remaining drive pass more quickly.

Wagner. Yes, something that would stir the blood. And do justice to this magnificent scenery.

No sooner had Dubois made his music selection than, to his annoyance, he could hear some racket pass overhead.

What was that?

Dubois' blood ran cold. Was it a police helicopter?

Then Dubois saw it go by and relaxed as he saw the helicopter's bright red and yellow colors.

Everyone knew what those colors meant. It was a rescue helicopter. Probably on its way to save someone dumb enough to go climbing in this weather.

The music's volume had gone up as the helicopter flew overhead. Now that it had passed, it was back to its original level.

Once again, Dubois was impressed. Too bad he'd have to leave this vehicle behind.

Well, wherever I go, I'm sure I'll be able to buy another one just like it.

WHAT IS THAT?

All Dubois could register was that something large had just appeared right in front of him.

Instinct took over. There was no time to brake.

No space at all to pass to the right.

Maybe to the left?

As he jerked the steering wheel to the left, Dubois knew it wouldn't work.

It didn't help that the icy road made the SUV skid out of control.

But in the end, it didn't matter.

Dubois turned out to be correct about one thing.

The guardrail didn't even slow him down.

The sound it made as the SUV crashed through, though, did make Wagner's Ride of the Valkyries rise to a truly impressive volume.

As the SUV hit the trees below, it swelled even louder for just a moment.

And then Dubois heard nothing at all.

CHAPTER FORTY-NINE

Paris, France

Anatoly Grishkov had dared hope that after succeeding in his mission for the DGSE, he would be allowed to return to retirement quietly.

Well, Grishkov could say he still hoped that. Former FSB Director Smyslov might have asked to meet him again in this café to offer some well-earned congratulations.

Grishkov sighed. It was really too bad that he was old enough to know better.

At least this time, Ivan gave him some decent Russian black tea to drink while waiting.

Fortunately, Smyslov didn't keep him in suspense for long.

"Grishkov! So good to see you!" the familiar voice boomed as Smyslov grabbed him in one of his traditional bear hugs.

One that Grishkov was surprised to feel had some real strength behind it.

Smyslov had rushed in so quickly that Grishkov hadn't been able to get a good look at him.

As Smyslov released him and sat down, though, Grishkov could see that Smyslov looked...much improved!

Seeing Grishkov's look of astonishment, Smyslov laughed.

"Yes, believe me, I'm just as surprised as you are," Smyslov said. "In many important respects, we remain far ahead of the French. Medicine, however, appears to be one area where they have pulled ahead."

"I'm glad to see it, for your sake," Grishkov said, meaning every word. "Does this mean you'll be able to return as the FSB Director?"

Smyslov laughed and shook his head. "No, thank you. Even if Director Kharlov were willing to step aside – which he certainly is not – I wouldn't want the job. First, though my health has improved, I don't know how long that will last. The French doctors say they're pleased with my progress, but they urge caution."

Grishkov nodded. Maybe the doctors were just covering themselves. But maybe not.

Smyslov was many things. But young was not one of them.

"More important, though, is that I feel no need to return to my old job. Kharlov has proved himself capable. And I am enjoying my time here in France. Enough that I think I may join you in retirement," Smyslov said.

Seeing Grishkov's expression, Smyslov laughed again. "Don't worry, my dear fellow! You won't be seeing me as your neighbor near the Mediterranean. As you might expect, the best French doctors and medical facilities are here in Paris. Besides, I'm enjoying the food and entertainment that this city has to offer. In some respects, I might prefer Moscow. But I must admit, here there are years' worth of experience still waiting to be explored."

"I'm happy for you," Grishkov said.

He meant that, too. But Grishkov knew that none of this was why Smyslov had asked to see him.

"Well, my friend, I must congratulate you on your performance during your latest mission," Smyslov said. "Our President told me it makes him sorry he agreed to my request to let you retire. But considering this mission sent you to the hospital again, he still agreed with my recommendation that you receive his customary reward of one million American dollars."

"That is very generous of the President," Grishkov said, trying to keep his voice as neutral as possible.

He could see from Smyslov's smile that he had failed.

"You suspect that the President wants more from you for that money," Smyslov said. "Or, perhaps, that I do."

"Am I wrong?" Grishkov asked.

Smyslov laughed and shook his head.

"No, you are not. But before I go on, tell me. Were you really content in retirement?"

Grishkov recalled his first months in France alone at home with Arisha. Much of that time had been very pleasant.

Raising two children and working first for the police, and then the FSB, had left little time for them to be together.

And the south of France near the Mediterranean was certainly a better place to spend the winter than either Moscow or Vladivostok.

But Grishkov couldn't argue with Smyslov's implied point.

It had been nice to feel useful again.

Seeing those thoughts pass over Grishkov's face, Smyslov nodded.

He knew he'd made his point.

"A problem that will again make the French ask for your assistance has come up. We don't yet have all the details, but..." Smyslov shrugged.

Grishkov groaned. "Really? How many nuclear weapons did we lose track of over the years?"

"This time, it's not ours!" Smyslov said with a smile. "It is French."

"Really? And how did that happen?" Grishkov asked.

"Again, we don't know all the details," Smyslov said. "But if you search the Internet, you'll find that the number of French nuclear tests in the Pacific was 'variously reported as 175 and 181.' Would you like to guess the reason for the variation?"

"Several tests were unsuccessful for some reason, I suppose?" Grishkov replied.

"Maybe," Smyslov said. "The truth is, we can only guess. But we do have reports that one of those unexploded nuclear devices has been found, washed up on an uninhabited atoll in French Polynesia."

"Uninhabited? Really? I thought a few hundred thousand people lived out there," Grishkov said.

"Correct," Smyslov said. "I'm glad you already know something about the area."

Grishkov made a face. "Arisha talked about going to Tahiti for a vacation, so I looked it up. When I saw how long it would take to fly there from France, I've done my best ever since to talk her out of it."

Smyslov nodded. "To answer your question, about two-thirds of the one hundred twenty islands constituting French Polynesia are inhabited. But dozens are not."

"Very well," Grishkov said. "But I'll be blunt. Why do we care?"

"A good question," Smyslov said. "I'll be honest. I'm not sure how much we do. But the Chinese have been sniffing around the area, which could spell trouble."

"Really?" Grishkov said with genuine surprise. "Why would we care what the Chinese do out there?"

"Again, I'm not sure we do," Smyslov replied. "But the new American government has become quite isolationist. In the past, we're sure they would have prevented any Chinese advance so close to Samoa and Hawaii. Now though?"

Smyslov shook his head.

"The Pacific as a Chinese lake may not be so good for our Far East fleet," Smyslov growled. "And as we've discussed before, we have a long border with China and few Russians living on our side of it. A China that has succeeded in building a Pacific empire may have its appetite whetted for one on land as well."

"Understood," Grishkov replied. "So, what resources do you think Russia will commit against this possibility?"

Smyslov smiled. "I could be wrong. But I think I'm looking right now at the effort the President will authorize."

"Very flattering!" Grishkov exclaimed. "You know that no matter how lucky I've been so far, there's no chance one person could make a real difference in something like this."

"I agree," Smyslov said. "I will use what influence I have left to get you some help. However, even if I succeed, I won't lie to you. It still won't amount to much. Frankly, I think the President and Kharlov want you involved mainly so we'll be kept informed of what's happening."

Grishkov nodded. "That makes more sense. If the Chinese can somehow use the reappearance of this lost French nuclear weapon to support their expansion, obviously, advance warning would be useful. But, tell me. How do you think the Chinese will proceed?"

"That's not yet clear," Smyslov replied. "I'll give you my best guess. Riots in favor of independence for French Polynesia last led to mass arrests and several deaths in 2024. If the leaders of the independence movement gained possession of that newly discovered French nuclear device..."

Smyslov shrugged and continued. "I can only speculate. Could the Chinese try to intervene as 'peacekeepers?' Perhaps sponsoring an independence referendum? Many things are possible. Until you are there, though, we can only guess."

"Well, there's only one thing I know for sure from our conversation," Grishkov said.

"Yes?" Smyslov replied with a smile. "And what is that?"

"I can now tell Arisha with a clear conscience that our vacation together to Tahiti will have to wait."

CHAPTER FIFTY

Dubai
United Arab Emirates

Khaled Madi hadn't become one of the wealthiest men in France by failing to prepare for all eventualities.

Madi didn't know in any detail why his plot had failed.

He just knew that it had.

Would that failure lead investigators to Madi?

Well, men from the DGSE had already been to see Tareq. Even though the DGSE Director had been well paid to be part of the plot.

Madi had, therefore, executed his contingency plan. A part of the plan he had never told Tareq about, of course.

Tareq had gone silent. Had he fled or been killed?

Well, it didn't matter. It was time to leave France.

Fortunately, the United Arab Emirates was willing to welcome anyone with Madi's wealth. Everything Madi could want was available, from excellent health care to many luxurious living options.

Even better, here, nobody would look down on him as a non-European.

For now, Madi had rented an entire floor at one of Dubai's many outstanding hotels. Just while he looked for a more suitable permanent residence.

Security would be a top requirement for that new home. Would the French try to extradite him?

Very unlikely. The government here would never cooperate with extraditing a wealthy Muslim like Madi to a Western country like France.

But Madi was sure the French might try to assassinate him. And at the moment, he knew he was vulnerable.

It wasn't just losing Tareq. When Tareq disappeared, many of his best men did too.

The truth was, Madi didn't know his remaining security guards that well. Or really, at all.

Madi was sure, though, that they weren't enough. Not when the French government could decide to send one or more of its highly trained agents after him.

Yes. Tomorrow he would have to make hiring additional security guards his top priority.

Madi shook his head. Right now, for example, he only had one guard on duty with him. The other three were all occupied with securing the stairs and elevator providing access to this floor.

That single guard was walking toward him. Madi thought furiously. What was his name?

Khaled! The same first name as mine! Madi was pleased that he'd managed to remember, and said, "Yes, Khaled?"

Without hesitating, Khaled drew his silenced pistol and shot Madi in the head at point-blank range.

Then twice more in the chest, just to be sure.

In a few moments, he would walk to the elevator. And tell the other three guards Madi had given him instructions that under no circumstances was he to be disturbed until the following morning.

By then, Khaled would have long since flown out of Dubai. Just as Madi had known, Dubai was one of the world's busiest airports.

Flights were available at every hour, to almost every imaginable destination.

Ironically, Madi's death had nothing to do with the French authorities.

Instead, ISIS had paid Khaled a small fortune in cryptocurrency to eliminate Madi.

For the millions ISIS had paid Madi, one collapsed Paris parking garage was not enough.

Not even close.

CHAPTER FIFTY-ONE

DGSE Headquarters
Paris, France

Captain Giraud looked up as Felix Weber entered the DGSE Director's waiting room. The Director's assistant waved him to one of the vacant seats without comment.

Felix chose to sit next to Giraud, who smiled.

"I know I said it before, but it bears repeating. From what I heard from Jacques, nice flying."

Felix returned his smile. "I should have my head examined for agreeing to do such a stunt. He could just as easily have driven into us."

Giraud nodded. "True. But even then, you must admit the mission's purpose would still have been accomplished."

Felix laughed. "Maybe so. But Jacques was smart not to explain that part beforehand."

The receptionist glanced toward them, clearly wondering what in the world they were talking about.

Giraud and Felix looked at each other and stopped speaking.

Henri Fournier walked in a few moments later, and was clearly surprised to see them.

Then he nodded. "Excellent! I'm sure the new Director called us in to congratulate us on the success of our last mission. Do you know who he is?"

Giraud said something swiftly that made Henri redden and sit abruptly beside the receptionist.

Felix grinned and said, "I don't know the expression in French, but we have something like it in German. We say 'when pigs whistle.' I think in English it's 'when pigs fly.' The animal and the verb may vary, but I'll bet a similar expression exists in many other languages."

"Very amusing," Henri said stiffly.

Just then, Anatoly Grishkov entered.

"What's amusing?" he asked. "I could certainly use a laugh!"

"Well, I think the joke is on us," Giraud replied. "I don't think it's a coincidence that we're back together against all my expectations."

The receptionist interrupted.

"Excuse me," she said. "The Director said that when all four of you were here, I was to tell you to go into his office."

With that, she gestured towards the heavy door to the Director's office. An audible "snick" told them all that it was now unlocked.

Giraud stood, followed by the other three team members.

"Once more into the breach," Felix said with a smile.

Giraud shook his head. "We're going to have to talk about your fondness for English expressions."

Felix could see, though, that Giraud wasn't serious. He thought, correctly, that his flying skills had earned him considerable credit with Giraud.

What Felix didn't know was that his courage had earned him quite a bit more.

As soon as Giraud entered, he saw Jacques Montand sitting on the sofa, which was the largest piece of furniture in the office. Larger, even, than the Director's impressive desk.

At the table in front of Jacques, there was an assortment of pastries and a large glass urn of black coffee.

Grishkov saw with approval that steam was rising from the urn. As for the pastries- well, Grishkov had to admit that this was one area where the French standard might exceed even the best efforts of Russian gastronomy.

"Good to see you, sir," Giraud said as they entered. "So, you'll be joining us for our meeting with the new Director?"

"Not exactly," Jacques said, gesturing to Grishkov to close the office door as he became the last to enter.

"Please, all of you, have a seat and help yourself to coffee and pastries," Jacques continued.

They all looked at Jacques curiously but did as he asked.

Only then did he say, "Actually, I am the new Director."

Jacques had to suppress a laugh, as all four were simultaneously dealing with surprise and either eating or drinking.

With varying degrees of success.

Giraud had more success than the others and was more senior, so replied first.

"Congratulations, sir. We had not yet heard of your appointment," Giraud said.

Jacques nodded. "My receptionist and the Deputy Directors are the only ones who have been told so far, earlier this morning. The official announcement will come from the President's office later today. In the meantime, though, a matter has come up that cannot wait."

"I see," Giraud said. "Do I guess correctly that we four are here because you have decided to keep us together as a team?"

"Correct," Jacques replied. "Perhaps the only operational decision made by my predecessor that I agree with now that I have seen you work together. I think you will all find it an interesting challenge."

Giraud's eyes widened, and he saw Felix had the same reaction. "Interesting" and "challenge" were not words especially welcomed by those with much combat experience.

Giraud was surprised to see that Grishkov looked...resigned?

Had he already heard something about this?

Giraud was not at all surprised, though, by Henri's reaction. The youngster looked like his girlfriend had just asked him to go on a tropical vacation.

Giraud quickly discovered that, at least in part, Henri's reaction was justified.

"You are all going to French Polynesia on a flight later today," Jacques said. "You will travel from Charles de Gaulle airport to Tahiti via Los Angeles on Air France. You will also be going to New Caledonia and...well, more details are in the briefing papers I will give you shortly. For now, I will just speak briefly about the purpose of your mission."

Giraud nodded and looked around him at the other team members. "I know all of us have been on mission in Africa. As far as I know, this is the first time any of us have gone to French Polynesia."

Felix, Henri, and Grishkov all nodded.

"I think I can speak for all of us when I say we look forward to the change of scene," Giraud said.

"Good," Jacques said. "I have been there, and indeed, the islands are quite beautiful. However, I doubt you will have much time to appreciate its beaches. As detailed in your brief, your goal is to locate a missing French nuclear test device. Reports say that it was recently discovered washed up on an uninhabited island."

"Do we know who found it?" Giraud asked.

Jacques shook his head. "No. But we have our suspicions about who has it now. Your first task upon arrival will be to coordinate with our security forces. They will give you the latest information on the Kanak and Socialist National Liberation Front, or KSNLF, which is dedicated to Polynesian independence."

Giraud's eyes widened. "And we think they may have it? That's bad news indeed."

"Yes," Jacques replied. "Though so far, nothing has been confirmed. But the bad news doesn't end there. The Chinese have recently been active in Polynesia. They've started with Tuvalu and Tonga. We think they may support whatever steps the KSNLF may take, or threaten to take, with our missing nuclear device."

"If the Chinese managed to establish a naval base in Polynesia, they'd be well placed to threaten the U.S. Pacific fleet in Hawaii," Giraud said.

Jacques nodded. "So far we have said nothing to the Americans about any of this. The President is not sure whether he wants them involved. As you know, they can be...indelicate. And the opposite of discreet."

"Yes," Giraud said. "I'm sure we don't want anyone to know about a missing French nuclear device. Though I suppose at some point, the KSNLF may announce it?"

"They might," Jacques said. "Even that would doubtless scare many tourists away from their dream Tahiti vacation. But we think they'll wait until the device is ready to use. If they're smart, they'll realize that the search for the device will involve all our security and military forces once announced."

"So, what can we do that they cannot?" Giraud asked.

Jacques nodded toward Grishkov. "The Russian drone proved quite useful in locating a nuclear threat the last time. We are negotiating with their government to have it sent to help again. Just as before, though, we're sure they'll want one of their people involved in the search."

"I see," Giraud said with a frown. "How soon before we know about the drone?"

"I hope, by the time you arrive," Jacques replied. "How long will it take for the drone and its support staff to arrive? That, I'm afraid, will be some days later."

Giraud nodded thoughtfully. "Well, we'll just have to do what we can in the meantime to narrow the scope of the search."

"The right goal," Jacques said. "Since French Polynesia occupies over five million square kilometers, reducing the search area should indeed be your first objective."

"Any idea whether we'll likely run across the Chinese during our search?" Giraud asked.

Jacques shrugged. "Our forces have yet to encounter Chinese agents. On the other hand, they are unlikely to advertise their presence. And if they are working with the local independence movement, they will probably have help remaining hidden."

"Understood," Giraud said. Then he looked around him at the other team members.

"Do any of you have questions for the Director?" Giraud asked.

They all shook their heads.

Giraud stood, followed by Jacques and the rest of the team.

"It seems we should all prepare for our departure," Giraud said.

Jacques nodded and shook Giraud's hand.

"Good luck," he said. "I have every confidence that you will succeed, just as you did last time, in protecting our nation."

Nobody on the team said a word until they were in a DGSE sedan on the way to the airport.

All of them were looking over their briefing papers when Grishkov asked, "Does anyone know whether they grow coffee where we're going?"

Giraud looked up from his folder and smiled. "Yes, as a matter of fact. The coffee is famous in France and very expensive if you can find it. They grow both Arabica and the much rarer Red Cattura coffee beans. Why do you ask?"

Grishkov smiled back and said, "Two reasons. One is that I'd like something to look forward to besides the mission. The other is born from experience."

Now, all three of the other team members were looking at Grishkov.

Giraud laughed and said, "Fine, out with it. What's the other reason?"

"Simple," Grishkov replied. "If I go halfway around the world, I'd better return with a present for my wife!"

Afterword

First, thank you very much for reading my book! If you have any questions or comments, please get in touch with me through my blog at https://thesecondkoreanwar.wordpress.com/

I'd really appreciate your rating or – even better – review on Amazon.

The continued atrocities carried out by Russian forces in Ukraine almost made me delete all references to the Russian Agents in this book. Why didn't I do that in the end?

First, I noted up front that this novel is set in a fictional near future like all my others. It's one in which Vladimir Putin is no longer the President of Russia, and the war in Ukraine is over.

Has the nature of the regime radically changed in my imagined future? Has democracy arrived in Russia?

No to both questions.

But it's not absurd to imagine that a Russia free of Putin might, from time to time, act in ways that are less evil than it does now.

Of course, Russia will always act in its interests. Just like every other country.

I think, though, it's believable that the leader of a post-Putin Russia could find it worthwhile to help prevent a dirty bomb from exploding in Paris. Particularly one a Russian scientist had a hand in creating.

Also, I have received quite a bit of feedback from readers of the eight-book Russian Agents series, all asking me to keep at least Grishkov in the new French Agents series.

I have to admit, he's my favorite character, too.

I've heard from many readers unhappy with my decision to end the Russian Agents series and begin a French Agents series instead. I think one of their reasons is worth an answer.

It is that France no longer counts in any real way as a world power. That while Russia still projects influence around the globe, France does not.

That in any conflict, Russia would easily overwhelm France.

In short, nobody should take France or its agents seriously.

Unlike those readers, I think a war between Russia and France is highly unlikely. But let's take a look at what the result would be, just for argument's sake.

A superficial look at the numbers seems to support the conclusion that Russia's military forces could easily brush aside the French.

French nuclear warheads number in the hundreds. Russian warheads probably exceed two thousand.

France has dismantled its land-based nuclear weapons. About eighty percent of its remaining warheads are designed for delivery by sea, and the remainder by bombers.

Russia can fire its nuclear weapons by land, sea or air.

In a nuclear exchange, though, it's arguable that French capabilities are enough to make Russia hesitate to strike. French *Triomphant*-class ballistic nuclear submarines are modern, highly capable, and some are always on patrol.

Could Russian attack submarines successfully target them?

Maybe.

All of them? I think that's highly doubtful.

And what if a single *Triomphant*-class sub survived?

Each carries 16 M45 or M51 missiles, each with six to ten TN 75-150 kt or TNO 100-300 kt thermonuclear warheads.

For comparison, the Hiroshima bomb was about 15 kilotons.

In other words, up to 160 nuclear warheads, each between five and twenty times as powerful as the bomb dropped on Hiroshima.

Would some of them be intercepted?

Certainly.

All of them?

I think enough would survive to make Russia regret starting a nuclear exchange.

What about combat aircraft? French Rafale fighters and Mirage bombers number in the hundreds. Russian fighters and bombers, in the thousands. Even after the many lost in Ukraine.

However, Russia could only commit part of its fleet of aircraft to combat against the French. Less than a hundred kilometers separate the Russian Far East and the U.S. Air Force.

Russia's border stretching for thousands of kilometers with China could never be left unguarded.

Also, which air force has more capable planes with better-trained pilots?

Many experts believe the answer is the French. If so, it's worth remembering what NATO planners called a similar Soviet numerical advantage during the Cold War.

Targets.

The Russian Navy is certainly larger than its French counterpart. However, Ukraine has repeatedly demonstrated Russia's capabilities are not nearly as impressive as they are on paper.

The sinking of the Russian Black Sea flagship cruiser *Moskva* by Ukrainian anti-ship missiles was only the best known of many losses.

And Russia's sole aircraft carrier, the *Admiral Kuznetsov*? It has been in drydock for years, always with repairs "nearly finished." Will it ever return to service?

The Russian Navy says yes. At this writing, though, much of its crew has been transferred to combat duty in Ukraine.

Geography suggests that a one-on-one battle between large detachments of the French Navy and the Russian Navy will never happen. But wherever ships from the two forces encounter each other, I think the French ship or submarine will prove more capable, with a better-trained crew.

Finally, there can be no denying the overwhelming numerical superiority of the Russian Army. However, many NATO countries like Poland and Germany stand between Russia and Paris. So, a one-to-one comparison is meaningless.

Ukraine has been resupplied by NATO countries but has been joined by no foreign troops. Yet it has kept the Russian Army out of Kyiv for years.

That says everything necessary about the capabilities of the Russian Army despite its numerical advantage.

Finally, what about the ability to project power globally?

Outside the countries that were part of the Soviet Union, how many host overseas military bases now operated by Russia?

One. Syria.

That's it.

Sure, a few other countries like Cuba and Venezuela will allow visits where Russian ships and aircraft can resupply. But they don't host Russian military bases.

France has military bases in Africa, South America, the Middle East, the Caribbean, and the Indian and Pacific Oceans.

In short, France can conduct global military operations on a scale no country besides the United States can equal or surpass.

Does that mean France has global ambitions? Do any French politicians dream of a return to the days of Empire?

Well, no.

But France shows no signs of abandoning its far-flung territories around the world. And as long as those remain, I believe the French Navy and Air Force will remain a factor all other countries need to respect.

Thanks again for reading my book! I hope you will enjoy the next entry in the French Agents series, *China Conquers Polynesia*, due in 2025.

CAST OF CHARACTERS

Alphabetical Order by Nationality
Most Important Characters in Bold

French Citizens
President Allard
Antoine Bertrand, DGSE Deputy Director for
   Technical Support and Financial Investigations
Secretary-General of the Élysée Blanchet
Raphael **Boucher**, Security Contractor for
   Société Générale de Transport International
Roland **Dubois**, DGSE Director
Sergeant **Felix** Weber, French Foreign Legion, DGSE Team Member
Captain **Giraud**, French Army, DGSE Team Leader
Henri Fournier, DGSE Agent, DGSE Team Member
Jacques Montand, DGSE Deputy Director for Operations
Khaled **Madi**, President, Société Générale de Transport International

Libyan Citizens
Samir **Ali**, Truck Driver
Ismail **Abdul**, agent of Société Générale de Transport International
Lieutenant Issa, Officer in Charge, Libyan border inspection detachment

Moroccan Citizens
Nassar Alaoui, Deputy Director, Tanger Med Special Agency
Lieutenant Berrada, Officer in Charge,
   Moroccan border inspection detachment
Saad, Truck Driver

Russian Citizens
Anatoly **Grishkov**, Retired FSB agent, DGSE Team Member
Boris Kharlov, FSB Director
Retired FSB Director Smyslov
Mikhail Vasilyev, FSB Agent in charge of Okhotnik drone

Made in United States
Orlando, FL
02 December 2024

54884427R00153